Praise

"Loaded with subtle emotions, sizzling chemistry, and some provocative thoughts on the real choices [Grant's] characters are forced to make as they choose their loves for eternity." —*RT Book Reviews* (4 stars)

"Vivid images, intense details, and enchanting characters grab the reader's attention and [don't] let go."
—*Night Owl Reviews* (Top Pick)

Praise for the Dark Warrior series

"The world of the Immortal Warriors is a thoroughly engaging one, blending powerful ancient gods, fiery desire, and touchingly human love, which readers will surely want to revisit." —*RT Book Reviews*

"[Grant] blends ancient gods, love, desire, and evil-doers into a world you will want to revisit over and over again." —*Night Owl Reviews*

"Sizzling love scenes and engaging characters."
—*Publishers Weekly*

"Ms. Grant mixes adventure, magic and sweet love to create the perfect rom

Praise for th

"Grant creates a vivid
the Celts and Druids tr

D1042011

merging magic and history. The result is a wonderfully dark, delightfully well-written [series]. Readers will eagerly await the next Dark Sword book."

—RT Book Reviews

"Another fantastic series that melds the paranormal with the historical life of the Scottish highlander in this arousing and exciting adventure."

—Bitten By Books

"These are some of the hottest brothers around in paranormal fiction." —Nocturne Romance Reads

"Will keep readers spellbound."

—Romance Reviews Today

THE HERO

DONNA GRANT

St. Martin's Paperbacks

This is a work of fiction. All of the characters, organizations, and events portrayed in this novel are either products of the author's imagination or are used fictitiously.

THE HERO

For information address St. Martin's Press, 175 Fifth Avenue, New York, NY 10010.

ISBN: 978-1-250-08339-5

Our books may be purchased in bulk for promotional, educational, or business use. Please contact your local bookseller or the Macmillan Corporate and Premium Sales Department at 1-800-221-7945, ext. 5442, or by e-mail at MacmillanSpecialMarkets@macmillan.com.

Printed in the United States of America

St. Martin's Paperbacks edition / December 2016

St. Martin's Paperbacks are published by St. Martin's Press, 175 Fifth Avenue, New York, NY 10010.

10 9 8 7 6 5 4 3 2 1

To all the men and women in uniform

ACKNOWLEDGMENTS

Starting a new series in a new genre is always tough. I have a lot of people to acknowledge for helping me make this book possible. My heartfelt thanks to:

Julia for your help with the Russian translations and making sure I get it all right.

Crystal and the SMP art department for the gorgeous cover that so rocks my world.

Brant, Marissa, Amy, and the others in the marketing and publicity department—y'all are the bomb!

Monique Patterson for continuing to push me because you knew I could do it.

Natanya Wheeler for believing in this series and me.

PROLOGUE

Late July

Natalie smoothed her windblown hair from her face as she entered the restaurant in downtown Dallas. Dakota's had superb steaks, and it also happened to be one of her favorite places.

She was seated at a table for two near the vast windows while she tried to contain her anxiety. Pulling out a compact from her purse, she checked her makeup and hair for something to do while she waited.

Ever since the phone call two days ago, she'd been antsy. She had no idea why she agreed to the meeting. Or why the hell she was a ball of nerves.

Liar.

Natalie briefly closed her eyes and sighed. Fourteen years hadn't dulled her feelings. Everyone said it was just a high school fling she would soon forget.

To help her get over it, her mother attempted to push her to marry into Dallas society. Natalie's answer was to leave Texas altogether for college. That's where her life took a drastic turn and opened a plethora of possibilities.

Somehow, she found herself back in Dallas. It still

made her shake her head in wonder. Though she loved her job. It was the only thing in her life she did enjoy.

"Natalie."

She looked up to find a tall man with cowboy boots, starched jeans, a white button-down shirt, and a gray tweed sports coat standing at her table. Atop his head of dark hair was a black Stetson. He hastily removed the cowboy hat and held it against his chest as he shot her a charming smile.

"Darlin', you've only gotten prettier, if that's possible."

She smiled and started to rise when he placed a kiss on her cheek. Natalie motioned to the chair. "Orrin Loughman, you're still a flirt. Please sit."

He pulled out the chair and lowered his tall frame into it before he bent and rested his Stetson, top down, on the floor. A quick glance showed that despite being in his fifties, Orrin looked better than most men in their thirties. When he straightened, his gold eyes caught and held hers.

The waiter's arrival halted any more talk. Once their drink order had been placed, the waiter walked away.

"I bet you're wondering why I wanted to meet," Orrin said. The smile slipped. His tanned face had more lines of strain and worry than she remembered. His hair, so dark brown it was nearly black, now sported gray at the temples.

But it didn't detract. If anything, it made Orrin even more handsome.

Natalie nodded at his statement. "It wasn't as if you were at the ranch a lot. We rarely talked in the year I dated Owen."

Orrin began to speak but hesitated when the waiter appeared with their drinks. He accepted his bourbon with a nod while Natalie slowly twirled the stem of her wine glass.

She hated that she'd brought up Owen. She'd sworn she wouldn't. But when it came to Owen, her mind and heart did as they pleased.

"My son was a fool to let you go," Orrin stated.

Natalie took a drink of the chardonnay and hated the flutter of happiness his statement caused. That joy she'd found so long ago was gone. She needed to remind herself of that.

"But that's not why I wanted to see you."

Of course, it wasn't. Had Natalie actually fooled herself into believing Orrin was attempting to bring her and Owen back together?

She hadn't seen or heard from Owen since the night of their graduation when he'd dumped her so suddenly. After spending the summer in tears, she'd left him and everything to do with him behind.

Or so she'd thought.

She met Orrin's gold eyes, determined to forget Owen. "Why, then?"

"I recently learned you work for the Russian Embassy."

That caused a small hesitation before she gave a nod. "I do."

"In the past year, have you seen or heard anything about Ragnarok?"

Natalie frowned as she leaned her forearms on the table. "You mean the tale in Norse mythology about the end of the world?"

"I wish." Orrin ran a hand across his chin.

She would never forget how often Orrin had been gone on some mission for the Navy SEALs, leaving his three sons behind with their aunt and uncle on the massive Loughman Ranch.

He never spoke about his assignments, but it wasn't difficult to guess that whatever Ragnarok was, it had something to do with a job.

"I can't help you if you don't give me more information," she urged.

Orrin's gaze narrowed. His look was intense, as if he were attempting to read her mind. "Why Russia?"

She blinked, taken aback by the question. "I learned I have a natural affinity for picking up languages. Russian and Italian are my favorites. I did so well, I was offered a job in St. Petersburg."

"And the embassy?" he pressed.

"As a Westerner, I wasn't always looked upon favorably in Russia. It became more and more challenging to work there. So, I returned to Texas. That's when the Russian Embassy contacted me. I've been there for the past seven years. Now tell me what the hell this is about."

Orrin pushed aside his bourbon. "You're sure you haven't heard of Ragnarok?"

"Positive."

"Do me a favor. If you do, call this number." He pulled out a business card with the Loughman Ranch insignia and slid it across the table.

Natalie picked up the card and turned it over to see a phone number. "Do I need to be concerned?"

Orrin blew out a deep breath. "We all do, darlin'."

That didn't help. If anything, it made dozens more

questions pop into her head. They all rushed in at once, and while she was sorting through them, finding which one she wanted to ask, he carried on as if he hadn't just mentioned a clue to something she suspected was highly classified.

Orrin tossed back his bourbon.

"Tell me more," she urged.

He opened the menu, winking at her over the top. "I'm starving."

That was Orrin's way of politely telling her she would get nothing more from him. There was no more talk of Ragnarok, missions, or Owen. For the next hour, Orrin asked enough questions about the past fourteen years to keep her talking nonstop.

But she didn't quit thinking about Ragnarok or what it could be.

By the time he walked her to her car, she wished she'd known Orrin better fourteen years ago. The time with him today had been beyond pleasant. It made her long for the past.

And worry.

Whatever Orrin knew was important enough to seek out the ex-girlfriend of his middle son. Not something Orrin would do lightly.

Two weeks later, Natalie walked into her boss's office to get a stack of files when she saw an open report on his desk. Her gaze landed on one word halfway down the page—Ragnarok.

CHAPTER ONE

September

The blades of the chopper cut through the air with a *whomp, whomp* noise that Owen Loughman had come to find soothing. He sat back with his eyes closed in the seat of the Blackhawk helicopter, trying to figure out why he'd been pulled from his mission with his SEAL team in Afghanistan.

Not surprisingly, he'd been told exactly nothing.

He cracked open an eye and glanced at the cockpit. The two men piloting wore solid black. No military designation. No adornment of any kind. Obviously CIA.

Owen had witnessed—and experienced—his fair share of craziness since becoming a SEAL. CIA agents thought they kept themselves under the radar. It was the biggest load of shit. Everyone recognized them immediately.

It wasn't the fact that he hadn't gotten details of why he and his team had their mission halted after a week in the desert. It wasn't that he'd been shoved onto a plane in the Middle East without explanation. It wasn't even that no one had so much as looked at him since he'd landed in the States and was promptly put on the Black-hawk.

He was a Navy SEAL. He was prepared for anything—any and all surprises. No, the unease had everything to do with the CIA. He didn't trust the government bastards.

The disquiet feeling that saved his life countless times began to stir. He blew out a breath and opened his eyes as he turned his head to look out the open door of the chopper.

Texas.

He would recognize his beloved state anywhere. He hadn't been back in . . . he had to stop and count . . . ten years. He couldn't believe it had been that long. Where had the time gone?

The last time he'd seen Texas was the day he'd graduated from the University of Texas and joined the Navy. From the time he was in junior high, he'd known he would make his life in the military. It was who the Loughmans were, dating all the way back to the Revolutionary War.

He'd been the only one to follow in his father's footsteps and choose the Navy, though. Wyatt, his older brother, chose the Marines, along with Cullen, his younger brother.

He couldn't recall the last time he'd spoken to his brothers. Their family wasn't close. He blamed it on their father, because it was easy. Though in truth, the fault lay with each of them.

The chopper began its descent. His gaze took in the rolling hills and the cattle scattering to get away from the noise. Then he spotted the two-story, white house with black trim that brought back a flood of memories.

Home.

He rested his hands on his thighs covered in desert-colored cammies, wishing his gun hadn't been taken from him in Afghanistan. Just what the hell was he doing back home?

The Blackhawk landed a hundred yards from the house. The pilot turned in his seat and looked at Owen through the tinted screen of his helmet. "We've reached your destination, Lieutenant Commander."

He unbuckled his seatbelt and grabbed his pack before jumping out of the open doors, his gaze perusing the area as memories flooded back. No sooner had his feet hit the ground than the Blackhawk was airborne again.

He glanced up, watching the chopper disappear. Then his gaze slid to the house. It looked . . . empty, desolate. Which couldn't be right since his aunt and uncle lived there.

Owen took a deep breath of the fresh Texas air. And stilled. He smelled death.

He hurried to the side of the house and squatted, flattening his back against the porch railing. Quietly, he lowered his pack to the ground before he cautiously looked around the corner.

Aunt Charlotte's numerous hanging plants that she lovingly cultivated still dotted the wrap-around porch, swinging in the breeze. An empty rocker teetered.

It was quiet. Too quiet.

He silently crept to the front steps. If anybody was

there, they were inside the house. He glanced behind him. The open landscape allowed him to see anyone coming. The scattered trees were large enough to hide a foe, but even they were too far away for someone to surprise him.

Except for the oak out back. He would have to tread carefully there.

He hurried up the five steps to the porch and flattened himself against the house beside the front entryway. Slowly, he opened the screen door. Just in time, he recalled the squeak if opened all the way.

Keeping away from the glass inset into the wood, he rested the frame of the screen on his forearm as he put his hand on the knob. Then, with a deep breath, he twisted and gave a slight push.

The heavy door opened noiselessly. When no gunfire erupted, he peeked inside the house. When he saw nothing, he quickly entered, his hand catching the screen to close it without a sound behind him. He moved to the side of the foyer and listened for any noise.

The house remained as soundless and still as before. On silent feet, he walked to his left. He glanced up the stairs but chose to look around the ground floor first. The front room, the one his mother had used as a music room, had been turned into a formal living area by his aunt.

His gaze searched the space. As if pulled to them, he spotted two holes in the wall. Bullet holes. A sinking feeling filled him.

For long seconds, he stared at the marred drywall, hoping it was his mind playing tricks on him. But there was no denying the truth that was before him. Had his father's work once more followed him home? It infuriated him that Orrin hadn't taken precautions to keep his family safe as he'd promised.

Moving to the wall, he touched the holes. The bullets had been removed, but by the size of the openings, he surmised they were 7.62mm. Military grade.

His eyes slid to the next room. He knew what he would find. His mind screamed for him to turn and walk away. The house had seen so much death, and as always, he was the one to find it.

He hadn't run away when he was a boy. He wouldn't do it now. Though his years with the SEALs had shown him unbelievable ways a person could kill—and be killed—nothing could compare to knowing it had struck your family.

Again.

Owen swallowed and walked through the doorway to the large living area with the eight-foot-wide stone fireplace. The first thing he saw was the blood. It coated the recliner, which was also riddled with bullet holes.

He clenched his jaw, anger kindling in his gut. His fears were confirmed. Uncle Virgil and Aunt Charlotte were dead. As he stood in the living room where he and his brothers had watched TV, opened Christmas gifts, fought, and played, the primal side of him—the beast the Navy had shaped and trained—demanded justice.

Justice his mother hadn't gotten.

He slowly turned the haze of rage and anguish into cold fury that could be directed with reprisal so horrible the screams of the men who had killed his family would reverberate in Hell.

Pulling his eyes away from the recliner, he slowly

moved around the living area. Debris from the gun battle littered the floor, making it so he had to carefully choose where to set his feet so as not to make noise.

He reached the arched double entry into the kitchen and felt his chest squeeze in fury. The shooters had found Aunt Charlotte there. By the dough still on the counter, she'd been making her famous bread. The blood pool on the floor was large, as was the pattern of splatter on the walls.

A floorboard creaked behind him. He whirled around, his arm jerking up and back to hit the intruder. At the last minute, he recognized the dark gold eyes and stopped his assault.

"Wyatt."

His elder brother gave a firm nod in greeting. "Owen."

He frowned as he looked at Wyatt's face covered with a thick beard. His dark hair was unkempt and long. Wyatt stood still as stone, his gaze moving from one place to the next.

Having gone undercover enough times himself, Owen recognized the reason for Wyatt's appearance. His brother had always been quiet. A loner. Only the Loughmans knew the cause.

And no one spoke of it.

Now, Wyatt appeared even more serious, if that were possible. He was leaner than Owen remembered, more lethal and vicious. Wyatt wore black camo with no insignia. So that's where his brother had disappeared to. Delta Force.

Despite Wyatt's icy demeanor, not even he could hide the anger that sizzled in his eyes or the way his hands clenched at his sides.

Men like he and Wyatt knew only one way to seek vengeance—blood. Whoever had done this to their family was about to see just what the Loughman brothers were capable of.

Wyatt stepped around him into the kitchen and stopped next to the pool of blood. His gaze remained on it for a moment before he met Owen's gaze. "There's nothing upstairs."

He opened his mouth to speak when the sound of another chopper filled the air. Both brothers hurried to the front of the house. Sliding against the wall, they peeked out the windows to see another man in green fatigues appear in the doorway of the Blackhawk.

"I'll be damned," he murmured when Cullen jumped from the helicopter before it landed.

Cullen's cap was pulled low over his face as he stood staring at the house. He didn't move even as the chopper took off, the sound fading quickly.

Owen looked at Wyatt to find a frown on his brother's face. Nothing ever changed. He pushed away from the wall and walked out the front of the house. The sight of his younger brother brought a smile. Too bad the reunion was tarnished with death. But that seemed to be the curse of the Loughmans.

Cullen dropped his pack from his shoulder and smiled when he caught sight of him. Owen jumped off the porch and met Cullen halfway, enfolding him in a hug.

They pounded each other on the back in greeting. He then held his younger brother at arm's length and looked into hazel eyes so like their mother's as Cullen removed his hat. If he thought Wyatt had changed, it was nothing compared to Cullen.

Cullen's gaze held a cynical edge, showing suspicion that only someone who had been neck-deep in war would understand. His hair was kept in the typical style of the Marines—high and tight—with the sides shaved close to his head and only a quarter inch spiked on top.

"Damn, it's been a while," Cullen said with a bright smile.

He playfully slapped Cullen on the cheek, but he couldn't hold his smile. Not when he knew what had brought them together. "You've grown up, little brother."

Cullen's laughter died as his gaze moved over Owen's shoulder. The grin was gone, the hardness back in place. "Wyatt."

Owen turned around to find Wyatt on the porch, watching them. Life as a Loughman hadn't been easy for any of them, but particularly Wyatt. Owen still remembered being a young boy, how people used to be envious of their ranch. For a few years, the siblings had lived a life of wonder and joy.

But it all shattered one stormy day.

None of the boys had been the same since. Owen looked between his two brothers, hating that the tension was already back.

"What's going on?" Cullen asked as his sharp gaze looked around. "Where are Uncle Virgil and Aunt Charlotte?"

Wyatt leaned against the post. "Dead."

Cullen's eyes become intense. "How?"

"I'd say at least five men," Owen said.

Wyatt added, "Six." He walked down the steps and pointed to the ground. "Two came in the front. Another two from the back, and I spotted two more sets of foot-prints around the barns."

Owen scrubbed a hand down his face. This was a hit. Pure and simple. But against his aunt and uncle, who were some of the best human beings he'd ever known? This wasn't about Charlotte and Virgil. This was about something else. He immediately thought of his father. But it could be because of one of them, as well. He and his brothers had enemies of their own.

That soured his stomach. Hadn't he sworn he wouldn't allow such things to touch his family again?

He walked back into the house and to the living area, followed by Cullen and Wyatt. He looked at the recliner where their uncle had been killed to the fireplace where one of the shotguns hung.

"It's untouched," Cullen stated.

Owen glanced around the room. "Virgil never got to it."

"He didn't stand a chance against such firepower," Wyatt stated.

Cullen strode to the kitchen and stood quietly for several minutes. When he spoke, his voice was low and filled with raw fury. "I'll not stop until I find out who did this."

"We feel the same," Owen said, fully understanding how Cullen felt.

Cullen released a breath and faced his brothers. "I was in the middle of a mission when my team was pulled. No way was I picked up and immediately brought here just because they were murdered."

"You weren't the only one, kid," Wyatt said. "I was on a mission, too."

Owen crossed his arms over his chest. "Make that all three of us. I can't think of any of my enemies who would know to track me here."

"Me either," Cullen replied.

Wyatt gave a single shake of his head.

Owen's anger burned brightly. "This involves Dad. It has to."

A muscle ticked in Wyatt's jaw. Owen ignored the telltale sign that Wyatt was furious and frowned when he heard the sound of an automobile approaching. The three instantly fanned out. Cullen took the back door while Owen positioned himself at the front. Wyatt squatted behind the sofa in the formal living room.

The motor shut off, and a moment later, a vehicle door closed. Owen glanced out the window and caught sight of the front of a dark gray BMW 6 Series.

Seconds ticked by without the sound of anyone approaching. Wyatt turned his head toward the back of the house when the front door was thrown open, and someone stepped inside. Owen stilled a second before he grabbed the slim form.

He had the intruder flipped onto their back immediately. In the next moment, Owen found himself on the floor, staring at the ceiling. He jumped to his feet and tried to look beneath the baseball cap of the person, but he couldn't make out anything.

Owen didn't waste any time getting the advantage and slamming the person against the wall. There was a gasp that sounded distinctly feminine as the air in the intruder's lungs was forced out.

That caught his attention. With a shove, he knocked the hat off. A wealth of light brown hair tumbled free.

All the breath left him as he stared into green eyes he feared he'd never see again.

"Natalie?"

"Hi, boys," she said off-handedly.

He frowned, suddenly furious to find her there. "What the hell are you doing here?"

"She's looking for me," came a voice behind them.

"Callie?" Wyatt asked in a strangled voice full of surprise and annoyance as he stood.

Callie Reed glared at each of them as she walked around Owen and nodded to Natalie. He released Natalie, and she moved to stand beside Callie. He exchanged a look with his brothers, though Wyatt couldn't stop staring at Callie.

"Someone please tell us what's going on?" Owen demanded.

Callie shrugged. "I work here."

Green eyes met his. "I came to help."

CHAPTER TWO

Natalie had known the black helicopters she spotted on her way to the ranch could be transports for the Loughman boys. It gave her a little thrill to think Owen might be on one.

Then she remembered that he'd left her. Suddenly, she didn't want to see him again. But things she couldn't change had been set in motion—and it was out of her hands now.

"I see it," Callie said through the speakers in Natalie's car. "It's a military chopper."

"I wanted to get to the ranch before them."

Callie grunted in agreement. "You don't want to see him."

"I really don't."

"Welcome to my world," Callie murmured.

She grinned but didn't comment as she continued driving at breakneck speed. "Where are you?"

"I should get there right behind you. Shit. Hang on."

Natalie grimaced when she heard the squeal of tires through the phone connection. She waited until she

heard Callie let loose another string of curses before she
released a breath.

"Dumbasses can't drive," Callie stated irately. "If I
didn't drive as well as I do, that could've ended up killing someone."

"Save it for those responsible for Charlotte's and Virgil's murders."

There was a pregnant pause before Callie said sadly,
"Yeah."

The days of Natalie going back to her house to have
a glass of wine and watch episodes of *Criminal Minds*
or *Doctor Who* were long gone. Ever since the day she
saw Ragnarok in that report and called the number Orrin
had given her, her life had changed.

That's when she and Callie had begun talking several
times a day.

The sound of another chopper flying low overhead
caused her to glance up. It looked like another military
helicopter, which immediately made her think of Owen.
Again.

She sighed. After all the wasted years, she thought
he'd be gone from her thoughts. It seemed she was forever wrong when it came to him.

"There's another one. I'm betting it's them," Callie
said.

"Think there's any way I can look around without
them knowing?"

"You mean without Owen knowing? Doubt it."

She knew Callie was right, but that didn't mean Natalie had to like it.

"How's work?" Callie asked.

Because she worked for the Russian Embassy, and she wasn't sure if they listened to her conversations, she and Callie never spoke of her work. The fact that Callie brought it up meant there was a reason.

"Busy. I had a hard time getting away."

"Time isn't on our side."

Of that, she was clearly aware. "How long do you think we have?"

"I don't know. Everything hinges on finding it."

It being Ragnarok—a bioweapon.

How different her life would be if Orrin hadn't contacted her in July. She wouldn't be embroiled in kidnapping, espionage, and murder.

And yet . . . it felt as if this were the exact place she needed to be.

Then again, that could be her heart trying to convince her this all led back to Owen. As far as she was concerned, men were pigs. She'd had enough of the lies, the cheating, and the bullshit that always went with dating.

She was happy living the single life, not having to clean up after anyone, share her closet, compromise on where to eat or if she got to watch her favorite shows. There was no one taking her covers, snoring, or—

"Natalie?"

"Sorry," she told Callie. "I was thinking."

"About Owen?"

"About all of it. The shit is about to hit the fan as soon as the boys learn what's going on."

Callie snorted loudly. "Then let it. Where have they been these last ten years? Have they even bothered to send a fucking text? No. They have no idea how badly that hurt Orrin."

"I doubt they think about it." She should know. In the year she'd been with Owen, there were two things never discussed—his mother's murder, and his feelings about his dad.

"Which just pisses me off," Callie said tightly. "If I had a dad like Orrin, I'd never be far."

"I know." Callie was another who didn't discuss her family. And with a family as infamous around Hillsboro as the Reeds, it was no wonder.

The Reeds were drunks and criminals of the worst sort. It had been Orrin who helped Callie escape all of that. And why she thought of Orrin as a father.

"We have to find him," Callie said.

Natalie slowed the car and put on her blinker as she prepared to pull onto the Loughman Ranch. "We will, Callie. We will."

"Even if we have to do it on our own. If the jackasses Orrin calls sons won't help, then I'll make sure they're not around to interfere."

That made Natalie smile. If anyone could do that, it was Callie. What she lacked in height, Callie made up for in intelligence and talking rings around people. Few could keep up with her.

"I just turned into the ranch." She felt a flutter in her stomach.

Excitement or dread? She wasn't sure she knew.

This wasn't the first time she'd been on the ranch since her breakup with Owen. In fact, she'd been there several times since discovering Ragnarok, but this time was different.

This time, Owen could be there.

"I'm close," Callie said.

The line disconnected. Natalie didn't see the black fence that lined either side of the drive, or the cows and horses that grazed peacefully.

Her gaze was locked on the white house that drew closer with each second. By the time she parked in front of the two-story ranch home with its wide, wrap-around porch, all she could think about was the dinner she'd had the week before with Callie, Virgil, and Charlotte.

She put the car in park and glanced around. There was no sign that anyone else was there. Since she expected someone to come out at the sound of her car, she assumed Owen and his brothers hadn't yet made it to the house.

Or perhaps, luck was on her side, and those choppers hadn't been bringing the brothers.

She got out of her car, but it was more difficult than she imagined making herself go up the steps to the porch. She might be involved in all of this, but she'd never witnessed a murder scene firsthand.

Frankly, she didn't want to.

But Orrin's life was on the line. Everything she and Callie could discover only helped their chances of learning who took Orrin and where Ragnarok was.

She reached the front door. At least she wouldn't have to see Virgil's and Charlotte's bodies. They had already been taken away.

That was her last thought as she walked through the doorway and found herself flat on her back. Natalie knew the instant the large hands grabbed her that it was Owen.

Her heart skipped a beat, even as she instinctively reacted and used her momentum to pull Owen over her head. She got up, but in the next heartbeat, he had her pinned to the wall.

The heat of him was the first thing she felt. Then it was his hard body trapping her. She felt herself softening, needing to feel him after all these years.

She thought he would threaten her. Instead, he knocked off her cap. His dark brown eyes widened in shock.

How she wished her heart didn't feel like it was about to explode out of her chest. He was . . . breathtaking. She drank in the very sight of him. Sharp, chiseled features that looked as if they had been fashioned from granite stared back at her. Gone was any hint of the teenager she'd known. Before her stood a man in all his masculine glory.

He'd always been tall, his muscles honed at an early age from working on the ranch. Now, however, Owen filled out his wide shoulders. His light tan tee stretched tightly across his chest, molding to every ripple of muscle in his arms and shoulders. The shirt was tucked into camo pants she imagined were for the desert by their sand and khaki color. His hair was longer, the dark strands shoved away from his face in long waves.

Her surprise at having Owen against her was quickly hidden. Out of the corner of her eye, she spotted two more figures. How she wished she would've waited for Callie.

"Hi, boys," Natalie said. It was the only thing she could think of.

Owen frowned, the irritation clear in his sensual chocolate gaze. "What the hell are you doing here?"

"She's looking for me."

At the sound of Callie's voice, most of the apprehension left Natalie. Now she wouldn't have to face the Loughman men on her own.

She barely paid attention to anything going on around her. She was too intent on staring into Owen's eyes. It was obvious that he was irritated to find her there, but he had yet to release her.

And she didn't remind him of that fact.

Her allowing him to keep her pinned was an indication of how long it had taken her to get over him. And how she hated herself for it. After all she'd suffered, she should be shoving him away.

Her body had other ideas, however. With her blood burning through her and her nipples hard, she ached for his touch.

Yearned for it.

His eyes dropped to her mouth. Her breath hitched, caught in her throat. Yes! She wanted his kiss. It didn't matter where they were or who was around.

Dimly, she heard Callie and Wyatt talking. Much to her annoyance, Owen released her. She was more hurt than she wanted to admit.

Perhaps it was for the best. She'd sworn off all men. Especially Owen. She quickly moved to stand beside Callie.

"Someone please tell us what's going on?" Owen demanded.

Callie shrugged. "I work here."

Natalie looked at Owen and said, "I came to help."

Owen's breath locked in his lungs as he stared at Natalie's long, brown hair streaked with strands of copper.

He wanted those deep green eyes of hers to land on him again, to fill with desire . . . again.

She was even more beautiful than he remembered. The years had transformed her into a seductress who left him breathless and needy.

The girl had become a woman, and what a woman she was. He knew the weight of her breast in his hand, knew how it felt to sink into her body and hear her scream in pleasure.

And yet, the woman before him now held a hint of wariness that hadn't been there before. What happened to her to take away that lighthearted girl he once knew?

He glanced down at her dark green flannel button-down, rolled up at the sleeves. The shirt hugged her breasts before drifting inward at her waist to fall, untucked, against light blue denim.

Never could he resist Natalie in a pair of jeans and cowboy boots. He bit back a groan. Owen wanted to run to her, to yank her against him and plunder her sweet lips until the world faded away. Instead, he remained where he was, realizing too late that he was screwed six ways from Sunday.

"Sucks to be you," Cullen murmured.

He didn't bother to respond because he could barely wrap his head around the fact that she was actually there. Beautiful, vibrant, confident Natalie.

"What the fuck do you mean you work here?" Wyatt demanded of Callie in a callous voice.

Owen watched Callie's blue eyes flash angrily. It was always the same between them. Ever since Callie was thirteen and Wyatt seventeen when she'd come to work at the ranch during the summer. They'd butted heads immediately, and rarely were they together when they weren't fighting.

He stepped in before Callie could tell Wyatt where to go and how to get there. "You'd think all these years away would change you two." His gaze then moved to Natalie, who now wouldn't look his way.

"I'm not the one with the attitude," Callie said with a cold look in Wyatt's direction.

He leaned a shoulder against the wall. "You came back after college to work at the ranch?"

"No." Callie shook her head and bent to get Natalie's cap. She handed it to Natalie and straightened. "I work for your father."

"Fucking wonderful," Wyatt muttered as he strode past them out to the porch.

Cullen shook his head as he came to stand beside Owen. "What do you mean, you work for Dad?"

"Orrin is running a private ops team here," Callie said, glancing at Natalie. "Whitehorse. He's been doing private, off-the-books missions for the government for the last several years."

Owen was staggered by the news. His father was no longer with the Navy? That wasn't possible. Just as it seemed improbable that Natalie now stood in his living room. "Dad would never resign his commission."

"He did." Callie sat on the arm of the sofa. "He and his men have been going on missions the government couldn't send any of its forces to do."

"Why?" Cullen asked in a soft voice.

Callie shrugged, her gaze lowering to the floor. "He had men taken captive in Yemen, and despite his rank, his orders to send in a SEAL team to get them out was shot down. The men died, and he'd had enough. He put in the paperwork to retire." She looked up at Owen. "Until the DOD came to him with an offer."

"The Department of Defense?" Cullen asked. "Dad said he'd never work with those assholes."

Callie lifted a brow. "Things change."

"How did you get involved?" Owen asked. He noticed that even though Wyatt had walked outside, his elder brother stood near the screen door, listening.

Natalie's soft smile as Callie glanced her way told him that she already knew this part. By how chummy the two women were, it was clear that Natalie had been a part of things to some degree.

Just how much, he intended to find out. Then he'd send her straight home. He needed a clear head, and he couldn't do that with her around.

"Your father found me at Quantico," Callie explained. "The FBI recruited me. I was about to join when Orrin told me what he was putting together."

Owen rubbed his eyes with his thumb and forefinger. He hadn't slept in thirty-two hours, and it didn't look like he was going to get any rest anytime soon. "You go on missions with Dad?"

"I've been on a few. Mostly, I gather intel, get the requests to decode from Washington, and hack my way into whatever is needed."

Cullen wearily shook his head. "Now I know why we're here."

"Yeah," Owen said tightly. "Something went wrong. Where is Orrin, Callie?"

She licked her lips and covertly slid her gaze to the door and Wyatt.

It was Natalie who stepped in. "We don't know. The mission went off without a problem. He and his men landed in Delaware at Dover Air Force Base."

"The plane that was to bring them back to Texas waited over an hour," Callie said, her eyes full of sadness. "That's when I called the base. They found the bodies of all six of Orrin's men. They'd been shot execution style."

"Shit," Cullen mumbled, running a hand through his short hair.

Callie got to her feet. "That shouldn't have happened. Your father handpicked those men. They are the elite of all the special forces."

"Where was the mission?" Wyatt asked from the porch.

There was a long pause from Callie. Once more, Natalie stepped in. "Russia."

Owen wanted to demand to be told how Natalie was involved, but that would have to wait for the moment. But not for too long. He met Wyatt's gaze through the screen door before he turned to Callie. "Have you heard from our father?"

"No." She put her hands on her jean-clad hips and took a deep breath.

"We believe he was taken," Natalie said.

Owen nodded. "Otherwise, they would've left his body. What was the assignment?"

Callie's gaze quickly slid to Owen. "A new biochemical created for the Russian military called Ragnarok."

"Dad retrieved it?" Cullen asked.

Callie looked at each of them before she said, "Yeah. Along with the formula."

"That's enough to kill for," Wyatt stated.

Owen turned his head to look at the two bullet holes in the wall of the formal living room. "The Russians killed Virgil and Charlotte."

"The only reason for them to do that is if they have Dad, and he's not talking," Cullen said.

Wyatt snorted. "He hid the bioweapon. That's the reason we've not found Orrin's body and why the Russians came here."

"Every government has bioweapons. What's so important about this one?" Owen had hoped distance would help the tension between Wyatt and their father. Obviously it had been wishful thinking.

Callie shrugged. "I don't know, but there's something different about it."

"We need to know what that is," Cullen stated.

Wyatt gave a nod of agreement.

"If it were just Ragnarok our government wanted, we wouldn't have been returned here. Dad is the other reason we were brought home." Owen clenched his jaw. "Our government wants us to find him."

Cullen crossed his arms over his chest. "We'll find Dad and the fuckers who did this."

"Actually, your orders are to locate and bring the formula to DC. I think bringing you home was to show you what we're up against," Callie said and held out a piece of paper written in a code.

Cullen grabbed the paper while Owen looked over Cullen's shoulder to read it. He recognized it as the code his father had created and taught them years ago. Callie already decoded it, writing the message below.

"Son of a bitch," Cullen muttered.

Owen read the message twice. It wasn't the first time the government had put an item before a person's life. But he wasn't going to do this without finding his father, as well. Orders be damned. "Looks like we're going on a mission."

"You can't seriously be thinking about finding that formula," Cullen said. "It's better left hidden, just as Dad wanted."

Owen slid his gaze to Wyatt, knowing what he was about to say wouldn't sit well with his older brother. "Ragnarok could be anywhere. There's only one person who knows the location. We're going to find Dad."

CHAPTER THREE

Natalie pivoted and began to walk from the house when Owen's voice stopped her.

"Don't leave the property."

She kept her back to him but nodded before she pushed open the screen door and walked onto the porch and past Wyatt. There was no need to be inside the house as the brothers began discussing how to find Orrin.

Natalie had her own opinions of the Loughman family, and they'd changed drastically since meeting with Orrin and establishing her connection to Callie.

Leave? He actually thought she was going to leave? That wasn't going to happen. She was caught in the middle of this whether she wanted to be or not. And it didn't matter what Owen or the others thought. She was well and truly connected.

She stood on the porch and looked out over the beauty that was the ranch. So many days she'd spent right there on the porch drinking sweet tea and talking to Charlotte while Owen worked.

Once his chores were done, they'd saddle horses and

go for rides that lasted hours. It was the freest Natalie had ever felt. There was something about the ranch that called to her, a feeling that it was where she belonged.

The Loughman name was well known enough for her mother, even if they chose not to be part of Dallas society. Their wealth and position gave her a reprieve from her interfering mom.

But that's not what kept her dating Owen all those years ago. It was the passion and love that blossomed swift and intense. He hadn't seemed surprised by it, but she sure was. That year with him changed everything. She saw the world differently, felt everything deeper. Things had been so simple then. The years ahead had looked bright and joyful.

She gazed at the big blue sky with a smattering of clouds. How many times had she lain upon the ground somewhere on the ranch and stared at that sky with Owen? They'd spoken of dreams and wishes. And plans.

Every one of hers had included him. Not once had he let on that he felt differently. It was under that same star-filled sky that he had broken her heart—and nearly broken her spirit.

The past no longer mattered. It was fourteen years ago, with a lot of water under that bridge now. She was there because of Orrin and Callie. She was at the ranch because she wouldn't be able to live with herself otherwise.

So, no matter how much being near Owen brought up those painful memories, she wasn't going anywhere.

Owen walked from the house and searched for a glimpse of Natalie. Her car was still there, which meant so was she. He was both relieved and terrified of that.

She always had a way of making him feel everything deeply—too deeply. With her near, he wouldn't be able to focus on anything but her. His mind needed to be engrossed in the mission, fixated on their targets, and, at all times, fully alert.

The sooner she was away from the ranch and going on with her life, the better.

Or was it?

Owen's steps faltered. The very sight of her earlier had taken his breath away. Even now, his hands could still feel the warmth of her, the softness. His body had been pressed against hers, his every breath inhaling her fresh scent that was burned into his memory.

He was happy with his life, with his career. Then Nat had to show up and shake him to his core. His blood still pounded from holding her, his cock was still semi-hard.

All for her.

He'd sacrificed everything once to ensure her safety. And he was about to have to do it again.

The first time had nearly killed him. But he was stronger now, more sure of his decision. That didn't mean it wasn't going to slice him in two to leave her a second time.

An image of her green eyes filled with desire flashed in his mind. His steps slowed from the crushing weight of longing for Nat that assaulted him.

He took several deep breaths and pulled himself together. Then he walked to the pasture to the right of the house and stood at the fence. There, he watched a mare and her days-old foal. The filly was still a little awkward on her legs, but by the way she pranced and galloped, she was going to be as good-looking of a horse as her mother.

The sight of the ranch brought back a rush of memories—most of them involving Natalie. Many times over the years, he thought of asking one of his friends to find her. But he never went any further than the thought because he knew she was probably married.

He hadn't needed confirmation of that. Besides, things were better as they were. At least he'd always thought that until he'd come face-to-face with her and saw her left ring finger bare.

Being back at the ranch stirred feelings he wished he could forget. There was no chance of forgetting how happy he'd been, how everything had fallen into place when he was with Natalie.

At eighteen, he'd known she was the woman for him. The only one who could quiet his soul and bring him the peace he hadn't had since his mother's murder.

Now here Natalie was once more.

His thoughts were interrupted by the sound of footsteps on grass. Callie strolled up and stood on the bottom rung of the fence as she watched the foal. "She's a looker for sure. Your father was anxious for her arrival."

"What happened on the mission?" he asked as he faced her, leaning one arm on the fence as he did. He needed something to turn his thoughts from Natalie, and this was exactly where his mind needed to be.

Callie's hair was back in a ponytail, the chestnut color startling in the sunlight. Her blue eyes were direct, penetrating as they returned his stare. "He should've returned. None of them should be dead. Whoever got the drop on them is good."

She was worried, he realized. "I need specifics. If it was Russians who killed Virgil and Charlotte to get information, they'll most likely come for us next."

"I think you're exactly who they want." She sighed and stepped off the fence. With her hands on her hips, she cocked her head to the side and squinted at the sun. "Orrin had plans to ask each of you to join him eventually, but he knew you weren't ready to forgive him. Not yet anyway."

He didn't reply. There was no need. The history between Orrin Loughman and his sons wasn't pleasant.

Callie dropped her arms, looking down.

He straightened from the fence and glanced at the house. Wyatt was on the phone, talking to one of his superiors in the hopes of learning more while Cullen gathered evidence around the house. These were the few quiet moments before everyone went into action.

And Natalie would be long gone by then.

"Spit it out, Callie," he urged.

"It *was* Russians."

"You know this how?"

"Who else would come?"

She had a point. But how did they know it was Orrin who stole Ragnarok? That's what kept nagging at him.

"The Russians found our base."

He raised a brow, a slow burning anger rising as he comprehended her implication. "You mean the base is here? Dad operated his group here? On the ranch?"

Callie couldn't look at him as she nodded.

"Didn't he learn anything?" he exploded, no longer capable of holding back his fury. "Wasn't my mother's death enough?"

Out of the corner of his eye, he saw Cullen round the side of the house, and Wyatt end his call. Both looked his way.

"What's going on?" Cullen called out.

He started to go to his brothers when Callie grabbed his arm.

"Wait," she said and licked her lips. Her gaze darted around, most likely looking for Wyatt. "I'd rather tell just you."

"Tell me what?" he demanded.

"Yes, tell him what?" Wyatt asked from behind Callie.

Owen had seen him move swiftly and silently to come up behind Callie. To surprise her or overhear, Owen wasn't sure.

Callie shoved her hands in the back pockets of her jeans and pretended she hadn't heard Wyatt. She withdrew a piece of paper and handed it to Owen. "This just came across the wire."

He glanced at Wyatt over her shoulder as he took the paper and opened it. It was a printout of a coded email. Owen read it and handed it to Wyatt as Cullen reached them.

"All information regarding the formula or Orrin Loughman must be shared with the DOD," Wyatt read aloud. He moved so he could see Callie. "When did you get this?"

"Didn't you hear me say just now?" she asked with a roll of her eyes. "It was in the coded emails," she answered, barely sparing Wyatt a glance.

Cullen's frown deepened. "Who sent it?"

"Dad's mission wasn't sanctioned," Owen surmised.

"It's why they brought us here. They've made it clear they want the bioweapon more than they want Dad."

"That's bullshit," Callie declared.

Owen had his own thoughts on that subject. It didn't bode well when the very department that sent Orrin on the mission was now leaving him swinging in the wind. Something was very wrong. And all of them knew it.

The problem was attempting to untangle the mess. Owen had been in a situation like this before. The deeper they dug, the more information and lies they would find. That's when it would become near impossible to determine who to trust or what to believe.

"Were all his assignments unsanctioned?" he asked Callie.

She shook her head and glanced at the barn where Natalie stood in the opening. "Only a few. Orrin was careful about which ones he accepted."

Wyatt shook his head in frustration and looked toward the mare and filly as the silence lengthened.

"Callie, who sent the email?" Cullen asked again.

Callie cleared her throat. "The murder of Virgil and Charlotte went out on the news last night."

Wyatt's head jerked to her. "Why?"

"The sheriff's department already did their investigation after a government team came in and collected evidence and took the bodies," Callie answered. "Mark called this morning to let me know they won't be returning since the investigation has been handed to you three."

"Mark?" Wyatt asked through clenched teeth.

Callie raised a brow but didn't look Wyatt's way. "Mark Cooper has been our sheriff for a few years now."

Owen remembered Mark. He was Callie's age, and everyone knew he'd always had a thing for her. Cullen gave Owen a shrug as he glanced at Wyatt.

"Why put it on the news and then send us in?" Cullen asked.

Owen rubbed his chin as he spotted Natalie. "I'd have liked to look around the scene before the local authorities came in. And why send them in at all?"

"A formality," Callie said.

Wyatt snorted loudly. "A government team isn't brought in to clean things up unless they're hiding something. Then they send in the locals?"

Cullen clenched his hands into fists.

Owen was ready and willing to go after the bastards for what they'd done. This was about a weapon that could affect the entire world, the murder of their family and a special ops team, as well as the apparent kidnapping of their father.

He felt Wyatt's gold gaze on him. Wyatt gave him a single nod, an affirmation that his thoughts were the same. Owen turned to Cullen.

"Fuck yeah, I'm ready to go after these assholes," Cullen stated.

Owen's gaze slid to Callie. In the furor, no one bothered to notice how upset she was. Their father had taken Callie on as a workhand not just because she was good with cattle and horses, but because Orrin saw something in her no one else had.

The ranch and the Loughmans became family to her. Orrin became a father figure, steering her away from the life her family tried to push on her repeatedly. Callie was torn up by the team's death and Orrin's disappearance, but as was customary Callie, she kept it locked tightly away.

That was something she and Wyatt had in common. Not that he would point that out to either of them unless he wanted to be punched.

Callie raised a brow at his silent question. "As if you need to ask. I've been ready to go after Orrin. Why do you think Natalie is here?"

Owen's gaze narrowed on Natalie. He still hadn't figured out how she was a part of all this, and that unsettled him in ways he wasn't yet ready to acknowledge. With the way Callie talked, however, she'd alluded to Natalie being involved.

That was about to change.

He then looked around at the buildings near the house. It appeared as though each of the barns was still being used for the animals. So where was the base?

"You said Dad used the ranch as his home base. Unless he's taken over part of one of the barns, I'm not seeing it," Owen said.

His head turned back to Natalie. Surely not. Surely his father wouldn't have put it so close to the house. With all the acres of property available, why there?

Callie motioned for them to follow her. The direction took them right to Natalie and the horse barn. And his ire grew.

As if sensing his thoughts, Callie said, "Just so you know, Virgil and Charlotte knew about this. It was their idea for Orrin to use the ranch. He picked out a spot on the back five hundred, but Virgil urged him to use something closer."

It didn't surprise Owen at all that Virgil would want

Orrin close. The brothers bickered often, but each one would do anything for the other. They were as close as Owen and his brothers weren't.

Owen felt the resentment rolling off Wyatt in waves. It was always the same whenever anything with Orrin was discussed. Owen kept pace with Callie until they reached the barn. Then he stopped next to Natalie as they moved inside. Only then did Callie shove aside a bale of hay and press a button.

Cullen jumped back as the ground emitted a small noise a second before a piece of earth slid back, revealing narrow, metal stairs. Owen glanced at Natalie to see she wasn't surprised by any of it. He sighed and walked down the stairs after Natalie. He hurried to the bottom, taking in all the computers and electronics as well as several rooms that branched off.

"This way," Callie said as the latch slid closed above and she moved past the four of them.

Wyatt followed her around the line of computers, past a conference room with glass walls and a large black table with plenty of chairs around it, to what appeared to be a wall of metal.

She halted before a steel door and punched in a code. It unlocked with a click. Callie pushed it open and held out a hand for them to take a look.

Cullen let out a whistle. As soon as Owen walked inside and got a glimpse of all the rifles, handguns, grenades, bullets, and other various weapons, as well as night vision goggles and communication devices, he understood.

"Damn," Cullen said with a smile. "A dream come true."

Callie sidled past them to a small laptop in a back corner where Natalie waited. "Take whatever you think you'll need. I need to let the DOD know you're going after Orrin."

"No one said we're going after him," Wyatt declared in a voice devoid of any warmth.

"He's your father," Natalie said in dismay.

Wyatt shrugged. "He got two more family members killed. He should've learned the first time."

Owen sidled between them and held Natalie's gaze for a moment. Then he looked at Callie. "First, Wyatt is an idiot, and we are going after Dad. Second, don't send anything. Whatever we do, we aren't taking orders from the government about this."

"That means we won't get their help either," Cullen pointed out.

Wyatt grunted behind them. "Perhaps that's for the best. We shouldn't trust anyone now."

Owen swiveled his head to Wyatt. "Agreed."

"Ditto," Cullen said.

Wyatt coolly turned away and began gathering weapons.

Owen released a breath and found Natalie watching him. They had yet to have a conversation alone. He wasn't sure what to say. Sorry wasn't nearly enough.

"I think it's time Natalie explained why she's here," Cullen said.

CHAPTER FOUR

Owen had wanted the conversation between him and Natalie done in private, but perhaps it was best that it be done now in front of the others.

That way, he wouldn't be so wrapped up in his conflicted feelings and aching to hold her again.

He waited, eager to hear how she'd gotten pulled into this mess. Once he knew, he could figure out a way to get her out and safely back to her life—as far from him and the danger as he could get her.

"Back in late July, Orrin asked me to meet him for lunch," Natalie began.

Wyatt put a clip in a pistol and turned to her. "Is that something he did often?"

"Never before. It was so odd, that I almost didn't meet him."

"But you did." And Owen wanted to know why.

Callie clicked a pen several times. "It was after we got the request for Orrin and his team to take the mission in Russia. There was something about the orders and Ragnarok that didn't sit right with him."

"How do you know?" Cullen asked. "Did he say something?"

Callie shook her head. "It was the way he acted. I asked him what was wrong, but he told me probably nothing. I saw him doing some research on Russians in the area. Natalie's name came up."

"Because I spent three years in St. Petersburg working before returning to work for the Russian Embassy in Dallas," Natalie explained.

Owen couldn't believe she had lived in Russia. What else had she done? And why did he feel as if he'd been left out of something important.

Because he had. He'd willingly walked away from her. *To keep her safe. To keep her alive.*

"Why Russia?" he asked.

"Orrin wanted to know the same thing," she said with a small smile. "I explained that during college, I learned I was able to pick up languages easily, which led to me changing my degree to linguistics. I favored Italian and Russian. When I was offered a job in Russia, I decided to take it."

Wyatt pulled back the slide on a pistol, letting it click back into place. "So you speak Russian fluently?"

"Yes," she affirmed.

Owen frowned. "Did Dad tell you about his possible assignment?"

"Not a word." Natalie sank onto one of the stools. "He asked me if I had seen or heard anything about Ragnarok."

Wyatt gave a nod of his head as he braced his hands on the table. "Norse mythology."

"It's an end of world scenario," she said. "I hadn't seen or heard anything about Ragnarok. As soon as I told him that, the rest of the lunch went pleasantly with no more such talk. Then, a few weeks later, I saw a report where Ragnarok was mentioned."

"That's when she called me," Callie said. "By that time, Orrin and the team were already in Russia collecting the bioweapon."

"So the bioweapon is Ragnarok," Owen stated.

Natalie glanced at Callie before she said, "Yes. After I saw the report and called Callie, I tried to do some digging into it. When I found nothing, I decided to ask my boss. He became agitated and closed off. The next day, I learned I wasn't allowed in his office without him there."

Cullen raised a brow. "He's got something to hide."

Owen's gaze didn't leave Natalie. He saw the way she fidgeted. There was more to her story.

But Callie beat him to the punch when she said, "That's not all. Tell them, Natalie."

"I learned they were tracking everything I did on my computer at the embassy," Natalie explained. "My clearance was restricted, and I soon found that I was being followed."

"Even outside of work?" Wyatt asked with a frown of worry.

She shrugged. "I don't know."

"Is that everything?" Cullen asked.

Natalie wrinkled her nose. "I wish. I almost didn't go into work today after Callie told me what happened to Virgil and Charlotte, but I decided to head there and do one last search for anything pertaining to Ragnarok.

I knew it couldn't be coincidence that Orrin asked about the very thing no one wanted to talk about. I didn't know about the mission. I only knew he was gone."

"But you put two and two together," Owen said.

She nodded, her green eyes meeting his. "I have a feeling I won't be employed much longer. I snuck back into my boss's office to find the report and read more. I didn't find it. But I did find a piece of paper with my name on it and the word Ragnarock below it. Underneath that was something else—the Saints."

"Who the fuck are the Saints?" Wyatt asked.

Callie shrugged. "I've not had a chance to dig. But she can't look anymore."

Owen couldn't believe Natalie had gone as far as she had. "Absolutely not. Did you find anything on Ragnarok?"

She swallowed loudly. "Before my clearance was lowered, I only found a mention of Ragnarok pertaining to something a scientist was working on in Russia."

"Too bad we don't know more," Cullen said.

Natalie looked at each of them. "I had to come. Not because the embassy knows I'm looking into Ragnarok, but because I might be able to help with the Russians."

"Shit," Wyatt stated in a low voice.

Cullen crossed his arms over his chest. "Dad felt something wasn't right, so he talked to Natalie. The Russians know Natalie is looking into Ragnarok. Our government is leaving Dad hanging in the wind as well as ordering us to give them all intel we come across. This is a shit storm of epic proportions."

"We trust no one but who is in this room," Owen said.

Everyone gave a nod of agreement.

Natalie pushed away from the wall. "If y'all are through with the house, Callie and I can start cleaning up. It won't be long before visitors begin arriving to pay their respects."

"And see another murder here," Cullen murmured.

Owen frowned then. "Where are the bodies?"

"More importantly, where were you two when Virgil and Charlotte were shot?" Wyatt asked the girls.

Callie lifted her gaze to Owen, her face going slack. "I took Master Ben for a ride, checking some of the fences as I did."

Owen couldn't believe the stallion was still around. He'd have to bring the horse an apple.

"I heard the gunfire," Callie continued as she sat straight, her eyes going unfocused. "I raced back as fast as I could, but I was too late. I usually keep to a strict schedule, but I was worried since I hadn't heard from Orrin after they reached Delaware. Virgil suggested I take a ride to clear my head."

Cullen walked to Callie's side. "It's not your fault."

"I might've been able to stop them had I been here." She swallowed hard, her unfocused gaze directed at the wall.

"If you'd been here, they would've killed you, as well," Wyatt pointed out.

Owen nodded slowly. "I'm glad you weren't. Without you, we wouldn't know half of what we do." He then looked to Natalie. "And you?"

"At my house. I was the second call Callie made."

"I'd like to know why she called you," Wyatt said.

Owen would, as well.

"We were doing our own research on Ragnarok here,"

Natalie said. "We were careful never to speak of it over the phone. Anyone listening would think we were just meeting for drinks to chat."

Before he got a chance to ask, Callie said, "Orrin gave me a number to call if anything ever happened to him. The man who answered had me explain the scene, as well as tell him about the last time I heard from Orrin. He ordered me not to touch anything because he was sending a team. Within thirty minutes, a chopper arrived."

"CIA?" Owen asked.

Callie shrugged. "They wouldn't talk to me except to tell me to get out of the house. I watched them take Virgil and Charlotte, as well as gather bullet casings and other evidence. Then they were gone. An hour later, Mark and his men arrived. Though they didn't seem surprised to discover the bodies missing. I didn't ask what he knew."

Owen looked at his brothers. "We will."

"We're going to need that phone number," Wyatt said.

Callie blinked and slid her gaze to him. "Orrin said it was for emergencies only."

"I think this constitutes an emergency." Wyatt's gaze narrowed as he looked her up and down. "Don't you?"

Just when it appeared Callie was about to launch into an argument, Owen said, "Let's all take a few to digest everything."

"And come up with a plan," Cullen added.

Natalie stood from her place on the stool. "I'll start cleaning up."

"I'll help since I'm finished gathering what little evidence was left," Cullen said after looking longingly around at the base.

Owen slapped him on the shoulder. "You'll be back, kid. Then you can play in here for as long as you want."

"Stop calling me that," Cullen growled.

After Owen and Wyatt had a look around the ops center and went through emails, they returned to the house to help the others.

For the next two hours, the five of them worked to remove any trace of blood from the residence while discussing different plans of attack. At one point, Owen looked up to see Wyatt helping Cullen take the recliner out behind one of the barns.

At the same time, a white Chevy Suburban drove up.

"Mrs. Turnbill," Natalie said as she went to the door.

CHAPTER FIVE

"We brought food," Mrs. Turnbill said as she handed Callie a large, covered dish.

The other three ladies followed Wanda and handed dishes to Cullen, Wyatt, and Owen, who were forced to step out onto the porch.

"Get the tea, Natalie," Mrs. Turnbill urged.

Natalie turned, her legs feeling wooden and her stomach unsure if it should remain in her throat or plummet to her feet. This was how she'd felt since first seeing Owen again.

It was worse when that chocolate gaze of his landed on her. Then she couldn't remember which way was right and which was left.

While they'd been cleaning, she'd had a task to focus on, something to do other than try to keep her hands off Owen. Now, there was company.

But that company made her think of those responsible for Virgil's and Charlotte's deaths. Were they lurking somewhere, waiting to strike again?

Her gaze landed on Owen. She didn't want him to know how frightened she'd been up until he arrived. To realize that she'd been followed made her sick to her stomach.

What was this Ragnarok that people would kill for? Surely this wasn't the only bioweapon Russia had. No. It meant that there was something special about Ragnarok.

"Natalie?"

She jumped, remembering that she wasn't alone. The bioweapon was quickly forgotten as Owen's eyes met hers briefly. She shot Mrs. Turnbill a smile, then the elderly lady said her name again.

It took everything she had to make herself walk to the back of the Suburban. Her hands shook so badly that it took two tries to get the doors open. Owen was the only man to ever make her so anxious. Even after all these years, he still had the same effect on her.

Natalie grabbed the two jugs of sweet tea and turned. She came to a halt when she found Wyatt standing there. She took in his thick beard, which hid most of his face, and his gold eyes trained on her.

There was a flicker of annoyance in those golden depths. "What are you doing here?" he demanded in a soft voice that did nothing to hide his anger.

"I explained that pretty clearly."

His gaze remained locked with hers. "Is that the only reason?"

"I know you never liked me, Wyatt, but you were gone when Owen left. He's the one who called it off. Not me."

"You think I don't like you."

She blinked. Was that a question or a comment? And

that's all he was going to say about her statement? "I know you don't like me."

"I've never given that indication."

Natalie shifted the gallon jugs. The handles were pinching her fingers. "Don't worry. I'm not here for Owen."

"Really."

Again, she wasn't sure if it was a question or not. Natalie moved around him. "Really."

She walked up the porch steps and tried to hand the sweet tea to Cullen, but the youngest Loughman merely smiled and opened the screen door for her.

Natalie was pretty sure they had all lost their minds. She just wanted to give the tea to someone and get back to searching for Orrin and Ragnarok.

Mrs. Turnbill was setting the dishes in the fridge when she saw Natalie. She then glared at Owen. "Don't just stand there, son. Help her."

Mrs. Turnbill had a way of inflecting her voice that could get anyone into action thanks to her years as a teacher. Owen was no different. He reacted instantly, reaching for the tea.

Their hands touched. A tingling sensation rushed up her arm and into her chest. She looked up at him. Their gazes clashed, held, as heat and desire simmered between them.

Fourteen years hadn't dulled the passion. It had only intensified it.

Natalie scrubbed her hands on her jeans and took a step back. She turned and found Cullen and Wyatt blocking the exit to the front door.

"I'm sorry about Virgil and Charlotte. They were good people," Mrs. Turnbill told the boys.

Cullen's smile was sad. "That they were. They were able to get a handle on all three of us as no one else could. They'll be sorely missed."

"I hope you find who did this," she said.

"Seen anyone around town out of the ordinary?" Cullen asked her.

The old woman shook her head of white hair before looking at her friends. "No, we haven't. Do you think whoever did this is still around?"

"We don't know," Owen replied.

Then it hit Natalie. She'd been young when Owen's mother was murdered, but it had been the talk of the small town for months. Everyone speculated that it was because of Orrin's work with the military, especially when the FBI showed up. As far as Natalie knew, Melanie Loughman's case had never been solved.

Now there were two more murders after Orrin had returned to town. Coincidence? She doubted it.

She made her escape from the house after a few minutes. She walked across the yard to the paddock and held out her hand to the filly. The foal wouldn't come to her, but the mare did. Natalie rubbed the horse's forehead. Owen had given her a love of horses. She'd always admired the beautiful creatures, but she hadn't known how much fun it was to ride until Owen.

"Nat."

Her hand stilled and her heart missed a beat at the sound of his voice. She glanced over her shoulder as she continued to pet the mare, the foal coming closer before backing off at the last minute.

"Hi," she finally answered.

"We haven't had a chance to talk alone."

She rubbed her cheek on the sleeve of her shirt. "I know." She turned to face him. "You look good."

His smile was warm. "So do you. I thought you were leaving this small town and never coming back?"

"Yeah," she said with a small laugh. "It's not as bad as I used to think."

Dark eyes watched her.

She lowered her gaze to his sun-kissed skin. He always had a golden glow about him, but his tan was darker, speaking of many days outside. It fit the desert camo.

"So, a SEAL?" she asked. She'd found out from Callie. It hadn't surprised her that he would be the one to follow in his father's footsteps.

"Yep."

That explained so much about him, from his bearing to his body and the way he surveyed things as if he were sizing everything up as a threat assessment.

Silence stretched between them, becoming almost awkward. She was searching for something to say when Mrs. Turnbill and the others walked from the house.

"Take care of yourself, Owen," Mrs. Turnbill called as she got into the SUV.

Natalie used their departure as an excuse to go back into the house. Anything to get away from the emotions she was struggling with regarding Owen. "I should help Callie with all the food."

She wasn't surprised when Owen didn't stop her. Though a part of her really wished he had.

It was hours later before she had a moment to herself. Her nerves were on end from the close proximity to Owen and the threat that hung over them.

Callie came up to her as she headed toward the front door. "The boys are in the living room talking."

Good. Nat couldn't handle another confrontation with Owen right then. "I think I'm going to head back to Mom's house and shower. After that, I'm going to grab a glass of wine and try to sleep."

"Stay here," Callie urged.

She looked around the house. "I don't think so."

"What about the group who attacked?"

She walked onto the porch and down to her car with Callie beside her. "It's just for tonight. I'll gather my things and stay at the ranch after that. I just need—"

"To be alone," Callie finished. "I understand."

Natalie had felt the tension between Callie and Wyatt, but she thought better of mentioning it. "It's just a few hours."

"A lot can happen in a few hours."

"I'm not that far, and I have my gun."

Callie shook her head and pulled out her cell phone. She dialed a number and put the phone to her ear. "Hey, Mark. Can you send someone to watch over Diane Dixon's house tonight." There was a pause from Callie. "That's right. Natalie will be there. Great. Thanks."

"You've got to be kidding me," she said.

Callie shrugged. "I'm not losing anyone else. Precaution is key, my friend. A deputy should be there by the time you arrive."

She could only smile as she got in the BMW. It was nice to have such a friend. She waved at Callie as she drove off.

After a long night of visitors, small talk, and fielding questions about when the service for Virgil and Charlotte would be, Owen walked out onto the porch hours before dawn with a cup of coffee.

Somewhere out in the night, Cullen kept watch. Owen stared into the darkness, recalling how vast the ranch was—and the many areas an enemy could hide.

As had been the case since the moment Natalie had come back into his life with all the force of a tornado, she crept into his thoughts and consumed him.

He wondered if she and Callie were together, talking about him. That was wishful thinking on his part. Natalie had done her best not to be alone with him again.

While he did everything he could to get her alone.

There was so much he wanted to know about their years apart. He wanted every detail, to see every picture, and hear her every thought.

After he'd left graduation night, he'd done everything he could to put her out of his mind. He'd gone on to have a life. In his mind, Nat had remained in Hillsboro. He'd never imagined her going off to St. Petersburg to work.

It made him realize that she'd also gone on with her life. In the back of his mind, he'd always known that. But he hadn't known what she was doing. Now he did.

And it was a reminder that he wasn't part of her life anymore.

The screen door creaked as it was opened, and Wyatt

walked out. He came to stand beside Owen, the two staring silently across the land.

"I'll take the next watch," Wyatt said.

Owen sipped his coffee. "There's a lot of land out there to cover."

"Callie's already thought of that. She was mumbling something about getting things in order earlier."

"Those bastards will be back."

"Without a doubt," Wyatt agreed. "I don't want anyone sneaking up on us. I don't know what Callie has planned, but we need to get it implemented ASAP. She was damn lucky not to be here before."

Owen was nodding his head when he recalled Nat mentioning she felt someone was following her. There was a high probability that she was being tailed, and Owen was going to find out tomorrow.

The screen door banged a second before the light switched on overhead. Wyatt whirled around, cussing as Owen took a step back out of the rays of light.

He looked to find Callie holding a leather bag that looked to be a cross between a briefcase and a purse. Her face was devoid of color.

"Callie?" Owen said, suddenly worried.

She swallowed and held up the bag. "This is Natalie's."

"So go bring it to her," Wyatt replied.

But Callie was already shaking her head. "I can't. She's not here."

Owen felt a stab of fear knife through him. "What do you mean she's not here?"

"She went to get her things at her Mom's. Natalie

planned to stay the night there and come back in the morning."

"Have both of you lost your fucking minds?" Wyatt demanded angrily. "Did you forget about all the blood we cleaned up earlier?"

Callie shook her head and gave him a withering glare. "Of course not, dickhead. I called Mark. He sent a deputy to keep watch."

That made Owen feel a little better, but he still wasn't happy that Natalie left. "What do you have?" he asked, nodding to the briefcase.

"She had some papers out earlier. I picked them up to put them back when I saw the file."

Owen's gaze dropped to the bag and the glimpse of pages he saw had been hastily shoved inside. "What did you see?"

"The bold red letters gave me pause. It's something in Russian I looked up, and I'm glad I Googled it. It's a classified document that isn't addressed to Natalie."

Wyatt lifted one shoulder. "It could be her work."

"Or it could be that she accidentally picked up something she shouldn't have." Owen's mind spun with possibilities, and he didn't like any of them.

Callie said, "She never should have left the ranch."

"I'm going after her," Owen said. He didn't need to hear any more. Natalie was in trouble.

After what had happened to his mother, Owen wouldn't allow the same fate to befall Natalie. Not if he could do something about it.

He'd left her behind for this very reason. Nothing was going to stop him from getting to her on time. She wouldn't die because of him or her connection to his family.

Wyatt tossed his coffee out, a grim look on his face. "They may be watching her house."

"It's time we put our skills to use then." Owen turned on his heel. Whether he wanted it or not, Natalie was back in his life—at least for the time being.

He'd keep her safe. Just as he would find the people responsible and end their miserable lives.

"If y'all hurry, you can get her out of the house and back here within the hour," Callie said.

Wyatt smiled. "My kind of mission."

CHAPTER SIX

The last time Natalie looked at the clock it was well after two in the morning. Ever since she'd left the Loughman Ranch, Owen's image and memories of their year together wouldn't leave her.

They churned through her mind on replay, reminding her of everything that had been wonderful—and everything that had gone so terribly wrong.

Research on Ragnarok—or any bioweapon—only jumbled her mind, bringing her thoughts right back to Owen. She didn't find anything useful anyway. Attempting to sleep proved just as ridiculous. Closing her eyes brought him into focus even more.

She thought about how close he'd stood to her just hours before.

How he'd touched her, and her body responded as if it had been fourteen minutes since he'd last held her and not fourteen years.

How deep his voice had been. That sexy, roughened Texas drawl had always made her stomach flutter. When they'd graduated, he'd been on the cusp of adulthood.

A man in all his powerful and masculine glory had stood before her earlier.

Owen hadn't been like most teenagers. He'd always been determined and motivated. He'd known what he wanted—and what he didn't. And just like his brothers, he kept most everything to himself.

While she'd been wondering what to do with her life, Owen had known all along what his future held. And it hadn't been her.

She'd thought they were so close. While she spilled every secret, wish, and desire, Owen had slowly been closing himself off to her. She'd been so absorbed with graduating and attending college that she hadn't noticed him pulling away. Until he was gone.

For years, she blamed him. It was only over the last five that she realized the fault lay with her. She was the one too blind to see the changes. Perhaps if she had, she would've been able to talk to him.

But in the end, it all would've turned out exactly as it had.

Owen hadn't loved her enough to stay. Not like he'd told her he had. The obligation running through all Loughmans to serve their country was stronger than anything else.

Even love.

Natalie must have finally dozed off to sleep after tossing and turning. She was dreaming of Owen. She knew it was a dream, because he was with her, whispering her name as he caressed her face.

Then they were racing across the ranch atop horses with moonlight cascading around them, carefree and in love. Laughing, with a future together waiting for them.

A hand clamped over her mouth. Natalie's eyes flew open as fear froze her in place.

"Nat."

Owen. She stared at the face hidden in shadows above her. Every shred of light was gone from the nightlight in the hallway to the streetlamp outside.

"We need to leave," Owen whispered, the urgency in his words forcing her to take in the situation.

Despite the fact that it had been years since she'd seen Owen, she knew him well enough to know that he wouldn't have broken into her house as a joke. He was here for a reason.

And that reason was the Russians.

She knew without being told that they must've been following her. Without asking questions, she rolled out of bed. His hand on her back pushed her low to the ground. How was she supposed to get any clothes on?

Natalie would figure something out. She crawled toward her suitcase, but Owen's arm wound around her waist as he lifted her and turned her to the window.

She halted, because she wasn't going out in her nightgown. But Owen had other ideas when he gave her a firm push. She looked back at him but still couldn't see his face.

There was an air of danger, of necessity she couldn't shake. Natalie decided against talking and did exactly as Owen wanted.

When she reached the window, she felt a cool breeze. This window was usually stuck. How was it that Owen had not only opened it but also did it so she hadn't heard?

She rose on her knees and peered out the window. In the next second, she was on her back with Owen on top of her. His weight reminded her of balmy nights spent beneath the stars together.

Of endless passion and never-ending kisses.

Of whispered promises.

Of love.

She closed her eyes and put the moment to memory. One of his legs lay between hers. She fought to remain still even as desire pulsed within her.

But he didn't move. She began to wonder if he was even breathing. Fear began to nestle uncomfortably in her stomach. Something was very wrong.

Seconds turned to minutes. Then she heard the call of a Hoot owl. Except it wasn't an owl. It was one of the Loughmans. She remembered how they'd perfected the calls of several native Texas animals while out hunting.

At the call, Owen rolled off her. In the next instant, she was once more in his arms as he lifted her out the window. Natalie bit her lip to prepare for her bare feet to hit the ground littered with pinecones and numerous other plants that were just waiting to puncture the sensitive skin on the bottom of a foot.

Except her feet never touched the ground. She found herself in Wyatt's arms while Cullen shoved a pair of boots on her feet. And they weren't cowboy boots. They felt heavier and much too big.

Then it didn't matter as Owen was suddenly beside her. She was set on her feet as Owen's fingers wrapped around her wrist.

They didn't take off running as she expected. They moved quietly and slowly from one tree to the other. Though the moon was out in the clear sky, it was only a fingernail and didn't allow much in the way of light.

But Natalie still saw that it was Wyatt who led them, and Cullen who brought up the rear. Natalie was plastered to Owen's body—her back to his front. His large hand was splayed over her stomach, guiding her.

Suddenly, a shadow came out of nowhere with a gun aimed at her. Owen shoved her aside. Natalie tripped over her too-large boots and fell to her hands and knees, scraping her skin. When she looked over her shoulder, Owen was locked in combat with a faceless man.

She waited for his brothers to join in, and that's when she realized all three were fighting. Natalie heard a grunt from her left. Then she heard a soft *pop, pop* that she recognized as a gun with a silencer, and the bark of the tree she was against splintered near her face.

Someone had tried to shoot her. With her heart pounding, she ducked her head and scampered to another tree. She flattened her back to it, her gaze darting around the area, attempting to peer into the darkness.

Every breath felt like an eternity as she waited for Owen or his brothers to finish and find her, but the seconds stretched endlessly.

She heard something off to her left and realized someone was coming around to her. Natalie wasn't going to sit and wait to be killed. They were going to have to work if they wanted her dead.

Slipping off the big boots, she used the tree to help her to her feet and glanced at the Loughmans. She couldn't take her eyes off Owen. It didn't matter how many movies she'd seen, witnessing such combat in close proximity was completely different.

And it drove home the danger.

Natalie bent low and moved to her right, toward

Owen and his brothers. She came to another tree and used it as a shield. Yet she couldn't find whoever was after her.

Her gaze returned to Owen. Each time a fist connected with skin, every crunch of bone, and every gurgle of pain she recoiled.

She winced when Owen got hit, and silently celebrated every strike he landed.

Then she heard something behind her. Her heart thumped wildly as she tried to dash away, but a big, meaty hand roughly grabbed her arm.

She was yanked around, and a gun shoved in her face.

"Now you die," said a voice in a thick Russian accent.

She fought the man with everything she had. He was tall, and his massive hands held her as easily as if she were a child. She kicked and clawed until he backhanded her across her cheek, snapping her neck back.

She thought she heard someone shout her name, but she was struggling to stay conscious as darkness crept into the edges of her vision. Then she was falling, landing hard on the cold ground.

Someone touched her hair, and she tried to roll away. They held her easily. "It's me, Natalie," Cullen said.

That's when she heard the loud grunts and the sound of bones breaking. Natalie raised her head to see Wyatt standing next to a dead body while Owen fought another.

It wasn't much of a fight. Owen stood over the man who was on his knees attempting to deflect Owen's blows to no avail. Then she saw the gleam of moonlight off something.

A knife.

She couldn't dredge up an ounce of pity as Owen

plunged the blade into the man's heart. If it hadn't been for Owen and his brothers, those men would've gotten her.

The deputy! "There is a—"

"They got to him first," Wyatt whispered. "Just knocked him unconscious."

"We're leaving now." Cullen helped her to her feet.

Owen was at her side again, leading her away from the scene. Cullen must have put her boots back on her, because once more, she fought to keep them on.

She lost track of time as she searched the darkness for anything to recall where they were while she stumbled her way around. Several times, Owen would halt while either Wyatt or Cullen disappeared, only to return a few moments later.

Natalie shivered in the night air. If only she still slept in her boxer PJs, she wouldn't be feeling so . . . exposed. Though she thought she knew her mother's yard and the surrounding woods well enough, Natalie became lost within minutes of leaving the house. She didn't even know which direction they were traveling in.

Of course, that could have something to do with having her head rattled after such a hit.

Fear and anxiety were taking a toll. Combined with her lack of sleep and the attack, the only thing keeping her on her feet was adrenaline. And when that faded, she was likely to pass out.

It seemed like hours before she felt Owen's muscles relax a little. Then she saw why when they crested a hill and she looked down on the Loughman Ranch. With a slight tug, Owen pulled her down as he squatted. She fell to her knees exhausted.

In all this time, none of them had spoken a word. She hadn't slapped at the mosquitos biting her or cried out when she swept against a bush with stickers that cut her arms and legs.

Cullen rested his hand on Owen's shoulder, and then he walked away, blending into the darkness as if it swallowed him whole. With a nod, Wyatt did the same in the opposite direction.

She and Owen remained where they were. In all the time they'd walked, Owen's hold on her hadn't lessened. He kept her tight against him.

Truth be told, it made her feel safe.

Then again, she'd always felt that way with him, even before he was a SEAL.

With the sounds of the night lulling her against the warmth of Owen's body, she snuggled closer and felt her eyes burn. She shut them for just a moment.

Owen knew the instant Natalie fell asleep. He kept her upright so she didn't fall while her head lolled to the side. Without thinking, he rested his chin atop her head.

He'd never been so scared as when he spotted one of the Russians with Natalie. Owen had reacted instantly—and with lethal force. They could've taken her away to rape, torture, or kill.

And it had set him off as few things could.

Later, he was sure his brothers would ask him about it. Right now, he just wanted Natalie at the ranch where he could keep her safe.

Being with Natalie in the dark reminded him of the

times they'd snuck out to make love under the stars. It didn't matter how many women came after her, he only ever saw her face.

Owen wished it wasn't a life and death situation that had them in such a position now. He wished he'd returned to Texas sooner. He wished he wouldn't have left that fateful night so long ago.

But he'd left because Natalie was the one thing that could've made him stay. He knew what they shared was something special, something that only came around once in a lifetime.

The sound of first one, then a second whistle from each of his brothers told him it was clear. He hesitated. He didn't want to wake Natalie. Once he did, the reality of the night would come crashing down around her.

"Nat," he whispered.

It took a moment before she raised her head and remembered where they were. He looked at her and nodded. Only when she returned the nod did they stand, their fingers linking as they walk from the trees.

Her back was straight, her gaze forward, but she held his hand as if her very life depended on it. Regardless of their past, at least she knew he would protect her.

The one thing Owen had always wanted to be was a hero in her eyes. Tonight, he'd gotten his wish. It was the circumstances that made his stomach turn. Natalie should never be involved in anything like this.

It was life and death from here on out.

Which meant her life was in his hands. It was a heavy weight he carried, but he did it gladly. Because it was Natalie.

Because she meant everything to him.

They ran across the yard toward the house. When they approached, Owen saw a shape step from the shadows. Callie opened the door so he and Nat could rush inside.

"I was getting worried," Callie said.

Owen checked out the window before he turned to Natalie. His mouth went dry as he took his first look at her in the light. She wore a skimpy gown that fell to the tops of her thighs, held on to her shoulders by thin straps. It was black silk with cream lace around the top and bottom.

His balls tightened as he realized that's what she slept in. That was the material he'd felt against his hand all night. It gave no more protection than a whisper.

Owen hadn't thought about what she was wearing. His only goal had been to get her out of the house before the Russians arrived.

His gaze took in the numerous scratches and bites on her chest, arms, and legs. Natalie wrapped her arms around herself and shivered.

Before Owen could pull his mind away from imagining stripping her out of the gown, Callie draped a blanket around her shoulders.

Natalie grasped it tightly, bringing it around to hide the black silk from view. "Thank you," she said to Callie.

"No problem." Callie then threw Owen a dark look.

He jerked his chin to the kitchen. "I'm sure Natalie could use some coffee."

"And clothes," Callie murmured as she walked past him.

Though Callie was curt with him, her hand was gentle when she turned to Natalie and guided her into the kitchen. He followed, standing in the doorway as Natalie sank into a chair at the table and Callie poured two cups of coffee. Owen declined the cup, which Callie kept for herself.

Natalie stared at the table after she'd fixed her coffee. Callie leaned her back against the counter while holding her mug between both hands, looking between him and Natalie.

"Are they all dead?" she asked and lifted her deep green eyes to his.

He wanted nothing more than to tell her a lie. He didn't want her dragged into the mess Orrin had created, but there was no way around it now. His father had put her there, and she'd willingly walked into it all.

In situations like this, the worst thing a person could do was lie. Natalie's life was on the line, and she needed to understand that.

Because there was about to be a drastic change she would more than likely fight.

"Yes, they're all dead," Owen told her.

Natalie took a sip of the coffee then nodded. "Thank you."

"It's what I do."

"How did you know they were there?"

Callie spoke before he could. "I found a file in your papers."

"A file?" A frown puckered Natalie's brow.

Callie pulled the folder from Natalie's bag and slid it

across the table. He watched as Nat's face paled as she opened it and read the pages. "Oh, my God."

"I know it's marked classified. That's the only word I looked up," Callie said.

Owen moved to stand beside Natalie in order to see the file. "What does it say?"

"No wonder they came after me. I grabbed this by mistake, but if I'd known it was there, I would've taken it anyway."

He drew in a deep breath and slowly released it. "What is it exactly?"

"Me." Her green eyes lifted to him. "This is essentially a hit taken out on me."

For a heartbeat, Owen could only look at her, his brain digesting the news. This couldn't be happening. He'd left Natalie to make sure nothing like this ever touched her, and here she was, smack dab in the middle of a pile of shit too tall to climb over.

"It lists my address, my mother's address, and all known associates," she continued.

Callie nodded. "Of course, they wanted to know where you might go if you happened to get past them."

"The ranch is listed, as well."

"Because you and Callie were talking," he said. "You set off alarms all through the embassy digging into Ragnarok." Owen could only imagine the things the Russians had seen and heard Natalie doing each time she spoke with Callie.

Callie ran a hand through her hair, pulling the ponytail out as she did. "I don't like this. We were careful not to discuss specifics on the phone."

"That doesn't matter," he said, waving away her words. "Nat's snooping made her a target. They let her live only because they hoped she might lead them to the bioweapon."

Natalie looked from him to Callie and back to him. "And now?"

"Now that my brothers and I are here, you're in the way. They've pieced together that you don't know anything."

Callie twisted her lip. "I really want to put an end to these assholes."

"We will," he promised. There was no other way. It had to be done. And they couldn't waste another second. "However, we can use them, as well."

Callie shook her head. "That's a dangerous game."

"Do we have a choice?" Natalie asked.

An image of the asshole backhanding Natalie flashed in his mind. "No, we don't. We have no idea where Orrin is or how to find him. The Russians are the best chance we have."

"And Ragnarok?" Callie asked.

He lifted one shoulder in a shrug. "We find Orrin, we find the weapon."

Callie sat her mug down next to the sink. "Let's get busy, then."

Owen couldn't take his gaze off Natalie. She hadn't yet realized the impact of what had happened tonight, but she would soon enough.

The first step was isolating her from everything. If the Russian group wanted her, they would have to go through him to get her. And that would never happen.

It was right that she was now staying at the ranch. She belonged there.

She belonged with him.

Always had. Always would.

CHAPTER SEVEN

Natalie could only stare at the paper that so casually called for her to be killed. It left her . . . shaken. Cold.

Terrified.

Had Owen not come, she would be dead now. All because she'd looked up Ragnarok. Whatever this bio-weapon was, she was glad Orrin had hidden it to keep it out of Russian—or US—hands.

She heard Owen talking behind her. Natalie didn't need to turn around to know he was speaking to his brothers. Now that she was safe in the house, the horrors that occurred earlier rushed back to her.

The sound of the gun, the spray of the bark. The sight of the muzzle of the pistol pointed at her face. Her cheek hurt from the hit, but it was nothing compared to running for her life.

Her mind drifted to Owen. He'd been calm, as if he experienced such things on a daily basis. And that's what saved her life.

She recalled how he'd fought ruthlessly and without an ounce of compassion. Natalie could never do such a thing, but then again, she wasn't a soldier like the Lough-mans.

Owen and his brothers did what they had to do for their country and those they loved. They didn't stop to think of the consequences or if it might get them killed. They reacted instantly.

"Oh, girl," Callie said as she sat next to Natalie at the table. "It's a good thing Owen isn't seeing this face of yours now. He'd have you in his bed in the next second."

In his bed. In his arms. Beneath the night sky. She'd take any of it. To be alive after coming so close to death.

"He made a choice. I wasn't what he picked," she said.

Callie eyed her. "But you still have feelings for him."

"I've had enough of men, and enough of coming in second."

At this, Callie snorted. "Men are pigs."

"Amen. How different my life would be if I hadn't married my ex."

"Wouldn't have's, couldn't have's, and shouldn't have's. It's safer to leave those out of conversations. You can't change the past. It's already done. Looking back only keeps you there."

She knew Callie was right, but it was hard not to go through her memories of Owen because there had been some truly wonderful times. "I'd be dead if it weren't for Owen."

"Do you regret your involvement in the whole Ragn-arok thing?"

Natalie shot her a wry look. "I told you from the first, no."

"They weren't following you or attempting to kill you then."

True. That was also before she comprehended how important Orrin's mission was. "It doesn't change anything. I'm in this now whether I want to be or not. And I don't want out. I want to find these guys and those giving the orders. Someone has to pay for the murders they've committed."

"These people have no idea who the Loughmans are. I almost feel sorry for them," Callie said. Then she smiled. "Almost."

Natalie returned Callie's smile. It hadn't taken them long to strike up a friendship. Even though Natalie remembered Callie from before, they hadn't exactly hung out.

As a young girl, Callie had been beautiful. The kind of gorgeous you saw on magazine covers or the movies. But Callie's was all-natural. She didn't wear makeup, and always kept her hair long so she could pull it back or braid it.

Natalie burrowed deeper into the blanket. "The Russians could be anywhere."

"They won't touch you, trust me. Owen lost his mother to such brutality. He just lost the two people who raised him in a heinous way. You won't be added to the list."

"I know he won't let anything happen to me or you, but I am going to help. He'd better get used to that idea."

Callie chuckled. "I'm sure you'll have no problem convincing him of that."

"I'm going to need some clothes. My bags are still at my mother's house, and I don't have time for a trip to Dallas."

"For now, there are some fatigues in my stuff that'll work."

"Not exactly my style, but it'll be better than what I'm wearing. I'd like to be more covered the next time I talk to Owen."

Callie laughed as she walked from the kitchen. "You might rethink that if you'd seen Owen's expression."

Now Natalie wished she had seen Owen's look. Flirting with that kind of passion again was setting herself up for heartbreak, but she couldn't seem to help it when it came to Owen Loughman.

He'd had her heart from the moment he asked her out.

Natalie rose and followed Callie, glancing to see that the brothers had moved out onto the porch. "You know, I held on to him and our love for a long time, and in the process, I ruined several relationships because I couldn't admit he was gone."

Callie walked up the stairs, glancing back as she reached the landing. She halted near a closed bedroom door. "How did you let go?"

"With difficulty," Natalie admitted. She stopped, memories flooding her. "I thought Owen was the one I'd marry, the man I'd spend the rest of my life with. His need to serve was stronger than any love we had. Discovering that, and allowing it to sink into my brain, was how I was able to slowly let go."

Callie slid her gaze to one of the doors farther down the hall—Owen's bedroom. "And now?"

Natalie twisted her lips. "It's like I never learned to let go. All those feelings are back again."

"Damn," Callie said softly.

Natalie shrugged. "I learned my lesson, though. I won't go down that road again."

"Good luck with that." Callie opened the door and waved for Natalie to follow. "I moved some of my gear up here last night."

"Moved? You mean you haven't been living in the house?"

Callie chuckled as she opened one of the bureau drawers. "Yeah, the brothers assumed the same thing. I live on the ranch, just not in the house. There're some old bunk houses that I renovated."

"The guys didn't like you out there alone, huh?"

"I didn't want to be out there alone." She grabbed a few things and pushed the drawer shut before she stood. "I may like to be on my own, but I like being alive."

Natalie smiled at her. "Smart."

"That I am. One day the guys will know that, as well."

There was more to the story, but Natalie knew she wasn't going to hear it right then. Perhaps later she might ask Owen.

"Here you go," Callie said and handed over the stack of clothes. Callie walked out and down to the next room, opening the door for Natalie. "It's just us here. The guys are guarding the place, so if you want to sleep, go ahead."

Natalie didn't get to respond as Callie left with a smile. Natalie walked into the room and closed the door behind her. After she set the clothes aside, she sank onto the bed with a sigh.

She fell back, her gaze going to the ceiling. At one

point, when she and Owen were deep into their relationship and talking about the future, she'd actually thought the house would be hers.

With how much Wyatt hated the ranch, everyone knew he would leave and never return. Owen was the next eldest, so would inherit. Natalie had envisioned their children running around, learning to ride horses, and helping work the ranch.

How naïve she'd been. Her mother even cautioned her not to get her hopes too high while shoving Natalie toward rich men from Dallas.

Natalie sat up and threw off the blanket. Then she removed her gown and began to dress. The only thing she was missing was a bra, but it wasn't as if she really needed anything. She never had much in the way of breasts. Ant bites her mother used to call them.

This was one time she didn't mind not needing a bra. She left the shirt untucked and looked down at herself. The black fatigues and shirt were just like the ones Owen had worn.

The boots they'd shoved on her feet were too big, so she left them off but put on the socks. A quick look at herself in the mirror and fingers combed through her hair, then Natalie left the room.

She folded the blanket and brought it back downstairs. She found Callie standing in the living room with the lights out, looking through the window.

"Three men can't guard this entire ranch," she said.

Callie shot her a look. "They're not going to be doing it alone."

With all the training Callie had gone through with the FBI while training to join and then working with Orrin, Natalie could well imagine how proficient Callie was to help the brothers.

The same couldn't be said for Natalie. She knew her way around a gun, thanks to lessons from Owen. Ever since then, Natalie made sure to keep up her training.

She'd also taken a few self-defense classes. A woman living on her own—in any country—needed to be able to defend herself. But none of her training meant much with what was going on. Yet, she wasn't going to sit by and do nothing.

Owen remained at his post high in a tree as lookout while his brothers finished putting the final touches on the plan they'd come up with as the sky lightened. He was farthest from the house, but he knew Wyatt and Cullen wouldn't let anyone near the girls.

He couldn't stop seeing Natalie lying on the ground with the big guy over her. In all Owen's missions and all the people he'd protected, not once had he ever lost control as he had then.

All Owen wanted was the Russian's blood, to feel the life draining from him for threatening Natalie. Never mind the fact that the man was probably part of the team that had killed his aunt and uncle.

Death was something Owen had gotten used to as a SEAL. It was part of his life, part of what he was trained for. He'd never taken pleasure in killing. Until last night.

Knowing there were more in the group out there had him on high alert. They had gotten onto the ranch without being detected before. That wasn't going to happen again. It didn't matter that it was just he and his two brothers watching over several thousand acres.

He would do what had to be done as he always did.

His thoughts then turned to Orrin. What had caused his father to seek out Natalie? Something raised a red flag, and Owen wished he knew what it was.

There was no doubt his father was good at what he did. Several of Orrin's missions were used as examples in the SEALs training of how to complete an operation successfully.

If there was one thing Owen knew above all else, it was to listen to his instincts. They didn't lie. For whatever reason, Orrin hadn't listened to his and had taken the mission anyway. It had cost Orrin his team's lives, as well as Virgil's and Charlotte's.

Would it end up costing Orrin his own?

Inevitably, Owen's thoughts returned to Natalie. In the years since walking away from her, he'd convinced himself that what he felt had been in his mind.

Then he'd come face to face with her again, and he realized how deeply he'd lied to himself. His love had only been dormant, waiting to see her again before it flared, consuming him.

That love teased him with glimpses of how his life could be with Natalie beside him. The more he saw, the more he wanted. And the longer Natalie was with him, the more it became clear that he was half a man without her.

It was a hell of a thing to realize fourteen years after leaving someone. The one good thing was that she wasn't married. That didn't mean she wasn't taken, though.

Jealousy roared within Owen. Natalie was meant to be his. And he was prepared to fight for her.

Then he recalled why he'd left her the night of grad-uation. It all came back to his mother's murder and Or-rin's part in it.

Natalie had always been full of life and laughter. She deserved a future with a man who was with her, not home occasionally in between assignments.

A whistle sounded, breaking into Owen's thoughts. He turned, thankful to see Cullen walking toward him with a black duffle bag over his shoulder.

Owen took one more look around for intruders and climbed from the tree. He landed beside his brother and nodded to the bag. "What's that?"

"Something to help out after we're gone. This is just the start of Callie's bag of tricks," Cullen said as he set the bag down and unzipped in.

Owen was impressed when he looked inside and saw multiple wireless cameras. "Wish we'd known about this yesterday."

"This will keep you alerted if visitors do drop by."

"Good."

"Let's get these set up," Cullen said.

Owen took a handful. "Has Wyatt told Callie?"

"Not yet." There was a smile on Cullen's face. "I think he's putting it off."

"He's probably waiting for me so we can tell both the girls at the same time."

Cullen nodded. "Probably. Natalie is at the base wait-ing for me to radio when the cameras are up so we can test them."

He paused at the mention of Natalie's name. He slung the strap of his rifle over his shoulder as they walked to the left. "All right."

"I got a look at the logbook Dad kept of the missions. Shit, Owen. They did everything. Some I'd have liked to have participated in."

Owen smiled. If there was one thing Cullen enjoyed, it was danger. The more of it there was, the more he wanted to be involved. Some things never changed.

"Where's Callie?" he asked.

"Seeing to the livestock with Wyatt covertly watching her."

Owen chuckled at the image. "That's not going to go over well."

"It will as long as Callie doesn't see him. And she won't."

No, Callie would never see Wyatt watching her, just as Natalie had never seen the Russians. Natalie. It always came back to her.

For the next forty minutes, he and Cullen set the cameras in hidden places in the area surrounding the house, barns, and several paddocks. Though they would take turns on patrol for a larger perimeter. The cameras were set to send an alert to their phones as well as the computers at the base if anyone walked near.

There was the potential of receiving a ton of alerts with all the wildlife and the animals on the property, but it was worth it to know if the Russian group got close again.

"They're all up and working," Natalie's voice came over the walkie-talkie. "That last one needs to be turned to the left and up just a hair."

Owen did as requested. A moment later, Natalie gave them the okay.

He and Cullen then headed back to the barn. He found himself wondering what Natalie thought about what he'd done the night before. She hadn't seemed outraged in seeing him kill the Russian.

Once they reached the barn, they made their way below to the base. Owen pretended to listen as Cullen spoke of his excitement at some of the weapons available to them.

He nodded, murmuring, "Yeah," when Cullen stopped talking.

"So you want to use it to shoot Wyatt in the ass?"

Owen jerked his head up from wiping down his gun. "What?"

"I knew you weren't listening. Your response just proved it."

"Sorry. My thoughts are somewhere else."

"You mean on *someone* else," Cullen said with a smile. "You were so intent on getting in the barn you didn't see her with Callie. They're on their way here now, food in hand."

No sooner had Cullen said it than Owen smelled bacon. He turned as the girls walked down the steps to the base. His gaze ran over Natalie's long hair against the black tee, and he smiled. The black fatigues were molded to her hips and beautiful ass to perfection. And he could honestly say in all his years in the military, no one—man or woman—had ever filled out a pair of fatigues like Natalie.

She placed a plate of biscuits next to the plate of bacon, smiling at Callie. He'd forgotten how it felt to have Natalie around all the time.

He fought back a moan when her gaze clashed with his. This was what he'd be seeing every day until Orrin was found.

God help him, because nothing had felt so right in a very long time.

CHAPTER EIGHT

"Good morning."

Natalie never thought she'd hear Owen's sexy voice say those words again. How many times had he woken her at dawn after a night beneath the stars with that same seductive voice? Too many to count.

"Good morning," she said and fidgeted for something to do. "It's not a lot, but it's food."

There was a beat of silence. "Thank you."

She looked at Owen. He'd been up all night, but he didn't look nearly as tired as she felt. She was on her fourth cup of coffee and was seriously considering switching to decaf. Then she smiled, because if there was one thing Virgil Loughman couldn't tolerate, it was decaf coffee.

How she missed him and Charlotte. Owen's aunt and uncle had been salt of the earth people. They were the kind of folks who would give you the shirt off their backs. And Charlotte always had food for anyone in need.

She moved out of the way for Cullen to get to the food, and when Natalie looked up, Owen was gone.

While nibbling on a biscuit, she heard his voice. A moment later, he stepped out of the back room with Wyatt.

Owen had changed into a pair of jeans and a white shirt. The urge to run her fingers through his long, dark waves was almost too much to resist. She hurriedly stuffed a bite of biscuit into her mouth.

"This is really good," Cullen said around a mouthful of food. "Thank you."

Owen lifted his mug of coffee to her while he chewed and swallowed. Then his gaze shifted to Callie. "The cameras are a much-needed addition."

Callie halved a biscuit and slathered it with butter that she'd pulled from a small fridge beneath her desk. "No one will be approaching without an alert."

Owen nodded and swallowed. "With the cameras as small as they are, we were able to hide them in places no one will ever know to look."

"That means all three of you won't have to stay out all night again, right?" Natalie asked.

Cullen glanced up at Owen before looking to Wyatt. "Uh, huh."

"What's going on?" Callie demanded.

Natalie had seen the looks passed between the brothers. And the way Wyatt tapped his watch as he and Owen stared at each other was a silent message.

"There's a chance the group might attack during the day, but most likely, it'll be at night," Owen said.

Cullen wiped his hand on his pants as he swallowed the last bite of his bacon and biscuit. "The Russians won't give up on finding Natalie."

"I'll be fine," Natalie said. "There are five of us now.

And I'm still a good shot." When Owen simply sat there, she replied, "You taught me to shoot, remember?"

"I remember," he said softly.

"You need me. I'm here and willing to help."

The one thing she did well was being a strong, independent woman. It infuriated her mother, who constantly told her she needed to play the weak, helpless female to get a man. Her mom played the part to perfection, and it made Natalie gag.

It was one of the many arguments that made having any kind of relationship with her mother impossible. Before their brief talk last month, a year and a half had passed since she and her mother had last spoken. With the Russians and Orrin missing, she was happy her mom was on a trip with her latest victim/boyfriend.

"I'm still better with a rifle," she told Owen. "But I've gotten a lot better with handguns."

"I'm happy to hear it." Owen's chest expanded as he inhaled. "But . . ."

Callie slammed down her coffee mug so that the remaining bit sloshed over the rim and onto the table. "Spit it out. We're not children."

"Those men after Natalie last night are just the beginning," Owen said. "There will be more."

Wyatt crossed his arms over his chest. "They won't stop until she's dead."

Natalie felt dizzy. She'd heard rumors about how vicious the Russians could be, but she had never seen or experienced anything like that in the decade she'd worked for them in St. Petersburg or the embassy.

But there was no denying the truth now.

"That group last night wasn't simple thugs. They were trained assassins," Cullen added.

None of this was making her feel any better. She sank into the nearest chair and gripped the sides to keep upright.

"We need to split them up," Owen said. "Make them wonder who Natalie is with."

Callie sighed. "Which means we're splitting up."

"It's the only way." Wyatt nodded after, to emphasize his words.

Natalie's stomach churned. "I thought I was helping. I've only made things worse."

Owen's chocolate gaze held hers. "You helped tremendously. You did it knowing your life could be in danger. That took a lot of guts."

And where did that leave her now? Scared and cornered. Fat lot of luck her "guts" had given her.

"So what have you three planned?" Callie asked, a brow raised.

"Natalie and I will remain here where I know the terrain and can keep her safe," Owen said.

Natalie looked at the others around the room. Cullen and Owen were both staring at Wyatt, who was apparently supposed to talk next.

"And me?" Callie asked. "What am I doing?"

The sound of beeping filled the room as three of the cameras alerted them to a presence.

CHAPTER NINE

Orrin came awake in an instant as cold water was poured over his head. He sucked in a breath as pain radiated from several injuries over his body. With gritted teeth, he opened his eyes.

From his position on the floor on his side, he could see the room was still dark and dank. Blood crusted one of his eyes shut from the previous beatings. His hands were tied behind his back, making sitting up difficult. But Orrin managed it.

He glared at the man standing before him. Major General Yuri Markovic. The bastard. Orrin couldn't remember feeling such hatred before. It was a good thing his hands were bound because he would've attacked otherwise.

In his camouflage uniform, Yuri stared balefully at Orrin. The fact Yuri felt safe enough to wear it meant that they might not be in America any longer. Which would be a very bad thing for Orrin.

Behind Yuri were two men, and two more waiting on the other side of the door—all wearing the same camo uniform and heavily armed.

There were few times in Orrin's life when someone had gotten the better of him, and Yuri had done just that. It stung Orrin's pride more than he wanted to admit. Mostly because Yuri was a friend—or rather, *used* to be a friend.

"You look like hell," Yuri said snidely, his Russian accent thick.

It was Orrin who'd helped Yuri learn English over seventeen years ago. Yuri was a quick study, but there were occasions when he still mixed up words.

Orrin shrugged. "It's the shitty accommodations and food."

"I can make it better. A steak, perhaps? A soft bed with a blanket."

Orrin smiled, cracking open his split lip. "I'm old, Yuri, but not so old that a soft bed will make me crack."

"You will crack. I have made sure of it."

For the first time since Orrin watched every man on his team executed, his gut tightened. The only thing that kept him sane was knowing that no matter what, Yuri would never be able to get to his sons.

They were all Orrin had left.

Yuri turned and pulled a laptop out of a bag Orrin saw sitting behind Yuri. He opened and turned the computer so Orrin could see it.

Silently, he watched the video from feeds attached to the helmets of Yuri's men as they arrived at the ranch and barged into the house. He didn't allow any emotion to show on his face as the men summarily killed Virgil and Charlotte. He pushed down the grief for his brother and sister-in-law as he realized his sons had just gotten pulled into this mess.

"Oh, you will break, *stariy droog*, old friend," Yuri said as he squatted beside him, careful not to get anything on his pants. "You will tell me where Ragnarok is, or I start killing your sons. Which goes first?"

Old friend. That's how Orrin had thought of Yuri once. Not anymore.

He watched picture after picture of his boys arriving at the ranch fill the screen. But if he'd done one thing for his sons, he'd taught them to survive.

He lifted his gaze to his captor. "Fuck you, Yuri."

The punch came from the side, slamming his head into the wall.

CHAPTER TEN

Owen stood in the doorway of the barn and watched Natalie on the porch as an old mail Jeep pulled up. A moment later, Callie joined Natalie.

The two stood side by side, while Gertrude, the mail lady who had delivered mail to their ranch for as long as he could remember, climbed out of the vehicle with a friendly smile.

Even from the distance, he heard Gertrude's "hello." He smiled because the woman had a whisper that could be heard for miles. And she could happily talk your ear off if you let her.

Gert was showing her age. Her hair was all white now and styled in a perpetual perm—flattened in the back from where she'd slept the night before. Her width had spread, and she wasn't as spry. But the smile never wavered.

Owen wondered how people lived like that. Did they never experience pain or heartache? They could get past things easier than him, that was for sure. Or perhaps they buried it with their smiles.

He observed Gert holding out the mail. Natalie walked down the steps and accepted the bundle—a grin tilting her lips.

God, she was gorgeous.

"Did I ever tell you that you were an idiot?" Cullen asked as he came to stand beside Owen. "At least you'll get some time alone with her."

"Shut up."

"Everyone wanted Natalie. I'm still not sure how your ugly ass caught her."

Owen wasn't either. He'd been so happy she accepted when he asked her out. That had turned into a second date, and before either of them knew it, they were only seeing each other.

Those had been the happiest months Owen had ever known. When he'd first left for the University of Texas, he often thought about what life would be like had he remained and married Natalie.

Would they have ended up like most high school sweethearts and gotten divorced? No. Not him and Nat. Even at that age, he'd known she was the other piece of him, his soul mate.

His mother had told him there was one person for everyone. She'd cautioned him to be patient and keep his heart open, because when it happened, he'd know it. And he had.

"If there's nothing more between you and Nat, I'd like a shot at her," Cullen said.

Owen sipped his coffee, never taking his gaze from Natalie. "Stop thinking about her. Right now, or I'll cut your balls off."

Cullen laughed and crossed his arms over his chest. "You had your chance. I'm going to take mine. She's only three years older than me."

He was getting ready to punch Cullen when Gertrude drove away. There was something about the way Natalie held the small box that alerted Owen.

Tossing down his mug, he started toward the house. He was halfway there when Natalie looked up at him. Her face was pale. Callie was talking to her, but Natalie didn't look away from him. Finally, Callie took the package from her hands.

"Oh, shit," Callie said.

Owen lengthened his strides and hurriedly reached the porch. He searched Natalie's face before he turned to Callie. She held out the box for him.

He took it and looked at the label. Even without a return address, he knew that handwriting. Perfect lettering, precise spacing.

"It's from Orrin," Callie said.

Owen returned his gaze to Natalie. "How did you know it was from my dad?"

"I didn't," she said. "I noticed the postmark. It's from Delaware."

"You two better come with me."

He returned to the barn with the girls trailing behind him. Cullen's cocky smile was gone. His face was impassive as he looked at the box. There was no need for words. Cullen saw the handwriting and knew just as Owen had.

The four then descended into the base where Wyatt waited. Callie took the box and went to her work area where she examined it for any type of explosives.

They all seemed eager to open it up, but Owen wasn't. As he looked for Natalie, he noticed her standing by the stairs. Her arms were wrapped around herself, as if she couldn't get warm. Then her green eyes met his. He wanted to go to her, pull her against him, and simply hold her.

Alone. With Natalie. For days, possibly weeks. The ideas that sprang to mind about what he'd like to do to her were many—and various. Then he remembered why she was there, and how close she'd come to death.

"Hmm," Callie said, breaking into his thoughts.

He turned his attention to Callie. She held a small, wand-like tool and slowly ran it over the package while she looked at the computer screen and the image that popped up.

"That's a vial," Wyatt said as he peered close to the monitor.

Callie set the instrument down and grabbed a box cutter.

Wyatt's hand on her arm stilled her. "What are you doing?"

Without looking at him, she shook off his hold. "This is from Orrin. There's nothing inside that could harm us."

"Except that vial," Cullen pointed out.

Owen agreed with Callie. It was time to open the package. "Dad is many things, but he wouldn't send a package to kill us."

"No, he endangers us just by remaining alive," Wyatt muttered.

Cullen immediately took offense. "That's enough."

"What are you going to do, kid?" Wyatt demanded as he spun around.

"Enough!" Owen bellowed as he got between the two of them, a hand on each of their chests. He looked at Cullen then at Wyatt. "Whatever Dad is, he isn't the kind of man who would kill us."

Wyatt raised a brow. "Really? He killed Mom."

The next second, Cullen shoved Owen to get to Wyatt. Owen did his best to keep his brothers apart, but punches were landed. When he was hit the second time, Owen had had enough. He rammed his shoulder into Cullen and slammed him to the floor.

Owen turned, ready to do the same to Wyatt, only Callie beat him to it. She stood and swiped her leg, knocking Wyatt flat on his back.

"Damn, that felt good," Callie said as she looked down at Wyatt with her boot on his throat.

Owen wished he could smile, but he was too pissed. "You two want to fight, then take it upstairs and out into the yard. Not here."

Callie removed her foot. "We're here to work. If you aren't going to help, then get your ass out."

Owen was surprised to see that during the commotion, Natalie had walked around them and opened the box. She had a letter in her hand that she held out to Owen.

He took it and opened it. There were just five words.

"What does it say?" Wyatt asked as he got to his feet.

Cullen straightened his shirt and walked over to him. "Read it, Owen."

He crumbled the paper. "You know what to do."

"Excuse me?" Cullen asked with a chuckle. "What's that mean?"

Wyatt shook his head and looked away. "That vial is

Ragnarok. Orrin sent the biochemical to us. He wants us to fix his mess."

"No." Every head turned to Callie. Her face was set in determined lines. "When was the last time any of you spoke to Orrin?"

There was a long stretch of silence. Then Cullen said, "It's been two years since my last phone call with him."

Callie turned to him, but Owen couldn't meet her gaze. "It's been around five for me."

"I won't even bother to ask Wyatt because I know," Callie stated in a harsh voice. "It's been ten years since he last bothered to even acknowledge he had a father."

Wyatt crossed his arms over his chest. "So we don't get along with our dad. What's your point?"

"My point," Callie said, looking straight at Wyatt, "is that none of you know him. You don't know how he thinks or how he operates. You certainly don't know what kind of operative he is. None of you have the right to think you know what his motives are."

"Um . . . just to point out something," Natalie said as she held the box.

Owen saw Nat with the box in one hand and the vial in the other. "What is it?"

Natalie handed the small bottle to Callie before she held up the box for them to see. "I noticed the postmark when I first saw the box. All any of you noticed was the writing. I think there's only one person who actually saw who it was addressed to."

Owen read the name. Then his gaze slid to Callie. "Why didn't you just tell us this was sent to you?"

"I may think of him as my father, but he's not. He's yours." Callie gently set the vial down. "The government obviously wanted you three here, so it was only right the contents belong to y'all."

"But it doesn't." Wyatt took a long measuring look at the vial. "It belongs to you."

It was the first time since Callie had arrived at the ranch that Wyatt spoke in what some might describe as a tender voice. There wasn't a gentle bone in Wyatt's body, so the fact that he took care with Callie said a lot.

Callie swallowed and looked away.

He ran a hand down his face. "Dad knew you'd be here, Callie. He recognized that you'd understand what to do."

"Owen's right," Natalie said.

"What we need to identify is if Dad knew something was going wrong before he sent the vial," Cullen said.

Natalie set the box down on the table. "That note could go either way. It could mean for Callie to hold it just in case, or it could mean that something did go wrong and she needs to take the next step."

"Either way, Dad wanted her to hide it," Owen said.

Wyatt's lip lifted in a sneer. "Just like him putting others in danger."

Owen shot him a warning look, as did Callie, but Wyatt saw none of it. He had the vial in his hand and was looking at it. The liquid was clear and innocent looking.

But something that two countries were willing to kill for meant something. They would only be able to hide Ragnarok for so long before time ran out for them, as well.

"Take us through the assignment," Cullen told Callie. She nodded and wrinkled her forehead as she thought back. "The job came across our coded messages, as they always do. I decoded it and gave it to Orrin."

"When?" Owen asked.

Callie looked at the calendar on the wall behind her. "It was Sunday afternoon. I did some digging into this biochemical to see if it was real, but found nothing substantial. Meanwhile, Orrin assembled the team and did his own research."

"Where was the team?" Wyatt asked.

"They live around the area," Callie responded. "It was part of agreeing to work with Orrin. They had to remain close for just such time-sensitive missions."

Cullen nodded. "Go on."

"It was three days later when I brought what I learned to Orrin. That's when I noticed something was wrong. He wouldn't tell me what. The next day, he went to Dallas to have lunch with Natalie."

"Was it normal for Dad to keep things from you?" Owen asked.

Callie shook her head, her eyes going to the closed door that was Orrin's office for a heartbeat. "He usually told me what was on his mind. When he returned from Dallas, he agreed to take the job. Two days later at dawn, a chopper arrived to take them to Sheppard Air Force Base in Wichita where a plane waited to fly them to Dover AFB in Delaware."

Owen listened with interest. "And from Dover?"

"A private flight from an ex-Air Force pilot who took them to Moscow via a brief landing in Dublin for fuel," Callie explained.

"Who's the pilot?" Wyatt asked.

Callie gave him a hard look. "Someone Orrin

considers family and trusts implicitly. I was in contact with Orrin when they left Moscow with the vial. He sent me a quick message to let me know they were back in Delaware. The return flight to Texas was going to be tight, so I waited until I knew they should've landed in Wichita before I called."

Callie cleared her throat and turned her head away. "When I couldn't get Orrin or any of the team, I contacted Carter, the pilot, but my call went unanswered. I was about to call our contact in DC when my phone rang."

"And?" Natalie asked when Callie paused.

Callie tucked her hair behind her ears. "Carter found the team executed in the hangar."

"Where was Carter during all of this?" Cullen demanded, his arms crossed over his chest.

"There was a problem with the engine. Carter took the plane to the mechanics' hangar to have them look at it. Carter notified Dover's military police when the bodies were found. Everyone was accounted for on the team but Orrin. Based on the type of ammunition used, it was the Russians."

"That, along with Orrin's kidnapping, had the government sending for us," Wyatt stated with a grimace.

Natalie then asked, "So, where does that leave us?"

"It means someone needs to talk to this Carter," Owen said.

Cullen glanced at the vial. "I'll go."

CHAPTER ELEVEN

Natalie did her best to keep her eyes open, but the lack of sleep was making it difficult. While the boys and Callie discussed the pilot, Natalie found a chair and sat.

"I've already spoken to Carter," Callie said.

Wyatt raised a dark brow. "Now we want to talk to him."

"Carter saw Orrin and the men walk from the plane to the hangar after they returned to Delaware. That's it," Callie argued.

Cullen's gaze narrowed slightly. "Why don't you want us talking to him?"

"There isn't a need. I've already done it," she insisted.

Owen shifted his feet as he widened his stance. "That's true, but we might hear something different. Or ask another question you haven't."

"Are you saying I can't do my job?" Callie demanded as she got to her feet. "Orrin had no problem taking me at my word."

"Oh, for fuck's sake," Wyatt said as he turned around.

Even to Natalie it seemed as if Callie was going to

great lengths so the brothers wouldn't talk to the pilot. Why?

Orrin was like a father to her. No way was Callie involved in the deaths of the team or Orrin's kidnapping. Though when it came to any of the Loughman boys questioning her judgment or her abilities, Callie tended to get defensive.

Not that Natalie blamed her.

These were Texas boys who were raised to treat women with the utmost respect, to honor and cherish them always. Overprotectiveness most times went hand-in-hand with such an upbringing.

It wasn't that the Loughmans didn't think Callie or Natalie were capable. They just felt it was their job to do, well . . . everything.

The Loughmans were the type of men who would stand by their women, supporting them in everything. They weren't the type who felt their manhood was threatened if their women made more money or had a better job, because the marriage was a partnership in all things.

Natalie blinked her scratchy eyes as she stared at Owen. He would never have held her back in anything she wanted. He would've encouraged her to take the job in St. Petersburg, and then he'd have found a way to be with her.

Just as she would've supported him in his need to serve his country. No matter the hardship, no matter the struggle, she knew to the depths of her soul that he would've urged her to go after whatever she wanted.

And he would've been there to root her on.

"Easy, Callie," Owen hastily said. "No one is saying

we don't believe you. It's called double-checking. That's all we're doing."

There was a long silence where she saw that even Wyatt was watching Callie. Wyatt's gaze was intense, as if he were holding his breath to see if Callie would cave.

"Sorry," Callie said and plopped back on the stool.

Natalie rubbed the back of her neck and stretched it. Then she quickly hid her yawn in her arm as she brought her legs up to her chest.

With every blink of her eyes, it became more and more difficult to lift her lids. She allowed her eyes to remain closed, and within seconds, she was asleep. Then she jerked as her head fell back.

She glanced at the group to see if anyone noticed. Fortunately, they were too intent on watching Callie dial the phone.

"Speaker," Wyatt ordered.

Callie sighed dramatically and hit the button to put the call on speaker. In two rings, the call was answered. Callie asked to speak to Carter. After she had been put on hold, Wyatt took the cell phone from her hand.

"What the hell?" Callie muttered in disbelief.

Cullen moved in front of her. "We want to talk to Carter. Fact checking, remember?"

Callie rolled her eyes. Natalie felt for her. A girl had no chance with three men like the Loughmans. They communicated without speaking aloud, so a girl had to stay on her toes to remain ahead of them.

Though that wasn't really possible.

The Loughman men were a brand all their own. They were as rugged as the Texas countryside, as fierce as the

Texas weather, and as constant as the sun rising in the east. They were also as stubborn as mules.

"Carter," came a very feminine voice over the phone.

Natalie covered her mouth as she chuckled at the looks of shock on all three men's faces. Callie turned to Natalie, a wide smile on her face.

Owen was the first to speak, "My name is Owen Loughman," he began.

But Carter quickly talked over him. "Orrin's son. Have you found out anything more?"

"Not really," Cullen said.

There was a slight pause. "I'm guessing you're another of the sons?"

"Cullen."

"Right," Carter said. "Let me make this easy. As I'm sure Callie has already told you, I saw nothing. The trip to and from Moscow went off without a hitch. Almost too easily, actually."

"Did Orrin comment on that?" Wyatt asked.

Carter said, "You must be Wyatt. In fact, Orrin did. He mentioned it after we left Dublin on our way back to the States. I asked what he meant, but he only shook his head. There was something troubling him, though."

Natalie saw all three of the boys exchange a silent look at Carter's statement.

There was a loud sigh over the phone from Carter. "I owe Orrin a debt that can never be repaid. He is one of the best men I know, and I want to help."

"You could've been in on it," Owen said.

Natalie could almost hear Carter roll her eyes with the snort that followed.

"If I wanted to kill the team, I could've done it in Russia or even Dublin. Why would I wait to return to Dover?"

"She's got a point," Cullen admitted.

"Damn straight. I normally get off with the team, but there was an issue with one of the engines getting enough fuel. I had another flight in a few hours, so I took the plane to the mechanics' hangar to have another pair of hands help me get it ready in time. It was the only reason I wasn't with Orrin."

Callie's gaze was on the floor as she fiddled with a pen. "It's the reason she's alive."

"Most likely," Wyatt admitted.

Carter went on, "This wasn't my first time working with Orrin, and we looked at every possible scenario where things could go wrong to prepare."

"Sounds like Dad," Cullen whispered to his brothers.

"We kept away from military zones and made sure to have all the documentation needed. The Russian government thought we were a news crew coming to do a story on the Kremlin. I never left the plane. It took six hours for the team to return from their mission. We took off thirty minutes later, and returned to Dover AFB."

"Walk us through what happened next," Owen urged.

"Orrin was in a hurry to get back to Texas. I let them off and took the plane to the hangar as I mentioned before. I spotted the readied plane that was supposed to take them back to Texas, so I assumed they were on it. That's the last I saw or heard from Orrin."

"And the rest of the team?" Cullen asked.

There was a long stretch of silence before Carter

continued. "It was close to an hour later when I returned to my hangar and discovered the bodies. There was no doubt they'd been executed."

"On a military base." Wyatt shook his head, a small frown in place.

"The base went on lockdown as soon as I notified them, but the culprits were already gone," Carter said.

Owen ran a hand over his jaw as he rocked back on his heels. "Has the base found anything?"

"Not a damn thing," Carter stated angrily. "They're keeping me out of it since I'm no longer military."

Callie jerked her phone from Wyatt's grip. "Thanks, Mia."

"Are you coming?" she asked.

Callie blew out a breath as all three Loughmans nodded. "Yeah."

"Let me know when. I want to be there when the assholes who did this are taken down."

Wyatt then spoke up and said, "The Russians might very well find you. Stay alert."

"Always," Mia replied. Her voice got soft as she said, "I owe him, Callie."

"We both do," Callie said in the same muted tone.

Mia cleared her throat. "Keep me posted."

Then the line went dead.

Natalie couldn't imagine being a pilot. She didn't especially like to fly, but Mia sounded like she fit right in with Callie and the men.

"If we believe Mia, she escaped certain death," Cullen said.

Callie gawked at him. "If? *If?* Of course, I believe her. You have no idea how close she and Orrin are."

Wyatt's gold eyes narrowed slightly. "Tell us."

"Not my story to tell," Callie replied with a dark look directed at Wyatt. "Suffice it to say that Mia would take a bullet for Orrin. She's an asset we're going to need."

Owen nodded slowly, his face lined with thought. "I agree with Callie about Mia Carter being an asset. I've a feeling we're going to need her. She was the last one who saw Dad."

"And she was there in Russia," Callie pointed out.

Wyatt didn't seem totally convinced, but Natalie couldn't decide if it was just because it was a habit to take the opposite path of Callie or not.

"I'll head to Dallas and catch a flight to Delaware to pay Mia a visit," Cullen said.

"I can call in a chopper," Callie said.

Cullen shook his head. "It's better to keep visits here to a minimum."

"Agreed," Owen said.

"Fine. What will I be doing?" Callie asked.

Natalie closed her eyes, wanting to rest them as she listened to different ideas being batted around. She could stay awake. It was just that her eyes hurt so badly.

"We need to know where the Russians are," Owen said.

The next thing she knew, she was floating. The fingers of sleep pulled her deeper, even as she knew she should wake. Somehow, she managed to crack open her eyes and she saw a firm jaw and a shadow of a beard.

Her head rested comfortably against a thick shoulder while strong arms held her. She knew without having to look that Owen carried her.

The room he walked into was dark, as light from the

other quarters barely filtered in. He sat, keeping his hold on her. And she was in no hurry to get away.

How she'd missed his warmth, his strength. He was silent. Natalie could hear the others talking, so she knew she was still in the base.

His shirt was soft against her cheek, his muscles incredibly firm. He held her as if she weighed nothing. His hold was gentle but secure while his heartbeat filled her ear. She took in the sight of his strong jaw and the wave of his hair.

She drew in a deep breath, letting his masculine scent fill her. He smelled of the outdoors, of Texas, and all man.

"I missed you."

Natalie wasn't sure if he wanted a response or not. She hadn't moved, so he could think she still slept, which could be the only reason he spoke.

Then he shifted and looked down at her. Their gazes clashed, held. "I never apologized. Leaving you the way I did, Nat, it was horrible. I'm sorry."

"Forget about it. It was a long time ago, and we were young."

"Not that young." He touched her cheek tenderly. "I never expected to see you again."

She briefly looked down at his mouth, then jerked her gaze back up. Because staring at those lips was a dangerous endeavor. "I assumed when you left that you'd never return."

"Fate brought us back together."

It would be so easy to allow her heart to get tangled in Owen's web once more. She wanted someone who would never leave her, who loved her and only her. And who would never stray.

But did a man like that even exist?

Damn, it was difficult to resist Owen. He'd always had power over her. It hadn't diminished over the years. In fact, it felt as if it had intensified.

His fingers caressed down to her neck before his hand slid around to her nape, delving into her hair. Natalie knew he was about to kiss her. She could halt everything by getting off his lap.

Yet she remained. Waiting—eagerly—for his lips to touch hers.

"Nat," he whispered and lowered his head.

Her heart missed a beat as his soft mouth brushed against hers. Then his lips were atop hers, firmly, his tongue sliding against them.

She sighed and flattened a hand against his chest. He kissed her softly, sensuously. He kissed her ruthlessly, mercilessly.

It was a kiss that claimed her breath.

A kiss that stole back whatever tiny piece of her heart had turned against him.

He moaned and deepened the kiss as she wrapped her arms around his neck. It was as if the past fourteen years hadn't happened, as if he hadn't left her behind.

The passion ran high, the fire rekindling quickly. She loved how he could stop her world with just a kiss. And she hated him for it, as well.

Why did she still want him? Why hadn't her heart forgotten him as she'd tried desperately to do? What was it about him that didn't allow her to move on? No other man had ever had such a hold on her.

He kissed her as if he were a starving man and she a feast. And it was glorious. She held him close—knowing deep in her soul that her heart would be hurting soon.

But to pass up something so wonderful was a sin. Whatever the past had been, and whatever the future held, the one thing Natalie knew was that she still cared for Owen.

Even as she sank deeper into the kiss, she knew that it wasn't worth the inevitable heartache and anguish she would endure when he left her again.

That's when she made a vow that *she* would be the one to leave *him*. This time, she would be the one in control.

The kiss ended all too soon. He looked into her eyes, but she couldn't discern his thoughts. He'd always hidden them well, but now there was a wall there, preventing even a glimpse.

"There's sadness in your green eyes," he whispered. "Please tell me I'm not to blame."

He was, but not for all of it. And it wouldn't be fair to blame just him. Her life had been molded because of the decisions she'd made—as hard of a pill as that was to swallow.

There was much in her life she was proud of, but there were some parts she wished had never happened.

Natalie put her hand on his cheek, feeling the scruff of his whiskers. "You have the most beautiful chocolate eyes, but they're dead. I don't know where you've been or what you've done, but it's taken your soul."

"Are you happy?" he asked, ignoring her statement.

Neither wanted to answer a question, which was why they kept changing the subject. "Are you?"

"I'm making a difference in the world."

She smiled. "That's not an answer."

"I gave you more than you gave me."

Natalie swallowed and ran her thumb over his bottom lip. "Happiness is a state of being. I've worked a long time to find mine."

"But someone hurt you."

Unable to help herself, Natalie slid her hand into his hair and let the thick, silky strands pass through her fingers. "The past is the past."

"The past shapes us."

She got the courage to climb out of his lap before she jerked off the black fatigues right then and there. She faced him with her decision made. His face was in shadows, but her eyes were adjusted to the dark. She saw the way he watched her carefully.

"I'm here with you because I called Callie that day when I saw Ragnarok. Orrin was always nice to me, making me feel welcome, as did your aunt and uncle. Even if the Russians hadn't been following me or come after me, I'd want to help."

"I know. You're very much like my mother in that regard." Owen slowly rose to his feet and gave her a soft kiss on her cheek. "Get some rest."

She watched him walk from the room. After a minute, she climbed into the cot where he'd sat and curled onto her side. Sleep was the farthest thing from her mind, though.

CHAPTER TWELVE

Owen ate some jerky and scanned the surrounding area from his post. It took all of his years of training to stop replaying his kiss with Natalie and focus. Remembering her life was on the line got him in gear.

"Owen," his name came over the comm in his ear.

The more he found in his father's base, the more he was impressed. Whether the gear was funded by the government—which wasn't likely—or his father had bought it himself, it was the best.

"Yes," he answered Wyatt.

"Just heard from Cullen. His flight for Delaware is about to take off."

"Good to know. Dad could still be there, you know."

"They didn't take him back to Russia. Not only did Callie check, but I also called in a favor from an old friend. No private plane or military plane has departed the east coast for Russia."

Owen considered Wyatt's words for a moment. "You know as well as I, they could've gotten out one way or another."

"That's true. Callie's going to continue checking flights that landed in Moscow and even St. Petersburg."

That was good news, at least. "It'll be easier to get to Dad here rather than in Russia."

"They want the vial. They'll use him as leverage if he's still in the States."

Owen frowned because Wyatt's voice was coming through the earpiece, but also around him. He looked down from his spot in the tree to see his brother.

"It's time," Wyatt said by way of explanation.

Owen climbed down from his perch. "You have everything?"

"Callie made sure of it. If I hadn't reminded her to get clothes, I think she'd have left without them."

Owen smiled at that. They started back toward the barn. Despite not having seen his brothers in years, once they'd come together, it felt good to have them around.

And though it was Owen's idea to split everyone up, he wasn't happy to see his brothers leave. There was no doubt they could all take care of themselves, but if he were honest, his hesitation was because they'd felt like a family again.

Something he hadn't realized he missed.

"The group that hit here are likely to be back," Wyatt said. "It's what I'd do."

He nodded. "I've set up guns at multiple locations for just such an event."

"Did you think it might be better to take Natalie away from here?"

"Briefly," he admitted. "I thought about the city where there are thousands of people, but any one of them could be her killer. We'd be trapped in a small space. Here, I have the advantage."

Wyatt checked his pistol—a Beretta M9—and returned it to the holster at his hip. "I can be back at any time."

"I know."

"We're the girls' only defense."

"That we are. You going to be all right alone with Callie?"

"Why wouldn't I be?"

He glanced at Wyatt. Then hesitated because he wasn't sure what to say. Even if he did bring it up, Wyatt would refute anything he said.

"I know you don't want Natalie to see any of this, but there's no choice," Wyatt said.

"It's going to get nasty. I don't want her to see the violence, the blood, and the death that are coming right for us. She's not involved in our life, and I want it kept that way."

"Do you?"

Wyatt asked it so softly, that Owen swung his gaze to his brother, frowning. "Excuse me?"

"Owen, you've always been smart. You constantly managed to remain focused on whatever it was you wanted. You didn't get derailed or change your mind. Few understand our family's need to serve our country, and that never bothered you. You had the right plan all along. You just screwed up one area."

He glared at his brother because he knew what Wyatt was getting at. "What?"

"Natalie. From the first time I saw that goofy grin of yours after you asked her out, I knew you two were destined to be together. She understood and accepted you like no one ever has. Or ever will," he added after a brief pause.

Owen looked away. He couldn't think of this. Not now. "She wouldn't have liked the places I had to go. She would've been alone more than she would've been with me."

"You'll never know. You left her behind without giving her a choice."

"I didn't want to repeat history."

Several minutes ticked by as they walked in silence before Wyatt responded. "You wouldn't let that happen. Orrin never thought his work would follow him home. You'd prepare for just such an occurrence."

"You give me too much credit." He removed his cap and ran a hand through his hair as they drew closer to the house and barns. "We can't do anything if we aren't there, now can we?"

"Did you know she got married?"

He clenched his jaw. Natalie wasn't the type of woman to spend her life alone. He'd always known she'd find someone. He just hadn't expected it to hurt so damn much.

"The divorce happened about two years ago," Wyatt continued. "She was married for four years and living in Dallas. Seems the asshole had multiple affairs."

So that was why she had that hint of sadness about her. How conceited of him to think he was the cause. Now he felt like an utter fool.

"She still loves you."

He didn't want to hear any more. "Enough. Just leave it alone."

"I saw the kiss."

He didn't respond. What was there to say? He hadn't expected to give in to his need to sample Natalie's sweet lips again. He just couldn't control the urge to see if she tasted as good as he remembered.

What was worse was that she tasted even better.

"Don't let her go a second time, Owen."

He glowered at his brother. "You really want to give me advice? The one of us who didn't date anyone? The one who rebuffed any and all women?"

"I'm giving advice. Take it," Wyatt stated in a hard voice so much like their father's.

Owen wouldn't mention that. If he did, he'd likely get punched in the mouth. They reached the house where three vehicles waited. Callie's red Dodge Challenger, Virgil's green Chevy truck that was older than Owen, and Orrin's new Chevy.

This was the part he didn't like. The time he had to leave Natalie alone. It wasn't for long, but a second was too long when someone wanted her dead.

He realized why Wyatt had given him that guidance as his brother watched Callie. "You wished someone would've given you that advice."

Wyatt looked his way and then turned his head away again. But the truth hung between them. While Cullen flirted with anything in a skirt, and Owen was smitten with Natalie, Wyatt put every waking moment into his studies, the ranch, and honing his shooting skills.

The only female he'd ever tolerated was Callie, but that only lasted a short time. Then Wyatt treated her worse than he did anyone else.

The hatred Callie had for Wyatt was deep and acute. That kind of loathing meant something had happened between them. He narrowed his gaze on Wyatt as he tried to recall memories of their childhood.

It all kept coming back to Callie.

Owen knew he would get nothing from Wyatt. He turned and headed to the base. The entire walk back, he searched his memories about Callie. She'd worshipped Wyatt, following him around as if he were the center of her world.

Wyatt had been annoyed, to say the least. Owen halted as an image of Wyatt teaching Callie how to throw a knife flashed in his mind. Callie had been laughing. And Wyatt . . . he'd been smiling, his gaze locked on her.

How could he have forgotten that? Wyatt never smiled. And yet, his brother had been grinning like a man smitten.

He would have to pay closer attention to Wyatt and Callie to see if his suspicions were on the mark. Wyatt wasn't exactly the type of man others enjoyed being around. He was sullen and closed off from anyone and anything.

Where had it come from? Owen had been beside him when they'd found their mom. He'd been sitting next to Wyatt when their dad came home. Owen had a scar on his soul that would never fade from the murder of his mother. And yes, in a lot of ways, he blamed his father.

But he didn't despise him as Wyatt did.

He'd hated him for a while, but it was hard to hold

on to that anger for his father when Orrin had been lost without his wife. Orrin forgot about his sons as he struggled to find his way.

Owen, along with Wyatt, kept Cullen away from most of that. They couldn't shield him from everything because they were all in the same house, but they'd protected him from seeing the worst.

Owen headed to the barn. There, he checked the two rifles hidden at either entrance. Natalie was a crack shot. If she needed them, they would be close.

His gaze moved to the house. So much tragedy had occurred within those walls that it was difficult for him to recall the times of laughter and happiness.

But those times had existed. His mother had made sure of it. Her entire life had been centered around her husband and her boys. She'd always had a knack for making an ordinary occasion special without even trying.

Memories long forgotten rose to the surface. Perhaps it was returning to the ranch after so many years. Maybe it was because of the death of Virgil and Charlotte.

He turned to the left and looked at the oak tree on the hill, its branches thick and stretching out wide in all directions. He remembered helping his dad and brothers set up a blanket and picnic as an anniversary surprise for their mother.

A smile formed as he recalled how he, Wyatt, and Cullen had been in charge of the fireworks. They'd nearly missed the signal because they'd been spying on their parents kissing, laughing, and cuddling together.

While Melanie had looked at the fireworks with a huge smile, clapping and oohing and ahhing, Orrin only had eyes for her.

Owen didn't recollect how the night had ended. Most likely, he and his brothers had run off since their parents were preoccupied. It was a nice memory, one he wished he would've remembered sooner. How could he have forgotten how much Orrin loved Melanie?

"What are you thinking?"

He turned at the sound of Natalie's voice. He hadn't heard her walk up. He pointed to the tree on the hill. "Dad surprised Mom on their anniversary with a picnic there once. We were in charge of the fireworks."

"That sounds so romantic."

"Yeah. It does."

Natalie chuckled and walked to stand beside him, looking at the tree. "You sound surprised."

"I never thought about it being romantic until now. Though I do recall how Dad couldn't take his eyes off her. Looking back, he went to a lot of trouble to make that night special."

"He loved her."

Owen turned his head to her as she looked at him. "Everyone used to say how much Melanie loved Orrin. She did. Without a doubt. But he loved her just as much. There were times I swear they forgot we were in the house."

Natalie smiled and crossed her arms over her chest. "How?"

"Dad would come home for leave. We'd have a family dinner and talk. It was afterward, when we were supposed to be in our rooms, that we'd sit on the stairs and watch them."

"Do what?"

"Dance. Dad would put on some music and stop her

from washing the dishes. In the middle of the kitchen, they would hold each other, swaying to the music."

"And the world would fall away for them," she finished.

He glanced at the house and swallowed. "Yes."

"That's a memory I hope you always remember."

He nodded. "Me, too. How's it coming in there?" he asked to change the subject.

She glanced inside the barn where the hatch was open to the base below. "Oh, good. Callie can multitask like no one's business. And she gives orders like a general."

They shared a laugh.

He swallowed when silence fell between them. "I won't be long."

"I know," she said, meeting his gaze. "I'll be locked in the base waiting. Nothing is going to happen."

"Don't come out for anyone but me. If the Russians arrive—"

She interrupted him, saying, "They won't. And if they do, they didn't find the base the first time. Wyatt and Callie are waiting for you. Get moving."

"Not until you're inside."

She smiled and turned on her heel. He waited until she was down the steps and the door closed, hiding the entrance, before he hurried to Orrin's truck.

Within minutes, the three vehicles traveled down the driveway, heading in different directions once they reached the main road.

If the Russians were watching, they wouldn't know which automobile held Ragnarok or Natalie.

CHAPTER THIRTEEN

Sklad (Warehouse)

Orrin lay on his side, his cheek pressed against the cold, damp concrete floor. His arms were numb from being bound behind his back. He was certain at least three of his ribs were broken from the last beating. There was also a chance his left wrist was, as well.

There were two things the Russians did well—drink and fight.

The sound of voices reached him through the metal door. They were muffled, and the Russian words were spoken quickly, but he was able to get the gist of the conversation.

One of the guards wanted to kill him. Immediately.

Another of the guards was quite happy with spending the time using Orrin as a punching bag.

It was Yuri who, with one word, silenced them. Inwardly, Orrin grinned. He knew his old friend well enough to know that the beatings weren't close to being done. He would suffer many, many more.

But Yuri was underestimating him. Yuri assumed he would give up the location of Ragnarok and the formula because of pain. Except none of them realized he'd been living the worst kind of pain for the last twenty-two years.

Nothing had erased Melanie's murder, the heinous way her life was snuffed out. There wasn't a second of any day that he didn't feel the loss, the helplessness of not being there to stop her killer. Not even sleep was an escape.

In his dreams, Melanie was still alive, and they were happy. The boys were at the ranch, and the love that held the family together was stronger than ever before.

Then he would wake, and cold, hard reality would intrude. His heart shattering all over again. The fact that his sons hated him only made things worse. They blamed him for Melanie's murder.

It was all right. He blamed himself.

"Are you ready to talk, *stariy droog*?"

Damn. Was he so lost in his thoughts that he hadn't heard Yuri enter? He couldn't afford something like that. He was alive because he kept his wits about him.

"No," he bit out.

Blood still caked one eye shut, so he had to shift his head slightly in order to see Yuri. The general stared down at him with contempt in his blue eyes. Gone was the camo uniform. In its place was a sports coat and trousers.

He wondered where the uniform was. It made Orrin miss his own. He'd outranked Yuri before he retired. Since Yuri was as competitive as they came, they'd once had a friendly rivalry of who could get promoted faster.

At least, he always assumed it was friendly. Now he knew the truth. He hated being blindsided. It was the second time in his life, and it didn't suck any less the second go round.

Yuri looked around the cell. "You look like hell, *starik*."

"Old man? I'm not the one with gray hair," he said. He wanted to sit up, but that would take too much energy to hide the pain of his broken bones.

"The formula you stole is not Ragnarok as you were led to believe. It is a new fertilizer."

He barked a laugh, sending pain from his ribs that he ignored. "Nice try."

"You did not test it, did you?" Yuri smiled as he bent down to see Orrin's face. "You did not have time. A pity. Had you, you would have known you chose the wrong lab."

"Then why kill my team and take me? Why keep asking for the vial? It's because I got the bioweapon your country intended to use."

Yuri tsked and went down on his haunches. "Orrin, your problem has always been your pride. You never liked to consider you were wrong. Your team was killed, and you were taken not because you stole Ragnarok, but because you broke into the Kremlin. And I took you at your word."

"We've both lied to each other when it comes to our countries."

Yuri shrugged. "That was before you put my job in jeopardy."

He went along with the scenario because he knew he'd stolen Ragnarok. There was a ring of truth to Yuri's story, however, which meant his job probably was on the line.

"If I didn't steal the bioweapon, then why do you keep asking for it?"

Yuri gave him a flat look. "You know how much our countries spend on things like that. It is a breakthrough we need for our crops, *stariy droog*. You understand this, *da*?"

Oh, he understood. He understood just what a liar Yuri was. Bastard. When he got out, he was going to take pleasure in bringing Yuri down.

"What's so important about Ragnarok? It's just another bioweapon you can remake."

Yuri's lips compressed.

"Your government sends men to find me because of fertilizer? Not buying it."

"Think whatever you like. I know the truth."

He grinned at Yuri as reality sank in. There were too many years under his belt in the Navy, too many missions as a SEAL to disregard such a sorry excuse for an explanation.

Fertilizer his ass.

It was Ragnarok that he and his men stole, but more importantly, he had a suspicion that the bioweapon was one that would end them all.

Unless someone had the antidote.

Sending the vial to Callie might have been the single worst thing he could've done. Yuri and his group wouldn't stop until they had it, which meant more deaths.

Then there was the fact that the vial could kill Callie and his sons because he hadn't bothered to look for an antidote while in Russia.

He'd known not to take the mission. Everything had

told him to let it pass, but the idea that he could save his sons from encountering such a weapon was what led him to accept the job.

How wrong he'd been. Now they would hate him more than ever.

"If you will not talk, you leave me no choice but to order another beating." Yuri stood, sighing loudly. "This brings me no pleasure."

"Get on with it," Orrin stated.

"See you soon."

"Yeah. See you soon."

As soon as Yuri walked from the small room, two men strode in. They yanked Orrin to his feet and shoved him into a chair. He took a breath and held it, right before the first punch landed on his broken ribs.

CHAPTER FOURTEEN

"This should be fun," Owen said to himself as a black Ford F-250 rolled to a stop in front of him deep in the woods on the backside of the Loughman Ranch.

The trees were thick enough to make finding him difficult unless someone knew the area. And there was no way anyone could come up on him without Owen knowing.

Which made it a perfect meeting spot.

Owen wished Wyatt were there. He and Mark had never liked each other much, and Owen suspected Callie was the reason.

The sheriff got out of his truck. Mark Cooper stared at him for a moment before he closed the truck door and strode toward Owen.

Owen looked the tall man up and down. Everyone in town knew Mark. He'd been the quarterback, and in Texas, everyone knew football—especially high school football.

"Expecting problems?" Mark asked as he nodded to the pistol Owen had strapped to his leg and the rifle he carried.

In order to see how much Mark knew, he said, "Seems you'd know."

"I actually know very little." Mark removed his felt, buckskin-colored cowboy hat and scratched his head of blond hair before replacing it. "I expected to hear from one of y'all sooner."

"We had some issues to take care of," Owen said.

Mark looked at him with intelligent blue eyes. "I don't suppose that involved my unconscious deputy and the blood at Diane Dixon's place, would it?"

"It might've." He wouldn't admit to anything. "How's your deputy?"

"Has a concussion, but fine other than that. The only reason we didn't send out a missing person's report for Natalie was because Gert saw her at your ranch. Was it the same sons of bitches who killed your aunt and uncle?"

"Possibly."

Mark rested his hand on the butt of his gun at his hip. "We found no prints we could match, and the blood came up with no match either. With there being no bodies, it's hard to have a crime."

Since Owen had already been out to the house, he knew the dead men were gone. No group as well trained as those Russians would leave their men behind.

"You got a phone call from Washington," he said. "What were you told?"

Mark looked away, gazing at the trees. He leaned his hip out and sighed. "The call was brief. I was told there was an incident at the ranch, and I was to bring five men and make a report."

"Did you know the bodies were gone?"

Mark gave a curt nod and looked back at him. "The man I spoke with divulged that the government was sending for you and your brothers, but in the meantime, they would be collecting the bodies and evidence."

"But why? The government could've kept this quiet without involving you."

"They had no choice. Someone contacted a news station," Mark admitted.

Owen didn't have to wonder who was responsible. The Russians. They wanted to create disarray, to make the government aware, and to guarantee each of the Loughmans understood what was at stake.

As if they didn't already.

"How's Callie?" Mark asked.

"She's fine."

Mark blew out a breath, shifting uncomfortably. "None of y'all might know this since you chose not to return and visit, but Callie is everything to Orrin and he to her."

"We know. We're looking out for her."

That seemed to pacify Mark. "There are many in Hillsboro who care about her."

"Have you told me everything?"

As if remembering what had brought him out there, Mark blinked. "My report was bare. Callie wasn't there to see anything. Since there were no witnesses, I had nothing to put down. Regardless, the next day, the file vanished from the office."

It had to be the government again. It still didn't make him feel any better about it, though. "Thanks, Mark. Appreciate you coming out here."

"Your mother's murder was never solved. I don't want to add your aunt and uncle to that pile. Or Callie."

"We take care of our own," Owen stated.

Mark nodded and took a step back. "Y'all have done a bang-up job of that." He turned and walked to his truck. As he opened the door, he hesitated. "By the way, where's Orrin?"

"Away," Owen replied.

Mark snorted. "Right."

He waited until the sheriff drove off before he said, "Shit. Did you catch all of that?" he asked Wyatt and Callie, who were on the phone.

"Sure did," Callie said.

"The Russians talked to the news station," Wyatt said crossly. "But why?"

Callie snorted. "To tell the government they weren't going to let Ragnarok go so easily."

"We have more facts now. Not a lot, but more than we had," Wyatt said.

Owen ran a hand through his hair. "Let's keep to the plan. I'm on my way back to the ranch. The keys are in the back taillight if y'all happen to need the truck."

"Be safe," Callie said. "Don't leave Natalie alone too long."

"Check in soon," Wyatt said.

Owen ended the call and tucked his phone into his pocket as he started walking toward home.

They seemed larger when the others were there, but then again, Natalie had visited each room several times to keep her anxiety at bay.

It felt weird to be there alone. And it was so quiet that she had to turn on some music when she found a radio. She kept the volume low, but the tunes helped to soothe her.

Several times, the cameras alerted her to something, but it ended up being a bird or livestock on the ranch. But each time made her heart pound and fear wrap her in its grip.

When she spotted Owen on one of the cameras, she let out a sigh of relief. It wasn't long before the door slid open and he walked down the stairs to the base.

She smiled at him, happy not to be alone anymore. And even happier to see he had her bag of clothes. She hadn't known he was going by her mother's. "Everything go as planned?"

"It did," he answered. "You?"

"Just peachy."

He set down the rifle and grinned. "It got to you, didn't it?"

"Yes, dammit." She blew out a breath and dropped the happy façade. "Crazy, huh?"

"Happens to everyone."

"Even you?" she asked with a raised brow.

His grin widened. "Even me."

When the conversation lagged, she grew uncomfortable. How was she going to survive time alone with Owen while trying so hard to ignore the attraction?

She had to say something because the silence was too disturbing. "I was searching through the base. I don't think Callie throws anything away that she believes could be useful. I found this." She held up the six-inch-long tube that was three inches in diameter. "The vial fit perfectly."

"Good thinking." He took the tube and examined it, tapping the glass. "I've seen something like this before. If its what I think it is, the glass is shatterproof. It's a great place to hold the bioweapon."

She couldn't look away as he turned the tube over and over, the muscles in his arms rippling and moving. His expression turned contemplative, a slight furrowing of his brow conveyed that he was deep in thought. "What is it?" she asked.

"We have no idea what this is made of."

"It's a weapon. That's enough for me."

His dark gaze lifted to hers. "It's not for me. Most countries have their own stocks of bioweapons, just as we have nuclear weapons. It's to show our strength, and alert the other countries that we have such capabilities."

"Okay. Your point?"

"What's so important about this?" He lifted the tube. "Why would Russia chance a war by sending their military after this? Because, make no mistake, those men we fought the other night were military. I know that kind of training."

She swallowed and suddenly wished Callie had taken the vial with her. "There must be something different about this bioweapon."

"Every bioweapon is designed to kill."

"Perhaps they did something different with this one."

"Maybe. If there's one vial, there could be more. Even if there's not, what happens if someone gets this? There needs to be an antidote."

"Good point." She'd been so concerned about her own safety and Orrin that she hadn't thought that far ahead.

Owen drummed his fingers on the desk. "Callie said Dad stole Ragnarok and the formula. He didn't send the formula to us, which means it could be anywhere."

"Or with anyone."

"No research I did on Ragnarok told me what it could be made of." She crossed one leg over the other. Then she recalled her friend Emily. "I have a connection at Baylor who might help."

"Baylor University?"

"She's actually a biology professor, but she might be able to aid us in finding someone who can discover what's in that vial."

"Call her," Owen said.

She hesitated. "My phone was left at the house."

"It wasn't there when I grabbed your clothes."

She turned to Callie's computer. "That makes things difficult, but not impossible."

Natalie typed in Emily Ashcroft at Baylor University. In seconds, several links pulled up, including Emily's number. It wasn't her private line, but it didn't matter as long as Natalie could get ahold of her.

She accepted Owen's cell phone he held out and dialed the number. The call was on the fourth ring when it finally picked up.

"Hello?"

"Emily? Hey, this is Natalie Dixon."

"Natalie," Emily said, a smile in her voice. "It's been ages. How are you?"

"Good. Listen, I've got a serious problem that I need your help with. I can't tell you much, but it's important."

Emily paused. "It sounds like it by your voice. Are you sure you're okay?"

"Yes."

"You need to learn to lie better. What do you need?"

She licked her lips and decided to put it all out there. "Access to the science lab and a chemistry professor."

"When?"

She looked at Owen and mouthed "when."

"Tomorrow," he replied.

"Is tomorrow too soon?" Natalie asked.

Emily blew out a breath through the phone. "Let me do some checking. I should be able to pull it off. I'll call you back with details."

She sent up a silent prayer of thanks. "Use this number. Don't call my old one."

"Gotcha. But I'm worried about you, Natalie."

The concern in Emily's voice made her lower her gaze to the ground. "I'll explain more when we get there."

"You better."

CHAPTER FIFTEEN

"Are you sure about this?" Natalie asked.

Owen looked at the vial that had begun this whole sordid mess. A few ounces that had the potential to wipe out the world. This wasn't the first time he'd been neck-deep in shit, but it was the first time he was in it with Natalie and his family.

Then there were the Russians. The fucking faction who were relentless in their objective. They had no idea where any of the group was, but with Callie looking, it wouldn't take long to find them.

"Owen?"

He lifted his gaze to Natalie. Her green eyes were clear and without fear. That's how he wanted to keep it. Going to Baylor could bring said shit storm right into their path. And it probably would.

But that's how someone got answers.

She blew out a breath. "You're the one who mentioned an antidote. And you were right. We need one. That can't happen until we know what Ragnarok really is."

"Leaving the safety of this base, the ranch. It's a risk, Nat."

"A risk we have to take. You know it. The only reason you're hesitating now is because of me."

He shot her a look. "Of course, it's because of you. Those Russians will come again. Here, we're ready."

"We can be prepared out there."

She was right, but that didn't stop his agonizing. If something happened to Natalie because he wasn't prepared . . . He couldn't even think of it.

Before he could answer her, his cell rang.

"It's Emily," Natalie said before she answered the call.

He hoped like hell Emily had managed to set everything up, because if she didn't, it was going to take them more time to find another place to get the tests run—time they didn't have.

He knew—just as Cullen and Wyatt did—that Orrin's time was rapidly ticking down. Callie might pretend otherwise, but she was aware of it, as well. She couldn't do the job she did and not be cognizant of it.

"Okay," Natalie said, a smile pulling at her lips. She gave him a thumbs up. "We can be there whenever. You tell me the time."

He began planning how he was going to get Natalie back and forth from Waco without any interference from those after her. The group would want retribution for their dead comrades. How long before they came for payback?

"See you tomorrow," she said and disconnected the call. "We need to be there at ten in the morning."

He scrubbed a hand down his face. Then he took his phone and dialed Wyatt, putting it on speaker.

"Yeah," Wyatt answered.

"We're making a trip to Waco."

"For?"

There was a loud snort that came over the phone. Then Callie said, "It must have something to do with this mess. If you narrow it down, there isn't anything in Waco that they couldn't get in Dallas. Unless . . . Nat, do you know someone at Baylor?"

He shared a look with Natalie, who was shaking her head while she smiled. The longer Owen was around Callie, the more he understood why his father had brought her onto his team.

"Yes," Natalie answered. "Emily is a biology professor, but she's managed to get us a lab and a chemist who is willing to look at the vial."

He hurried to add, "They don't know what they're looking at, and won't until we get there."

"Owen pointed out that we need to have an antidote," Natalie said.

He couldn't take his eyes off her. Working alongside Natalie was a reminder of how well they'd once fit together. It was yet another indication of what his life could've been with her beside him.

"I'm glad y'all called," Callie said. "I've been tracking down the group who attacked. Nat, I found your phone in Dallas at the embassy."

Natalie made a face. "They're not trying to hide it anymore."

"There's no reason for them to," Wyatt said.

Owen sank onto the stool nearest him. "Did you find anything else, Callie?"

"Did I find anything else?" Callie said, her voice laced with sarcasm. "That would be a definite hell yes. I put myself in Orrin's shoes. If he had such a mission, he would send only a few of his men to go after Natalie."

Owen nodded. "The rest would be for a second or third round."

"Exactly," Callie exclaimed.

Wyatt said, "There were six men at Natalie's. It was a job for no more than two."

"They wanted to make sure they got her," Owen replied.

Natalie had gone quiet, her gaze on the floor as she listened. Owen wasn't a stranger to having enemies after him, but what Natalie was going through was different.

"Y'all must have missed one of them," Callie said. "Because how else would Natalie's phone get to Dallas?"

Owen propped his arm on the table. "Damn."

"I did a sweep. I didn't see anyone," Wyatt stated.

Which meant the bastards were *that* good. They couldn't stand to underestimate the group again.

"Give me a sec," Callie said.

Owen could hear the sounds of her typing on a keyboard. It wasn't long before he heard Callie sigh.

"Okay, folks. I searched flights into the area that had anyone from Russia aboard," Callie said.

Natalie leaned toward the phone. "You really think they would've landed in Dallas?"

"Yep," Callie said. "No one wants to drive across the country."

He wished he could see what she was doing. It was people like Callie that saved lives while people like him were on the ground.

"You're assuming they know Orrin's base is here," Owen pointed out.

Callie didn't stop typing as she said, "Tell me, Owen. How many times have you traveled—around the world and even in the States—and everyone knew you were from Texas as soon as you spoke?"

"Shit," Wyatt said. "She's right."

Natalie met his gaze and nodded. "All three of y'all have been gone for a while, but Orrin hasn't. His twang is just as thick as it's always been."

"So they know he's from Texas," Wyatt said. "They couldn't know his base is here."

Owen blew out a breath. "It wouldn't take much digging to learn of the ranch and Dad's relatives. Though I don't think the Russian unit knew the base was here. I'm guessing they wanted to deliver a message."

"To who?" Nat asked.

Wyatt's voice was grim. "To Orrin. And us."

"Got it," Callie shouted through the phone. "There were eight Russians who boarded a plane from Moscow that landed in Los Angeles. Four of those eight got on the same plane to Dallas. The next day, the remaining four boarded a flight to DFW."

Natalie leaned her hand on the table. "It could be coincidence."

"Each group sat together," Callie replied.

"Ah," Nat said with a twist of her lips. "Perhaps not."

Owen drummed his fingers on the desk. "Eight landed in Dallas over two days. One got away with Nat's cell phone and is in the city. We got five of them. Makes the odds a little better."

"We need to prepare in case there are more," Callie added.

Wyatt grunted. "There seems to always be a supply of them. Hang on. Callie's making a face. Not sure what that means."

"It means we have a problem," Callie said.

Natalie sat straighter, worry lining her expression. "Problem?"

Difficulties were part of what Owen took care of on a daily basis. But then again, those "problems" hadn't ever been directed toward someone he cared deeply about.

"What is it?" Owen asked.

Callie blew out a loud breath. "I expanded my search. Add four more to the original eight. I have their passport photos, and I'll text them to you, Owen."

"Wyatt's right. There's an endless supply of them," Natalie said.

Owen hated that she was scared. He didn't want her frightened, because things had only just begun. It was about to get a lot worse very soon.

Wyatt's voice faded for a second as he spoke to Callie. Then he stated closer to the phone. "Callie found that the first four landed in Dallas a week before Orrin and the team left."

"There's no way they could've known about the mission," Callie said.

"Of course, there is," Wyatt declared harshly. "People share secrets all the time."

Callie's voice lowered in resentment. "It's never happened before."

"I'm betting Orrin never stole a bioweapon from Russia before either," Owen chimed in. "Am I right, Callie?"

"Yes," she answered grudgingly.

Wyatt said, "Let's assume someone told the Russians Orrin was coming for the weapon."

"If I was informed, I'd have moved it to a different location," Owen replied.

"Exactly. If Russia knew it was being stolen, they would either move it someplace else, or they'd replace the biochemical with something different to allow Orrin to think he stole the right thing."

"Something isn't adding up." Owen rubbed his chin as he widened his stance. "If Dad didn't steal Ragnarok, why kill Virgil and Charlotte? Why kill his team and kidnap him?"

"Then Orrin did steal the bioweapon," Natalie said.

Wyatt let out a sigh. "Not necessarily. We need to talk to Orrin's contact, but this is also another reason we need to know for sure what's in that vial."

"I'm the only one who handles communications with them," Callie said of Orrin's contact.

There was a moment of silence where Owen could imagine Wyatt and Callie glaring at each other.

Finally, Wyatt said, "Not anymore. Our government took all three of us off assignment and brought us to Texas. If they want us to fix this mess, we need details."

"All of them," Owen added.

Callie relented reluctantly. "I'll let them know."

The line disconnected. Owen looked to Natalie. "You should get some rest. Tomorrow is going to start early."

He thought it would be easier if she were out of sight,

but the knowledge that he was alone with Natalie only made him ache for her even more.

How the hell was he going to keep her safe? Not to mention, how was he going to keep his hands off her?

CHAPTER SIXTEEN

The next morning, Natalie stood in front of the mirror in the small bathroom of the base and stared at her reflection. She hadn't slept much. Not all of it was because there could be men waiting as soon as she and Owen left the ranch.

No, the major reason was Owen himself.

After that kiss, he and it occupied the majority of her thoughts. Alone. They were alone. It didn't matter for how long. The simple fact was that it would be just the two of them.

No one else to talk to or help her push aside the growing desire that threatened to break her apart.

She swallowed, the coffee she'd managed to drink rolling in her stomach. Fourteen years was a long time. Why then did it feel as if she were still eighteen, and it was the day after graduation?

He had gone on with his life. And so had she.

She rested her hands on either side of the sink and dropped her head. The truth was, she hadn't gotten on with her life—at least her love life. She'd been stuck, perpetually waiting for a man who could never be hers.

What had it gotten her? Nothing but heartache. These past few years had shown her she didn't need a man in her life to be happy. She quite liked it on her own.

Someone pounded on the bathroom door. Then Owen's voice asked, "You about ready? There's a storm headed this way."

Natalie took a deep breath and turned to the door. She opened it to find Owen still there. He held her gaze for a moment before he turned to the side to allow her to pass.

She'd been grateful for the clothes Callie had lent her, but she felt more herself now that she was in her own clothes—a pair of jeans and a cream sweater with gold threads shot through it. She zipped up her brown suede booties, added a long, gold necklace, earrings, and a set of bangle bracelets in addition to her watch. The fatigues might be practical, but they weren't her style.

"You might want to bring those boots for later. Wear the combat boots Callie gave you."

Natalie raised a brow. "Why? What haven't you told me?"

"We've got a walk ahead of us."

"A walk?" she asked in confusion.

He nodded. "The truck is parked on the back of the property. No one will see us leaving the ranch."

He was nothing if not careful. She changed into the combat boots and held her booties. When she stood, their gazes clashed.

She stared into his chocolate eyes and wondered what he thought of her. Did he think she'd changed as much as she knew he had?

"Ready?" he asked as he adjusted the backpack he'd put on and grabbed a rifle.

"As I'll ever be."

He grinned before opening the door of the base and slowly making his way up the stairs. She waited, watching the cameras.

"Come on up," Owen called.

Natalie grabbed the .9mm left on the desk and made her way up the stairs. When she reached the top, Owen closed and locked the base doors.

"Here," he said and handed her a rifle.

She recognized it as the one he'd taught her to shoot with. She put the pistol in her purse and grasped the larger weapon. "Thanks."

They crept from the barn and dashed across the field to a copse of trees as dawn streaked the sky. She was grateful that he'd mentioned her changing her boots. Though he hadn't done it to be kind to her feet. He'd done it because it was the rational thing to do.

They said nothing as they steadily made their way over the Loughman Ranch property. She had forgotten just how big the ranch was. It looked vastly different on the back of a horse versus walking.

Once they were in the thick forest of trees, she said, "It looks as if there's more livestock."

"I believe there is. Virgil must be keeping up with the demand for good Texas beef."

Owen stayed a few steps ahead on constant alert. She learned quickly to keep notice of him at all times. If he stopped, she immediately did, as well.

When she spotted the truck through the trees, she let out a sigh. Her feet were killing her. There was no denying that it had been a long time since she'd hiked any-where other than to a department store.

Owen held up a hand. She halted and watched as he slowly ventured from the trees, his rifle up and ready. He walked around the truck twice, checking tires, doors, and even under the truck.

Finally, he lowered the gun and motioned her forward. Natalie jogged to the vehicle while Owen retrieved the keys and unlocked it for her.

Once inside with her seatbelt strapped, Natalie rested her head against the seat. One ordeal finished—a million to go.

She tried to quiet the thoughts in her head. Impossible with a man as imposing and gorgeous as Owen sitting a few feet from her.

Natalie surreptitiously glanced his way. He looked as rested and refreshed as she wished she was. Then again, he was used to this kind of life. And thank God for that.

The engine roared to life. The backpack was in the seat behind them, holding the vial. Never would she have imagined weeks ago that she would be sitting next to Owen, attempting to rescue his father, save herself, and save the world from a bioweapon.

It was the blurb for a movie. Except there was no guarantee that the good guys would win or that she would still be alive at the end.

"You all right?" Owen asked as he drove.

She turned straight ahead. "I think so."

Out of the corner of her eye, she saw him glance at her. She forced her hands to relax and loosen the grip on the seatbelt.

"It's going to be fine, Nat."

"Okay."

They soon drove out of the trees to what might pass for a road. The only indication was the tracks of another vehicle.

She turned her head to find him leaning forward, his hands covering the steering wheel as he stared at her while the truck slowly rolled down the path. "What?" she asked.

"Don't you think I can keep you safe?"

She winced. "Sorry. I'm nervous. Of course, I do, Owen. The closest I've ever been to this kind of situation was reading a Steve Berry novel."

Owen suddenly smiled, making the corners of his eyes crinkle. "You never liked anything remotely scary. I couldn't get you on a hayride during the Halloween festival. You wouldn't even get on the Ferris wheel at the fair."

He remembered that? A curious feeling began to spread through her. Damn him. She'd forgotten how charming he could be, but no amount of sweet talk would ever make her forget how he'd casually left her behind.

Even if he'd left to follow his dreams and a code that only the Loughmans understood.

He sat back with a sigh, a resigned expression on his face. "You're uncomfortable alone with me."

"A little." There was no use denying it or lying. If they were going to spend any amount of time together, he needed to know how she felt.

And it was a reminder for herself, as well.

"I suspected as much." There was no heat to his words. Just resignation.

The radio was on, playing George Strait. She hadn't listened to country music in years, and it was another reminder of her time with Owen. How could it not be? She was with him, on the ranch, in his father's truck. Where did the memories end?

Natalie forgot how nice it was to ride high up in a truck. She leaned her head back against the seat again and stared out her window for the next twenty minutes as he navigated through a maze of "roads" until finally they found pavement.

It was a back road with minimal traffic. Owen pulled out and pointed them toward Waco. She looked at him and smiled when she spotted him driving with his right hand at the top of the steering wheel while his left elbow was braced on the door.

He did a double take in her direction. "What?"

"You drove in exactly that same position when we were eighteen."

He smiled widely, laughing as he did. "I never noticed."

But she had. She turned her head forward. Why had she said anything? *Distance, remember, Nat.* She needed distance.

"You don't have to be nervous," he said.

"I'm not."

He grunted. "You are. You're looking out the window and fiddling with the seatbelt. That was always a sign you were anxious."

Natalie could only stare at him. He'd never told her that he'd noticed those things in the past. "It's all the memories," she confessed.

"Yeah," he admitted. He was quiet for a second. Then

he said, "You know, throughout the years I wondered what you were doing, and if you were happy."

"Really?" She wanted to say that she hadn't thought of him at all, but it would be a lie. She'd had enough lies throughout her life. There was no need for more.

He glanced at her, his chocolate gaze intense and filled with regret. "Leaving you that night was one of the hardest things I've ever done."

"They why did you do it?" The words were out of her mouth before she knew it. She'd sworn she wouldn't ask. It was over, water under the bridge and all that.

But being with him brought it all back in crystal clarity.

He blew out a breath, a muscle ticking in his jaw as he clenched his teeth. "I thought it was for the best. I knew you'd ask me to stay, and I wasn't sure I could deny you."

"I don't know what I would've done. You didn't say anything to me leading up to graduation about going off to UT. You didn't even tell me you applied or were accepted. Since I thought we shared everything, I can't tell you how much that hurt."

"I'm sorry."

"It's too late for sorrys."

Her harsh words silenced any more conversation. She was fine with that for a while. Until she recognized they couldn't continue this. They were going to have to talk to get through the next few days or weeks.

"It's done and over," she said. "There's no use reliving past mistakes."

Owen nodded but didn't respond.

She'd ended the conversation, so it was up to her to

start it back up again. "Was the Navy everything you thought it would be?"

For several long minutes, Owen didn't act as if he'd heard her. Then he said, "In some ways. Not so much in others. It's my life. I serve my country, protecting the land and citizens."

"Always the hero," she whispered.

He shot her a frown. "I'm not."

"I could list everything, but you'd deny it all and say you were just being a gentleman. The truth is, Owen, you look after people. It's part of you, just as you followed the need to serve your country."

Owen continued driving without commenting.

Natalie shifted in her seat. She rolled his words over in her mind. Would she have tried to convince him to stay? Definitely.

Owen had been her life, the very foundation that molded her future. When he'd left, she hadn't been certain what to do. There was no doubt, that had he stayed, she wouldn't have gone to Wheaton or to Russia to work those years.

She liked the life she'd led, except for marrying the wrong guy. Then again, who did have the perfect life?

"I had news for you graduation night," she said. "I found my letter of acceptance from Southern Methodist University that Mom hid. She'd told me nothing ever came and showed me the letter of acceptance from Wheaton College that she had applied to for me."

"Your mom," Owen said with a loud snort.

That was all that needed to be said. He knew what kind of woman Diane Dixon was. There was no need to go into her craziness.

"So you went to SMU?" Owen asked.

Natalie hid her grin and watched him for his reaction. "No. I decided on Wheaton."

His eyes widened as he shot her a surprised look. "Really?"

"I got my MBA in foreign languages."

"I always knew you were going to do great things."

She lifted her shoulders to her ears and held the pose for a second as she stretched her back. "It felt nice to be so far from Mom and out on my own. I think it's exactly what I needed."

"You definitely needed out from under Diane."

Natalie laughed. "Being away from Mom had something to do with my decision. No one knew my business, though. I could get lost among all the people. I didn't have to hide anything or fear that someone would see me and run back to tell Mom. I was truly independent."

She smiled, remembering how that had felt. "I was terrified of being on my own, but at the same time, it was so exciting."

"I know what you mean."

There was something in his voice that drew her gaze. He looked sad, but the emotion quickly disappeared.

"All of that, including a stint in Russia, and you still returned to Dallas."

She realized where this was going. She also guessed that Owen already knew about Brad. But he was being his usual self and letting her decide if she wanted to talk about it.

"Odd how things turn out," she answered. "I hadn't intended to remain in Texas. I was looking at a job in Italy a friend had told me about when the Russian Embassy in Dallas contacted me. The money was good, and I liked that I would be working closely with other embassies and governments."

"That's good," he said with a slight nod.

She hesitated for a second. "I also got married. And divorced."

CHAPTER SEVENTEEN

Owen gripped the steering wheel tightly. Every time he thought of the jackass who'd dared to hurt Natalie, he wanted to do physical damage to him.

Then he recalled that he'd also hurt her.

"I'm sorry, Nat."

She forced a slight laugh. "I was devastated at first. I couldn't believe that he'd cheated on me multiple times, but then I realized that I wasn't happy. I'd married him because it felt like the next step, not because I was madly in love with him. It's as much my fault as it is his."

Owen jerked his gaze to her, meeting her deep green eyes. "That's bullshit. You didn't make him cheat."

"I know. Watch the road."

He turned his attention back to driving. "Don't you dare blame yourself."

"I blame myself for the marriage. I could've called it off. I should have, but I really thought I could be happy with him."

"If he hadn't cheated, would you still be with him?" He quickly cut his eyes to her to see her reaction.

Natalie nodded slowly. "I've never believed in divorce. You know that. You marry because of love and work to keep the marriage going. So, yes, I would've stayed with him. But . . . he broke my trust with the cheating. It was only after I filed for divorce that I grasped how badly I wanted out of the marriage. Perhaps I pushed him to have those affairs."

"No. No," he repeated it more forcefully. "People get married for all kinds of reasons. It doesn't matter what one spouse does or doesn't do, none of it justifies an affair. None of it."

She reached her hand out and laid it gently on his arm. "Thank you."

"Just speaking the truth." He really wanted to break both of the bastard's arms. And possibly his legs.

"What about you?" she asked. "Were you married?"

"No." No one could ever compare to the best thing that had ever come into his life—Natalie.

"Did you come close?"

He glanced her way. "Once. Fourteen years ago, to my high school sweetheart."

She didn't smile. Her green eyes were shrewd as they stared at him. "You wanted to marry me?"

"It's why I left without talking to you. I knew if I saw you, I'd propose."

"Huh."

That's all? He expected more from her. But if he wanted to see some kind of compassion or even—dare he say it?—love, he would be waiting a long time.

He'd really hurt her. And he hadn't been the only one.

He couldn't continue this conversation while driving.

He pulled off the side of the road and put the truck in park. Then he turned to her.

"I knew what I was getting into, Nat. I knew the life ahead of me in the Navy. I also knew I was going to be a SEAL. I saw firsthand what kind of life my mother had as the wife of a SEAL. The worry, the waiting. I didn't want to put you through that."

Natalie's green eyes looked at him as if he were from another planet. "That was my decision to make, not yours."

"No," he said firmly, with a shake of his head. "You would've made your decision based on your feelings. You would've never listened to the facts about military life."

"It was still my decision."

"And mine." He ran a hand down his face. "A marriage takes two people. Do you think I wanted to come home to find you bitter that I'd been on yet another mission? Or demanding that I give up the life because I got wounded or was sent away after only just returning?"

She held up a hand to stop him from talking. "Did your mother ever demand your father quit?"

He paused as he sorted through memories. "Not that I recall."

"But you fully expected me to be the kind of woman who would do that?"

"I didn't say that."

"You certainly did."

"It's a hard life, Nat!"

"But we would've been together!"

That's when it hit him square in the chest like a 50mm

bullet. She was right. They would've been together. He wouldn't have been alone all these years.

Yes, they might have fought, but they would've worked to keep their love alive and their marriage going.

"There's no sense in rehashing this. We've both moved on," Natalie said and faced forward.

He wasn't so sure after that kiss. He looked out the windshield and felt as if he'd just lost her again. That wasn't possible, though. He'd let her go the first time, and this time, she hadn't even been his.

But he'd had hope.

A hope he hadn't fathomed was growing within him until she snuffed it out so indisputably.

He put the truck in drive and pulled back onto the road. The rest of the ride was done in silence. Though their conversation continued to play over and over in his head.

By the time they were on the highway, he had noticed a beige car that stayed the same distance from him regardless whether he slowed or sped up. He'd suspected something like this might happen.

When he drove onto the Baylor campus, he was ready to get out of the truck and get on with their task. He found a parking place and checked his cell phone. Nothing.

It wasn't as if he'd expected anything, but he'd hoped Callie and Wyatt had some news. Or even Cullen, who should've made it to Dover AFB last night.

Owen shot Cullen a quick text before his gaze went to the rearview mirror.

"What is it?" Natalie asked.

"Three rows back and to the right is a beige Ford Taurus."

She turned and looked. "I see it."

"I spotted them on the freeway quite some time ago."

Natalie swung her head to him. "The Russians?"

"Possibly."

"Should we leave?"

He shook his head. "No. This is important. I'll get you in and out without incident."

"So, what's the plan?"

"Act normal. Put the container in your purse. Then we'll head into the building."

Her eyebrows rose. "That simple?"

"That simple. Look around. There are a lot of people. Those men will stand out." As long as they didn't have someone on campus blending in with the students, but he kept that worry to himself.

There was no need to put more anxiety on Natalie than there already was.

She unbuckled her seatbelt before turning and leaning between the seats. The sound of a zipper opening filled the truck. Then Natalie was facing forward, stuffing the container in her handbag. Owen was glad she carried a large purse.

"Ready," she said with a nod.

"We're going to get out and unhurriedly make our way to the science building."

She took a deep breath. "Sounds easy enough."

"It is. Ready to find out what this is all about?"

"Yes," she said emphatically.

"Don't look at the car," he cautioned her as his hand rested on the handle.

He opened the door, and she followed a second later. They exited the truck and walked around to the front. Together, they then made the trek to the science building.

Several times, he looked in the windows and glass doors as they passed and spotted the two large men who got out of the Taurus in the reflection.

Only when they were in the stairwell making their way up to the second floor did he pull out his phone and send a text to Callie, Wyatt, and Cullen that the Russians had tracked them to Waco.

"They're still following us, aren't they?" Natalie asked in a whisper.

He tucked his phone into his back pocket and gave her a nod. "They'll be looking for us, but they're keeping their distance."

"But they know we're here for a reason and not a social visit."

He grinned. "That's true. Most likely, they'll think we came to see if anyone has any information on the biochemical."

"I thought they kept the making of it private."

"They did. That means someone let the information leak to our government."

Her eyes widened. She tucked a long strand of light brown hair behind her ear. "They don't know who betrayed them, do they?"

"Probably not. They'll look for anyone who seems suspicious. Usually, if they can't discover the culprit quickly, house cleaning is done."

"So innocents are killed."

He nodded solemnly.

"That's wrong."

"That's life."

They walked down a long corridor and turned left. Out of the corner of his eye, he saw Natalie's posture change. Her smile was huge as she hurried to meet a petite woman with black eyes.

Emily Ashcroft was nothing like Owen had pictured. She wasn't the typical professor one might encounter at a university. Emily had streaks of purple in her short, midnight hair that was spiked all over.

She wore an AC/DC shirt that was cut up and a red tank beneath. That was paired with a black leather mini skirt, black tights that had skull designs barely visible, and tall, black boots.

The hairstyle fit her narrow face and frame. With large black eyes, full lips, and a body that would have his younger brother on his knees, Emily was a pleasant surprise.

She pulled away from Natalie and looked to him. Her dark gaze ran up and down, taking in his black tee, jeans, and black boots.

"Military," Emily said.

Owen smiled. "SEAL."

"Of course." A thin black brow lifted as she glanced at Emily. "Natalie, where have you been hiding him?"

"He's the one who's been hiding."

He snapped his gaze to Natalie, but she was smiling down at Emily. So that's what she thought? That he'd been hiding?

"Come on inside," Emily said as she motioned him to follow.

He waited until the door to the lab closed behind Natalie, then he looked down the corridor, waiting for the men. After five minutes without a sign of them, he strode into the lab.

CHAPTER EIGHTEEN

Natalie smiled as Emily talked a million miles a minute. It wasn't because Emily was nervous. It was mostly due to the fact that she was highly caffeinated, which was normal.

"Missed you at the party this weekend. They're simply not the same without you." Emily walked around the tables and stools to the front of the lab. "Brad looked awful. He kept asking if I'd call you for him. I refused, because frankly, honey, you're better off without him." Emily then threw a look at Owen and wiggled her brows as she grinned.

She should've known Emily would bring up her ex-husband. Emily had never been a fan of Brad's.

"Now he, on the other hand," Emily said and pointed to Owen, who stood by the door, "is a different story. He's a hunk."

Words wouldn't budge past her throat. All she could do was nod. Because he was exactly that.

"Is he single?" Emily leaned in close to ask in a whisper.

"I believe so."

Emily's gaze narrowed as she stared at her. "There's history between the two of you."

"How can you possibly know that?" Now she wondered if it was written all over her face. She thought she was doing a better job of hiding her feelings.

Emily shrugged. "By the way he keeps looking at you, it's obvious. Now, spill. I want all the juicy details. Because, sweetie, I'm not sure how you could've let that go."

"I didn't. He left me." She cringed when it came out louder than she'd expected.

She didn't bother to look behind her. She could feel Owen's presence approaching by the way her skin prickled with awareness.

"Yes," he said in his deep baritone. "It was my fault."

She thought she was past all the hurt and resentment, but apparently, she'd been wrong. Having Owen with her, kissing her, touching her, was bringing back feelings she wasn't prepared to deal with.

"Interesting," Emily said with a wide smile. "Very interesting. Now, let's get to work, shall we?"

"Please," she mumbled.

She started to walk away when Owen's hand grasped her wrist and kept her in place. He leaned in so close she could feel his breath on her neck, which made her heart race with anticipation and delight.

"Look at me, Nat. I won't bite." There was a long pause before he said, "Hard."

She stopped the moan before it passed her lips. Damn him for tempting her in such a fashion. But she kept her back to him.

"Look at me," he demanded softly.

She could never refuse him when he used that smooth baritone filled with sensuality and the promise of exquisite pleasure.

She gazed into his dark eyes and melted under the flagrant desire she saw there. His hand slowly caressed down to her fingers. Breathing became difficult as her blood pounded in her ears.

She attempted to swallow. No matter how she tried, she couldn't look away from him. A thick black line encircled his irises, and his pupils were dilated. Their bodies were touching so that every bit of his heat soaked through her clothes and into her skin.

Unable to help herself, she gripped his fingers. "Don't do this," she begged. She wasn't strong enough to deny him. She couldn't do it as a teenager—and she certainly couldn't do it now.

Not with the imposing, commanding man who held her immobile with the promise of ecstasy she knew he could deliver.

"I don't have a choice," he whispered. "I've never had a choice with you. I see you, and I have to have you."

The urge to give in, to melt in his arms was overwhelming. She'd dreamed of it so many times. Now, he was offering himself.

How could she refuse?

How could she accept?

It took her years to get over Owen—if she ever really had. She was beginning to seriously doubt that. But she knew there was no future together. He had his life where he thought she didn't belong, and she had hers.

Granted, she was now out of a job, but once the Russians no longer wanted her dead, she'd find something else. A job could be replaced. Her life couldn't. So she wasn't going to give her position at the embassy much thought for the moment.

Owen, on the other hand, stood before her. It would be so easy to lean into him and let him hold her, to let him take care of her. He did it so effortlessly.

But for how long? That's what kept her from giving in, but that argument was wearing thin when his heat and words kept pulling her closer.

Somehow, she found the wherewithal to pull her hand from his. Then she took an intentional step back to guard her heart. "I thought you said I didn't fit in with your life."

"I was wrong."

"Will you still think you're wrong once we find Orrin and stop the group after this?" she asked, holding up her purse.

"Yes. And I like your faith in me," he replied sarcastically.

"I'm basing it on past experience." She didn't give him time to respond. She turned and started toward Emily, who stood watching with unabashed curiosity.

"Damn," Emily said when Natalie reached her. There was a hint of sadness and even a little envy in her black eyes. "I've looked for that kind of passion my entire life. Don't be a fool and let it go."

"He nearly destroyed me once. I won't go through that again."

Emily touched her arm in comfort. The moment was broken as one of the doors at the back of the room opened and a man in a white lab coat entered.

His dirty blond hair was pulled back in a ponytail.

Vivid blue eyes behind black-rimmed glasses took in the room. He held Owen's gaze the longest.

She noticed how Owen remained where he was, closest to the doors. Were the men out there? She hoped they'd walked on, but she doubted that was the case. Owen would know. But she didn't ask. Sometimes the not knowing gave a person a measure of desperately needed peace.

It was an illusion. She knew that. Yet, she grasped what little she could and held on tightly. Because the worst had yet to come.

Emily's welcoming smile as the man approached was genuine and reflected in her black eyes. "Simon. Thank you for agreeing to do this."

"I don't know what I'm doing, and until I know for sure, I won't be *doing* anything."

She wasn't offended. She would be just the same in his shoes. She held out her hand to him. "Hello. I'm Natalie Dixon, and we're in a bit of a bind. Your help would be greatly appreciated."

"Simon Moore," he said as he took her hand and shook it.

Natalie set the purse on the table between them and took out the container that held the vial. "As much as we'd like to tell you the entire story, it's classified."

"You talk as if you work for the government," Simon said, glancing at Owen.

Owen crossed his arms over his chest. "We do. I'm a Navy SEAL. The few facts I can give you are that a vial was stolen from another country because our government wanted it, and those people want it back."

"Needless to say, that country is furious," Natalie added.

Simon braced his hands on the table, eyeing the tube and the vial within. "How angry?"

"They killed my aunt and uncle," Owen stated. "They'll go after anyone associated with whatever is inside that vial."

Simon turned to Owen. "What's in it?"

"That's what we want you to tell us."

Simon snorted and shook his head as he once more looked at the cylinder. "It's dangerous, isn't it?"

"We think so," Callie answered. "It's why I put it in this tube."

"Smart thinking," he told her. Then he held out his hand.

Her heart leapt. "Are you going to help us?"

"I'm a chemist," he told her as he turned the cylinder over and over in his hands. "My curiosity won't allow me to walk away without knowing what it is."

"Even if it puts your life in danger?" Owen asked.

Simon swung his gaze to Owen. "Even then. Someone has hurt your family for this. Tell me, why not ask the government for help?"

"Time," she replied.

With a nod, Simon walked back through the door he entered from. The top portion was glass. There was also several tempered glass windows looking into the room.

"It's his lab," Emily explained. She then swiveled her head to Natalie. "They're after you, too, aren't they?"

"I'm just helping some friends," she lied.

Emily raised a black brow and cocked her head to the side. "Nice try. Is there anything I can do?"

"How much control do you have here?" Owen asked.

Emily said, "Quite a lot. What do you have in mind?"

"There are two large men looking for us. They'll make their way into the building, if they haven't already. Think you can get rid of them?"

Emily winked. "Give me a second, sugar."

"No," Natalie said. "I don't want anyone else involved."

"They won't know I am," Emily assured her and exited through a back door.

She pulled up a stool from another table and sat. Her gaze swung to Owen. He watched the door in case the men came through.

She'd used to joke that he had eyes in the back of his head. No one was ever able to come up behind Owen and scare him. He always knew when anyone ever tried.

And she had attempted it many different ways.

Suddenly, his eyes slid to her. She recalled his words, and chills raced over her skin. She wanted him with a desperation that was all too familiar. Not even the long years apart could make her body forget him.

Once Orrin was found—because she knew they would find him—Owen would return to his unit of the SEALs. And everything would go back to the way it was.

He was so sure she wouldn't like the military life. What irritated her was that he was right. She wanted her time with him, and to have that reduced to just a few weeks a year wasn't much of a relationship.

How could she stay angry with him for protecting

their country? He risked his life every day for their freedom. He was a hero in every way possible.

He wanted her. It was there for the world to see. He wasn't hiding it. But she refused to allow him back into her life—and her heart.

Even if being with him was pure, unadulterated bliss.

"What's Simon doing?" Owen said.

She blinked and looked away from him. "I don't know. I always hated chemistry."

He moved to stand near one of the windows and looked inside. "He's trying to figure out the compounds within the liquid."

She glanced at the biosuit Simon wore and wondered how safe they were in the lab next to him. Would walls and glass stop Ragnarok?

Probably not with a name like that.

The door opened, and Emily walked in. "The men following you are out of the building, but they haven't left the campus. They'll be waiting."

CHAPTER NINETEEN

"They won't just follow us back will they?" Natalie asked.

Owen looked at his watch. "No."

"I suppose that means you're going to take care of them?"

"Yes." He had been waiting for this since they decided to go to Baylor. It was time he had a face-to-face with the Russians.

And take two more off the list.

That would leave only the remaining four. An easy target to take out.

Easy.

"Too easy," he mumbled.

"What did you say?" Natalie asked.

He shook his head. "Nothing."

What were they missing? Callie had checked. There were twelve men from Russia. Just twelve. But why would they put themselves in a position to only leave four to find the vial?

They wouldn't.

"There's more," he said as he faced Natalie.

Her forehead furrowed. "More? More what?"

"Men."

"But Callie looked."

He nodded as he strode to her. "I know. Maybe they were already here."

"We need Callie."

His lips compressed as he sent off a coded text to Wyatt.

Meanwhile, Natalie turned to Emily. "Is there a computer I can borrow?"

Emily left the lab and returned almost immediately with a laptop. "It's my personal computer. The campus can't track whatever you're going to do."

Natalie opened the laptop and began punching keys as he looked to see what she was doing.

"There's a group of expat Russians in Dallas. I didn't even think about them yesterday. I should have," she told him.

"We've had a lot going on."

Emily's eyes widened as she pieced it together. "Natalie, you work for the Russian Embassy."

"Did. I'm pretty sure I no longer have a job," she said.

Seconds later, a website pulled up for the Russian expat group. Natalie went to every link, but there was no way to know how big the group was.

"I'm not a hacker," she said as she met Owen's gaze. "Callie could find out all there is to know with little effort."

"It's a good place to start. There has to be a contact name," he said.

He looked over his shoulder at Dr. Simon Moore, who was still sorting through the ingredients of the vial.

He'd likely be there for some time. And there was no telling how long it would take Callie to get their information.

All they had now was time on their hands. Which made Owen uneasy.

"Umm," Emily said. "I might know someone who could get into the website."

Natalie was shaking her head before Emily finished. "No. You're doing too much already."

He pointed to the contact name on the screen. "Perhaps your hacker friend could give us information on Irina Matveev?"

CHAPTER TWENTY

Sklad . . .

Orrin had no idea what day it was or the time. The small room had no windows. Then there was the fact that he'd been knocked unconscious so many times he could've slept for days and not known it.

Yuri was becoming impatient. The torture sessions were coming more frequently, but he could take them. He would tell Yuri nothing.

He dimly heard something. He cracked open his good eye and saw that the door wasn't shut all the way. He saw the boots of one of his guards.

But that crack allowed in sound. The two guards were talking. Or rather, one was giving his not so pleasant thoughts about someone in power while the other merely grunted in response.

He was about to disregard them when he heard mention of the Saints. That name had come to his attention years ago when he was on another mission. He'd learned nothing about the faction, and sadly, soon forgot.

But, apparently, the sect had quietly worked behind the scenes.

A thread of unease wound through him. Shadow

organizations were always the hardest to bring down, because finding the head of such a nefarious group was nearly impossible.

Orrin closed his eyes and concentrated, blocking out the closest voices. Until he picked up another voice, one that he recognized—Yuri's. Yuri was speaking in Russian, and by the profanity-laced rant, things weren't going well.

"What are they doing at Baylor?" Yuri demanded, half in Russian, and the other half in English. It was a habit of Yuri's when he got upset.

The question caught Orrin's attention. So the boys were at Baylor. Most likely, they were attempting to discover what was in the biochemical. It was the smart thing to do.

He knew without having to wonder that Callie was right in the mix of things, as well. She was like a daughter, and he worried endlessly about her. Callie was strong, but she had a soft heart and a driving desire to be wanted and needed. She was more than competent in the field, but he knew firsthand what could happen to people in their profession.

He hadn't wanted it for Callie. It's why he'd turned her from the FBI. It was also why he kept her at the base, away from the danger.

Not so much now.

Yuri was speaking again, but it was too fast and fading in and out, as if he were pacing, for Orrin to hear everything. He did pick up a few things, though.

Whoever Yuri spoke with must be in Texas. He also heard something about Dallas and Russians dying. He inwardly let out a shout. His boys were doing damage to the group and taking them out one by one.

It wasn't until he heard Yuri say the name Natalie Dixon that Orrin drew up short. She must have found something about Ragnarok. That's the only reason she'd be involved.

He knew the boys and Callie would take care of her, but it was another life he had to worry about. Still, he wondered how Owen was taking it. Perhaps it would force his middle son to realize one of his biggest mistakes and rectify it.

The men were coming at his boys from every angle. Not that it would slow his children down. If only he could be there, helping them kick some Russian ass.

His sons were prepared, though. All three were the best of their branches. They hadn't gotten there by chance. They did it because it was in their blood—and because no Loughman knew how to fail.

Yuri ended the call and then proceeded to yell at anyone near him. That temper of his was going to get him one day. Yet Yuri played the political dance within the military excellently, enough to get him where he was.

Orrin had enjoyed that dance once. Now it sickened him. All the deceit and backstabbing left a bitter taste in his mouth.

A phone rang. Yuri stopped yelling mid-sentence. The quiet told Orrin that whoever was calling wasn't someone Yuri wanted to speak with.

"*Da*?" Yuri's voice was filled with reverence. And a heavy dose of anxiety. "I understand, sir. It is perfectly clear. I know how important it is. I will find Ragnarok."

Orrin wished he knew who it was on the other end of the call. He made a mental list of all the officers who outranked Yuri. There had been a couple through the years who didn't exactly like Yuri.

But which one?

"He is not talking," Yuri said. There was a long beat of silence before Yuri replied, "I will get it out of him one way or the other."

If Orrin had the energy, he'd snort. Yuri was good at what he did, but Orrin's family was at stake. He hadn't been able to protect his wife, but he was going to make damn sure his sons, Natalie, and Callie were spared.

The door to his room slammed open and hit the wall. Yuri's heavy footsteps stopped inches from his face, but Orrin didn't so much as flinch.

"Wake him," Yuri ordered.

Water was unceremoniously poured atop his head once again. Orrin blew out, spraying water. He rolled his head so he could look up at Yuri with his good eye.

"I have been nice," Yuri said. "That stops now. I know you are hurt. I know several ribs are broken as well as your wrist."

Orrin didn't bother to tell him that his right shoulder was dislocated from falling on it at the last beating. It wouldn't have happened had his hands not been bound.

"I can end your misery. Just tell me where the vial is," Yuri urged.

Orrin closed his eyes. He couldn't be too eager, lest his plan not work. Yuri had to think he'd managed to get the information on his own.

"No matter how good your sons are, Orrin, they will

not be able to withstand what I am sending their way. Three men can only do so much against a dozen of my men."

He had faith in his sons. He'd seen them in combat situations. He'd seen them training, and he'd seen them on missions. He knew just how good they were. They were ten times as good as he was at his best—which had been damn good.

"One more punch to your ribs and you could have a punctured lung," Yuri said. "Do not go out like this. The vial does not belong to your country. It is ours. Give it back, and I will leave your family alone."

He knew that for the lie that it was, but he opened his eye and met Yuri's gaze. "You swear no one will come after my sons?"

"I give you my word."

How many times had Yuri said those words to him? And how many of them had been laced with the same lie? He didn't want to think about that now. He'd consider it later once Yuri was dead.

"Tell me," Yuri said. He squatted down beside him and smiled. "We share a lot of good memories, *stariy droog*. Let us be friends again. You were only following orders, as am I. There is no reason this has to end badly for either of us. This is for our countries to bicker about, not us."

Orrin hesitated, darting his gaze away from Yuri. He had to make it look convincing. Because the one thing Orrin wasn't was a traitor to his country or his family.

He'd had plenty of beatings before, and he was prepared to withstand much more of the torture Yuri had already doled out. But if he could give his sons even a few more hours, then it was worth what this small lie was going to cost him.

"Come, Orrin. Your sons will be spared."

He released a long breath. "I have your word, right?"

"*Da.*"

He swallowed hard, then let a lengthy pause stretch between them. Finally, he said, "I sent the vial to Mitch Hewett at the Pentagon."

Yuri's smile was tight. "See? That was not so hard."

"What now?"

"Now I check what you have told me."

CHAPTER TWENTY-ONE

If Natalie had felt helpless at the ranch, it was worse while they waited at the lab. Though Owen didn't pace, his impatience filled the room like a dark cloud waiting to unleash its fury.

He walked from the windows to the door every few minutes, checking to make sure the men after her weren't there.

Her thoughts shifted just as quickly from wondering what Simon might be discovering about Ragnarok to how Orrin fared to Owen.

Each time, her mind halted at Owen. Despite telling herself not to, she thought of the future—a future with him. And one without.

She observed him when he wasn't looking, trying to picture what life would've been like as his wife while he joined the Navy and became a SEAL.

She tried to envision all the missions he'd been sent on. Then she wondered if he'd been injured, and if so, how badly. Natalie saw firsthand what life as a SEAL had done to his soul.

It had changed him, but not the core of him. Not yet,

anyway. Orrin had managed to have a wife and children while a SEAL, but for some reason, Owen felt differently.

She rubbed her eyes, stifling a yawn. The quiet of the lab was driving her insane. And the hard stool wasn't making things any better. She didn't even have her cell phone to play games. All she could do was stare at the walls, trying to think of anything other than Owen.

And failing epically.

It was an hour later when Emily finally returned. Natalie almost hugged her she was so glad to have a distraction. The stress of the current situation was giving her a headache at the base of her skull.

"Well," Emily said. "I was able to get some intel on Irina Matveev."

Owen's strides ate up the distance until he stood beside Natalie. "And?"

Emily placed a stack of papers before them. "See for yourselves."

Natalie scooted the pages out one by one. That's when she spotted a foreign seal on one of the papers. "Did your friend hack into the Kremlin?"

"It appears so," Emily replied with a grin.

Natalie saw a picture of Irina Matveev. The woman was in her mid-fifties with black hair beginning to show signs of silver.

The woman wasn't smiling. Nor were her eyes. She looked like a soldier with her hard stare and the rigid set of her jaw. Irina was attractive, and Natalie imagined she was quite a beauty when she was younger.

A look through her financials showed that Irina was wealthy, with strong ties in Russia. She was active in the

Dallas community, serving on the council of her church, and volunteering for several charities.

Everything looked normal until Natalie reached the papers with Russian seals. She read one after the other. When she finished, she lifted her gaze to find Owen watching her.

Owen jerked his chin to the papers. "What is it?"

"Irina Matveev," Natalie said. "She was a low-ranking KGB agent."

He shrugged as he set aside the papers he was looking at. "I'm not surprised."

She put her hands atop her stack. "I'm not an expert on the military, much less one from another country, but it says Irina was low ranking. However, with all her credentials, the missions she was sent on—including a stint in East Germany before the wall came down—and her accommodations, shouldn't she have been ranked higher."

"She's a woman. That likely explains the discrepancies."

"Except she suddenly vanished for a short period when the KGB was dismantled."

Owen frowned deeply as he took the paper and studied it. "Vanished? The KGB retired many of their operatives in an effort to put their best face forward when they put the Federal Security Service of the Russian Federation—or FSB—in place."

"Did the FSB take on any KGB?"

"I'm sure they did, but I'd wager there weren't many. Let me guess. Irina was one of them."

"She was," Natalie said, impressed. "Irina went from a low-ranking KGB agent to a very high-ranked FSB officer." She handed the papers to Owen so he could see the evidence.

Owen rubbed a hand over his lower face. "After ten years with the FSB, she abruptly quit and moved to Texas."

"Odd, isn't it?"

He gave a nod. "Very. Especially with all her commendations and her advancement. There's something strange, for sure. Makes me curious."

"We need more information."

Emily motioned to the set of papers. "My friend found all there was. Whatever happened in Irina Matveev's life, it's not on record anywhere."

While Owen continued to reread the papers, Natalie couldn't stop thinking that there was a connection with Irina somehow. Whatever the former KGB and FSB agent was hiding, the only way to get it was by talking to her.

It was a risky gamble, one that might be Natalie's last stop. But it wasn't as if they could call up one of Irina's friends to find out what they wanted to know.

"I think we need to question her."

"We have no authority. She has no reason to talk to us. I certainly wouldn't in her shoes."

That was a point Natalie hadn't considered. She rotated her shoulders, trying to work out the kinks in her neck.

"There is one avenue I can try. An acquaintance at the CIA," Owen said.

She widened her eyes. "An acquaintance?"

He made a face. "I wouldn't exactly call him a friend.

I helped him out a few years ago. He said he'd do me a favor in return. I'd forgotten all about it until now."

"If you were ever going to use that favor, now seems the time," Emily stated.

Natalie gave Owen a nod of agreement. He wasted no time pulling out his phone and dialing a number as he turned and moved out of earshot.

This was just another example of how clandestine and dangerous Owen's life was. She had a feeling the image she had of missions from watching movies was nothing compared to the real thing.

And that frightened her. While she was stressed to the max about her predicament, the bioweapon, and Orrin, Owen was able to look at it all objectively. It was how he'd been trained, and how he saw the world.

More proof that they lived vastly different lives. He was right earlier. She hated anything that upset her order. She detested anything scary.

Yet, she had walked right into the situation because she'd known deep in her soul that it was the right thing to do. She hadn't known a hit would be taken out on her, or that Orrin would be kidnapped.

She hadn't known that a group of assassins would come after her. Or that she would have to run for her life with Owen protecting her.

She hadn't known she would be thrown into a world of intrigue, secrecy, and deception that made her question everything.

But she'd never felt more alive.

There was no doubt she was terrified of dying, but there was a bigger picture she saw. Ragnarok. That bioweapon—regardless of what it did—could be used against another nation. That blood would be on her hands if she didn't do all that was possible to keep it hidden.

Emily's hand rested on her shoulder. "This is some shit storm you've gotten into, Natalie."

"I know," she replied with a wrinkle of her nose.

"But if anyone can keep you safe, it's him," Emily said as she looked toward Owen.

"He already has."

Owen turned back to them as he lowered his phone, the call obviously over. "I suspected the CIA might be watching Irina. The former agent still has contact with the FSB, though she's not technically working for them anymore."

"How is that possible?" Emily asked.

He lifted his shoulders in a shrug. "My contact was able to tell me that Irina left the FSB right after her husband died in mysterious circumstances. That's also when she left Russia."

"They obviously didn't try to stop her," Natalie said.

"That's the thing, after her husband was buried, Irina went into hiding. No one saw her for a month. The next time she appeared, she was in the States."

Emily's eyes widened. "Lots of secrecy involved."

"Though my contact didn't confirm it, there is a suspicion that the CIA helped her escape. He was hesitant to give me too much, which means Irina might be working for them in some capacity."

"It would explain why the Russians didn't send someone to kill her," Natalie said.

"Or it could all be a trick and Irina still works for the FSB," Owen pointed out.

Natalie looked down at the picture of Irina Matveev and wondered if she was the one controlling the Russians who'd tried to kill her. Could she face the woman who—potentially—wanted her dead?

"I still think we need to talk to Irina," she said.

Owen blew out a breath and walked to her. "I think you're right. Though, I don't like the idea of any of this."

"If it's her, she'll know my face," Natalie pointed out.

"There's no doubt it'll be dangerous. If it is her, she'll know all our faces."

Emily pointed to a piece of paper on the top of the stack. "Her address is here, as well as her itinerary for the next week."

Natalie looked over Irina's schedule. The woman was on the move constantly. But there was a lunch in two days that Irina had planned, right after a meeting downtown.

"I know this place," she told Owen. "I know the route she'll take. The building for her appointment is only a block from the restaurant."

"So she'll walk," Owen said with a nod.

Natalie glanced at the papers. "We could try to catch her on the way to her lunch appointment and have a little chat."

"If you speak Russian, she'll talk to you."

"And possibly kill her," Emily pointed out.

Owen's gaze narrowed. "She can try."

Hours of nothing. At least the last hour had been filled with something to do. Owen focused on Irina's file. There was something about her going from KGB to FSB and the missing years.

He flipped to the pages that listed her KBG file and looked at Natalie. "Something is missing. Her KGB file doesn't start at her recruitment as it should. It picks up in the middle after she's already been on several assignments. There's a reason some of her file is missing."

"What would cause something like that?" Natalie asked.

His gaze slid to Emily before it returned to Natalie. "It means someone wanted to hide something. I've done something similar for one of my men. He changed his name, and I helped the Navy bury any documents with his old identity so he could go undercover."

"Then Irina has something to hide," Nat said.

He shrugged. "She or the government. Her recruitment into the FSB and her rank tells me she was in the thick of things for many years."

"Why move to Texas?" Emily asked.

Natalie held up Irina's picture. "That's a question I'd like answered."

The more he thought of Natalie talking to Irina Matveev, the more he felt it was a bad idea. "Say Irina is running the Russians. You won't be able to change her mind about calling off the hit."

"The hit?" Emily repeated, her voice pitched higher. "Natalie?"

Natalie put a hand on Emily's arm. "Look who I'm with, Em. A SEAL. Like you said, he will keep me safe."

Emily didn't say more, but she wasn't as convinced as Natalie. At least Nat believed he'd keep her alive, and that's exactly what he planned.

"What if it isn't Irina?" Natalie asked. "What if she knows something that could help us?"

He conceded that she had a point, but it wasn't worth putting her so close to danger. "That's a lot of 'what ifs.' "

"The sooner we learn who is controlling the group, the more leverage we have. And right now, we need some of that. We're flying blind, and while I might not be a SEAL, even I know that's not good," Natalie said.

They needed to know who was in charge of the Russian assassins. She was right, leverage was something they required in order to retrieve Orrin. He just didn't like the fact that Nat was going to talk to a woman who could've decided to end her life.

"If we're going to do this, we need to have a plan and several escape routes.

She smiled. "Of course."

He went back to examining Irina Matveev's life on paper. She appeared to be a normal citizen, but looks could be deceiving.

He caught Natalie staring at him. When he met her gaze, there was something in her deep green eyes. He felt her observing him often, and he wished he knew what she was thinking.

Natalie always cloaked her feelings, and time had only made her a master of it. She'd shut him down quickly enough earlier, but the memory of their kiss still lingered on his tongue.

If only he knew what to say to break past the walls she'd erected to keep him out. At times, he felt he was close, but mainly it seemed as if she would never be his again.

He knew what he asked. At least, he thought he did. He desired her. There was no denying it, even if he wanted to. Seeing her, touching her, inhaling her intoxicating scent were all reminders of why he'd fallen head over heels for her in the first place.

He didn't care what he had to do, but he wanted Natalie with him. Always. Owen wasn't sure how it would work with his part in the SEALs or her work, but he was willing to find out.

He looked away from Nat and through the glass toward Simon, while making a mental list of everything he needed to do to get ready for Natalie to speak to Irina—as well as get away.

To his surprise, Natalie came to stand beside him. She fidgeted, showing her nervousness.

"We could screw this up."

He nodded. "But we won't."

"Irina could be the key."

"I hope she is. I also hope that she'll give us something, but in all likelihood, she won't."

"Thanks for bursting my bubble," she said as she faced him, smiling.

He grasped her shoulders and looked into her eyes. "Do you want to know why I think this will work?"

"That would be very helpful, because I'm beginning to second-guess myself."

"You have a kindness about you, Nat. An openness that people gravitate toward without even realizing it. We can use it to our advantage."

A small frown formed on her brow. "Openness?"

"If Irina is controlling things, you'll surprise her with a visit. If she isn't, we might learn some information.

Either way, I'll be watching. Nothing is going to happen. That I swear."

"Where will you be?"

He grinned, unable to help himself. "Somewhere I can get a clear shot off at any target who looks as if they're coming for you, and somewhere I can get out of quickly to get to your side."

She paused, considering his words. "That sounds like a good plan."

"This is what I do." He wondered if she realized she'd moved closer to him. He gently rubbed his thumbs in circles on her arms.

Her guard was lowered. He didn't know why, nor did he question it. He forgot Emily was in the room as he tilted his head. He'd been craving another kiss ever since the first. The hunger to taste her again was driving him mad with desire.

Natalie's lids slowly lowered and her head leaned to the side. His heart leapt as she leaned into him. Their lips were about to touch when Simon banged open the door to the lab.

Natalie jerked out of his arms. He gritted his teeth and faced Dr. Moore, whose hair was no longer tidy. It hung loosely about his shoulders in waves.

"I think I've discovered what's in the vial," he announced.

Owen faced him. "What is it?"

"It's new," Simon said. He ran a hand through his hair.

Emily shrugged, her arms crossed over her middle. "I thought it might be, based on what Natalie told me."

"Normally, we in the science community hear through

the grapevine when someone is working on a new bio-weapon, but I've heard nothing." Simon shook his head as he looked at the floor in obvious distress.

Owen crossed his arms over his chest. "We told you it wasn't from this country."

"It doesn't matter." Simon ran his hand through his hair again as he lifted his head to look at them. "No matter how secret the endeavor is, it leaks. Nothing stays quiet. It takes years to develop a weapon of this magnitude, and nothing has been said. That's not normal."

Natalie moved toward Simon. "Are some countries more secretive than others?"

Simon gave her a wry look. "None want it leaked, but scientists talk. They like to tout their findings and creations. It's hard to keep us quiet."

"A government should be able to," Emily replied.

Simon shrugged indifferently. "Not necessarily."

Owen tucked that bit of information away. "So, what is it?"

"Biological agents are made up of microorganisms, bacteria, fungi, and viruses. Along with their toxins. I've tested the liquid in the vial against all known agents such as anthrax, Ebola, ricin, and even the plague. It matches nothing in the CDC database."

Natalie exchanged a glance with Owen. "What does that mean?"

"It means, Ms. Dixon, that whatever was created is entirely new." He paused and gave a shake of his head. "I have no way of knowing what this weapon might do if used."

That wasn't good news at all. Owen had hoped they

would discover what Ragnarok did. Instead, they were leaving just as they'd come in regards to the weapon.

At least they had something, though—Irina Matveev.

"What about a cure?" Natalie asked Simon.

"I'd have to know what it did first," he replied.

The news was going from bad to worse. Owen watched Simon run his hand through his hair yet again, a nervous tick. He then asked, "Can you make an antidote?"

"If I had a few years," Simon answered acerbically. He pointed into his lab behind him. "None of you seem to understand what is sitting in there."

Owen took a few steps closer to Simon. "We know exactly how potentially dangerous it is. What we need to know is what went into designing such a weapon, and how it might be used."

"I . . . I don't have those answers." Simon shook his head as he dropped his arms to his sides. "I'd have to do extensive tests. As it is, I've put this entire campus in jeopardy by analyzing the vial without the proper containment protocols in place."

"You wore a hazard suit, gloves, and a mask," Natalie said.

Simon waved away her words. "I don't know if the liquid is supposed to be administered by ingestion, touch, or through the air. I'd need—"

"To do more tests," Owen said over him. "We understand."

Simon moved against the wall and pointed to the vial through the door. "Please, take that and leave."

Natalie gathered the papers while Owen collected the

weapon and tube. He walked from the lab and checked the hall for the men.

"Thank you, Emily," Natalie said while stuffing the papers in her purse.

Emily smiled and gave her a quick hug. "Stay safe. And let me know if I can help with anything else."

"You've done enough." Owen looked to Simon. "Both of you. Thank you."

He handed the container to Natalie, who put it in her purse. Natalie then looked up, giving him a nod that she was ready.

"How do we get out of here?" she asked.

He motioned to the map of the building on the door. "See those exits?"

"Yep. And we're parked here," she said, pointing to the parking lot.

"If we encounter the men, and I tell you to run, make your way through the building and around to the truck."

She flattened her lips. "Wish I'd known this earlier. I could've been studying a map of the campus."

"All you need to know is this building. Look at the map. Remember where the exits are."

He gave her a few seconds to put it to memory. Then Owen opened the door and peered first one way, then the other. Natalie was right behind him when he exited the lab.

Though he wouldn't say it aloud, he was ready to kick some Russian ass.

CHAPTER TWENTY-TWO

Natalie's stomach was a ball of nerves. It churned viciously to the point where she thought she might be sick. Fear gripped her in its iron fist, refusing to loosen its hold as they walked down the stairs.

Right toward the assassins.

"Remember the exits," Owen said.

"That's only if we run into the men." Then she understood. They would definitely be facing off with the assholes.

"If they approach us outside, run to the truck." He handed her the keys.

Truck. He wanted her to go to the truck. Right. She could do that.

While he fought the men.

The same ones who'd tried to kill her.

The same faction who'd murdered Virgil and Charlotte.

The same group who'd kidnapped Orrin and killed his team.

Natalie kept her gaze straight ahead. It was everything she could do to put one foot in front of the other.

For the first time, she truly understood the whole "fight or flight" thing.

Because she fought the urge to turn and run the other way.

Owen was confident they would get away. There was no reason for her not to think he was right. Except for the whole Russians-wanting-to-kill-her thing. And to think, she'd lobbied to talk to Irina Matveev.

She inwardly shook her head. What had she been thinking? Being with Owen gave her false bravado, but the reality was right before her. And she was scared shitless.

Her eyes locked on Owen's fine ass as he walked ahead of her. He fought with conviction and confidence, knowing he would win. Not once had he shown an ounce of fear.

It made her wonder how many people he'd saved as a SEAL. How many times had he been in such scenarios where he had to get past others trying to kill him?

Probably too many to count. But he was still standing. He was the one beside her.

She took a deep breath, her terror easing its smothering hold. All she had to do was follow his instructions to get to the truck. The rest would be on him.

Her hand went to the strap of her purse. It was up to her to ensure that no one got their hands on Ragnarok. Her chin lifted. She could do this.

She *would* do this.

As they passed a hallway, she glanced up and saw the cameras. They were everywhere. Not to mention people about campus. And lest she forget, the men after them most likely had weapons. All of it pointed to the possibility of Owen getting hurt.

Owen was an imposing individual with his wide shoulders, intense stare, and don't-fuck-with-me manner. His upbringing made him strong, honorable, and resilient.

His years in the SEALs had tempered him like a piece of steel. There was a fierceness that hadn't been there before. A savage, brutal side honed in war.

It was in his walk, in the way he thought. In his very being. He was a warrior through and through. A man who fought for his country and his family without hesitation or thought for himself.

That's who had saved her from the Russian assassins.

That's who was going to get her safely back to the ranch.

He halted at the doors of the science building and turned to her. "Get to the truck while I hold them off."

"Do you want my pistol?"

He gave a shake of his head.

She kept forgetting that Owen *was* a weapon. But he still couldn't stop a bullet.

"Look around. We're in a public place. They're going to have to watch themselves not to bring attention."

She gave a nod he was expecting. "Right."

"Ready?" he asked.

She might not have seen pictures of Orrin's team being executed. She hadn't seen the men surrounding her mother's house before Owen came for her.

But one of the brutes had gotten his hands on her. They had killed Virgil and Charlotte.

They had orders to kill her.

The group would do whatever it took to find the vial. That meant the odds of someone getting injured—or even killed—were elevated no matter how highly trained Owen was.

She'd felt safe on the ranch. Ever since they'd left, she'd been looking over her shoulder, waiting for the men to find her.

There was nothing like having your life threatened to put things into perspective. Like admitting what she craved.

Years ago, Owen had walked away without explanation. It didn't matter what had intertwined their lives again. He was risking his life to protect her instead of finding his father.

Life could be snuffed out so easily. She wasn't going to walk out those doors until she gave in to what her heart desired most.

She grabbed his shirt with both hands. He frowned down at her, his chocolate gaze searching hers. Before she changed her mind, she pressed her lips against his.

In the next heartbeat, his arms wound around her, holding her firmly. He slanted his lips over hers. She might have begun it, but he quickly took over.

He groaned and deepened the kiss. The taste of him was erotic. Her body came alive in an instant, opening and readying—for him. Her breasts swelled, aching for his touch. Her sex throbbed with need as her blood heated.

It was her turn to moan when his hand delved into her hair, gripping it to hold her head still as the kiss heated. Excitement burned through her.

His large hands ran down her back to her waist and hips before he pulled her against him. His arousal pressed into her stomach, causing passion to sizzle through her.

The kiss turned fiery, scorching her with the hunger she tasted—and felt. He was everything she'd ever wanted. This was what they were supposed to be. Owen was always supposed to be her happy ending.

Was it fate that sent them on different paths only to bring them together again?

He ended the kiss and looked down at her with tenderness and passion. "Don't pull back now. Not after that." His gaze dropped to her lips. "I missed your kisses and your taste."

She ran her hands over his thick shoulders, unwilling to talk. He wanted what she couldn't give, and she couldn't tell him that now.

"Don't think. Feel what's between us. It's swallowing me whole, Nat, and I can't be going down that road alone."

She pulled out of his arms, but he didn't let her get far. He cupped her cheek. A heartbeat later, he dropped his arms and faced the exit.

Then he pushed open the doors without another word about the kiss or his desires. They strode out of the building side by side. She spotted the Taurus's car doors open, and two Russians unfolding their large frames from the vehicle. They stood tall and daunting with their gazes locked on her and Owen.

Owen gave her hand a squeeze for encouragement. "Let them get close."

Pretending not to know the men were walking their

way, she and Owen continued toward the truck. The closer they got to the vehicle, the better she felt. Until she saw another man come around the truck.

He was taller than the others, with sandy blond hair and black eyes. She imagined he was cut from granite, there were so many bulging muscles.

While her steps faltered, Owen's didn't. He kept walking as if nothing was out of the ordinary. "Can I help you?" Owen asked the third man.

He smiled coldly and jerked his square chin to the building. "You had a long visit."

She'd hoped the man was just someone from the campus, but the Russian accent put a vicious, brutal end to that. She looked around to find they were alone with the men.

"Stay calm," Owen mumbled under his breath.

She almost snorted at the absurdity of his comment. There was nothing relaxed about the situation, or any way for her to remain that way since she'd never been calm to begin with.

She'd been on pins and needles since she saw Ragnarok mentioned in the report. Calm seemed as far away as the moon at the moment.

"And what business is it of yours?" Owen asked as he came to a halt ten feet from the truck.

She stopped beside him, her heart thumping so loudly she was sure everyone could hear. She glanced behind her and saw the other two men closing in.

"Do not play innocent," the giant stated with a warning look in her direction. "Give us what we want. Perhaps then the Saints will allow your father to live."

"I don't know what you're talking about," Owen replied.

The mention of the Saints caught her attention. She didn't have time to think more on it as her attention shifted to Owen when he gave her hand a squeeze. He didn't seem deterred by the giant or his questions.

"Ragnarok. Give it."

Owen threw out his hands before letting his arms fall to his sides. "I don't know what you're talking about. What is Ragnarok? Is that why my father went missing?"

She wanted to applaud. She was so thrilled at how easily Owen turned the questions on the man and made himself look innocent and ignorant of the facts at the same time.

But it infuriated the giant. His face went red and his lips twisted. "Three sons were brought to Texas."

Owen nodded slowly. "Our aunt and uncle were killed, and our father is missing. Obviously, you had something to do with that."

With eight little words, Owen's entire attitude changed. He went from unassuming to hardline. The change happened while he spoke, shocking even the giant.

The smile that Owen wore was cold and deadly. "I've been waiting for you."

That was her cue. She took a few stumbling steps back as Owen rushed the giant. She chanced a look over her shoulder to see the other two men rush to help their comrade.

It was a melee of fists, elbows, kicks, and grunts. The crunch of bone echoed in her ears. She gave Owen and the giant a wide berth.

Owen was quick, and his punches landed accurately, but the Russian was a good foot taller with an extended reach. She winced when the giant's fist connected with Owen's face.

The other two joined in on the fight. She wanted to help, but she wouldn't be any use. She wrapped her hands around the grip of the pistol in her purse. But she didn't draw it.

Instead, she raced toward the truck as Owen had told her to do, clicking the unlock button on the key fob. She threw open the door and jumped inside. Only then did she look toward Owen to see him holding his own against the three big Russians.

To her surprise, the sound of sirens rang in the air. The men broke apart, and without a word, they rushed to their respective vehicles.

Natalie started the engine and drove toward Owen, who hopped in with the vehicle still rolling.

CHAPTER TWENTY-THREE

Sklad . . .

Yuri stormed into the room with a red face, radiating anger that nearly made Orrin smile. He watched Yuri from his position on the floor, leaning back against the wall. The subsequent beating was worth his lie.

"There was no package delivered to Mitch Hewett!" Yuri bellowed.

Orrin held Yuri's gaze for a long, silent minute. "Even if you asked Hewett himself, he wouldn't tell you. This is the Pentagon, *stariy droog*."

"How do you think we knew you were coming to Russia?"

That stopped him. He'd suspected, but to actually have it confirmed left him furious. And cold. There was a traitor in Mitch's office. Orrin somehow had to let Mitch know so he could get it taken care of.

If Orrin got away from Yuri. The likelihood of that happening was dwindling quickly. If he couldn't contact Mitch, he would have to find a way to leave clues for his sons. They would be the ones to ferret out the mole and bring him before Mitch.

It wouldn't make up for the execution of his team or Virgil's and Charlotte's murders, but it would help. It was really too bad that he wouldn't be there to help his boys.

"You have nothing to say?"

He was really tired of hearing the Russian accent butcher his language. "You could be lying. Why spend time arguing with you?"

"Because you know I speak truth. I could tell you who told me." Yuri's lips turned up in a triumphant smile.

"I sent the vial to Mitch Hewett," Orrin repeated. He had to wonder why no one mentioned the formula. Did Yuri not know about it? That was certainly a possibility.

Yuri motioned his men out. He glowered at Orrin until they were alone. "It was a nice try, *stariy droog*. I have men ready to take out one of your sons. By now they have him."

"Good luck with that."

That drew Yuri up short. "It is one man against three."

"It could be thirty, and it still wouldn't matter." He smiled until he felt the wound open on his lip. "Your men are no match for any of my sons."

"We will see about that. I wonder if you will sit so confident when you listen to the screams of your offspring as he dies," Yuri said and held up his cell phone.

Orrin held his smile until the door closed behind Yuri. Then he released a breath and raised his eyes to the ceiling. "God, I know you and I haven't been on speaking terms since Melanie died, but these are my sons. I've already lost my wife, my brother, and my sister-in-law. Please don't take my sons, as well. Please. Watch over them."

CHAPTER TWENTY-FOUR

Owen was happy to be back at the ranch. He'd take the truck and hide it again later, but for now, he wanted Natalie in the base where the Russians couldn't get her.

She'd driven the entire way back, silent with both hands on the wheel. He hadn't disturbed her solitude, mainly because he was pissed at having had a chance at the group and not taking any of them out.

Then again, he hadn't expected the third man. The Russians landed punches with the force of a wrecking ball. He tested his jaw, amazed it wasn't broken.

The mention of the Saints also had him on edge. He sent a quick text to Callie to see if she'd discovered anything yet, but it wasn't coincidence this was the second time they'd come across that name.

They needed to find out the link between the Saints and Ragnarok—and quickly.

When the truck pulled up at the ranch, Natalie parked it in front of the house. She cut the engine and sat there.

"You did good," he told her.

She swiveled her head to him. "They could've killed you."

"And I could've killed them. We got away."

"They'll know we came back here."

He looked at the house. "We're going to go inside and turn on some lights. Then I'm going to sneak you into the barn and down to the base. After I know you're there, I'm going to take the truck back to where it was this morning."

Natalie opened the door and slid from the truck. He reached the porch first and held up a hand for her to wait. Only after he did a check of the house did he allow her inside. She turned on the kitchen lights while he flipped on the switch in the living room.

Almost immediately, he ushered her out the back door into the growing darkness. They kept low and ran to the barn. Within minutes, they were locked inside the base.

He decided to remain for a few hours. While the coffee brewed, he rubbed his eyes with his thumb and forefinger. It had been a long day, and it was going to be an even longer night.

Especially after another kiss from Natalie.

That had been completely unexpected. It rocked him to his core, and he yearned for more.

"You were really going to kill those men right there?" Natalie asked.

He poured coffee into two mugs and handed her one. "They think we have the bioweapon. If they get us, they get the vial. Our only choice is to be rid of them."

"In front of anyone who happened to look out a window?"

"I was only thinking of protecting you."

She smiled sadly and shook her head. "Don't use me

as an excuse. You wanted revenge for Virgil and Charlotte, the team, and your father."

"That was part of it, but not all." He flexed his fingers, working out the bruises in his knuckles. "I've seen what those men can do. The thought of them laying their hands on you again makes me insane."

"You saved me once already."

"Until the vial is in other hands, Orrin is back, and the group of assassins are gone, you're still in danger."

She wrapped her hands around the mug before taking a sip. "We managed a win today."

He smiled. He liked having Nat at the ranch. There was a tingling of exhilaration every time he thought of her there. It made him realize what he'd missed by leaving Natalie.

And how much he wanted to change things between them.

"You kissed me." All thoughts of the Russians and the bioweapon vanished as he recalled how she had pulled him against her. The craving to make her his intensified the longer he was around her.

She held his gaze. "I did."

"Don't deny the passion between us."

"I'm not," she replied. "But there's no point in talking about it."

"Why? You wanted the kiss."

"It was a kiss. Leave it at that, Owen."

She rose and walked away. He thought of all the things he wished he would've said that might have had her in his arms. But once again, he was too late.

He wanted to follow her, carry her to a room and

make love to her until the sun came up. He was desperate to let go of the past and get lost in all that was Natalie.

To have a future that consisted of more than death and loneliness.

It would be so easy. She made it so easy to love her. He wanted—*hungered*—to feel her in his soul, to know they stood together once more.

That's when he decided he wasn't going to give up so quickly.

CHAPTER TWENTY-FIVE

Natalie blew out a breath in the steam-filled bathroom. She'd taken an extra long shower after such a grueling day. She let the silk nightgown glide over her body as she put it on. After combing out her wet hair, she gathered her clothes and returned to the bunk area.

Natalie stopped at the bed she'd claimed and dropped her shoes. There was only the one light on at the bedside table because she liked the soft glow of it.

She felt a prickle of awareness on the back of her neck before heat spread over her. She knew without turning around that it was Owen.

And God help her, but she was glad he was there.

There were soft footsteps as he padded across the concrete floor. She let the clothes slide from her fingers to the ground. Her breath locked in her lungs when she felt him come up behind her.

She found it difficult to form a thought as she waited for his touch. He stood so closely, his shirt brushed her arm. The heat of him surrounded her, cocooning her in desire and expectation. Her blood pumped faster, and awareness sizzled around her.

Long fingers moved her hair to one side. His head bent, lips skating along her skin. She leaned her head to the side to give him better access.

One arm wrapped around her waist, just below her breasts. He held her tightly while his lips and tongue tantalized her skin. Her eyes slid shut, even as he molded his body to hers.

He teased a spot on her neck that drove her wild. A breathy sigh rushed past her parted lips as he gently nipped. Her sex throbbed with need—a need only Owen could quench.

Chills raced along her arm when his fingers caressed from her wrist up to her neck. Her head rolled onto his shoulder. She bit her lip when one of his fingers hooked the thin strap of her gown and tugged it off her shoulder.

He continued to pull until the gown snagged on her nipple. She gasped when the silk scraped the turgid peak. Then his fingers were there, rolling her nipple between his digits.

She wrapped her fingers around his wrist as pleasure rushed through her as quick as lightning.

His hands were everywhere. Her neck, her cheek, her hair. He caressed her hip, cupped her butt, and massaged her exposed breast.

All the while, his mouth was on her skin, kissing, nipping, and using his tongue to lick and lave. Her legs buckled, but he managed to keep her upright.

Suddenly, he spun her around to face him. She clung to his wide shoulders. Their gazes locked then held while he slid the other strap from her shoulder. The silk nightie fell to a puddle at her feet.

Owen knelt before her. He cupped a breast in each

hand, teasing her nipples. Then his lips wrapped around one peak. Natalie moaned, her fingers shoving into his thick hair.

He moved from one nipple to the other, touching nothing but her breasts—yet her entire body was on fire. For him. Hunger mixed with desire inflamed her.

When he stood, he lifted her in his arms. She wrapped her legs around his waist and smoothed her hands over his face. She gazed into his eyes, her fingers sliding into his dark locks once more.

He walked to the bed then slowly lowered her. The feel of his weight on her again was delicious, intoxicating. She wanted them skin-to-skin, with nothing but the night around them.

She sighed when his lips found hers and kissed her as if there were no tomorrow, as if they were the only two people on the planet.

Owen was in heaven. He knew because he'd been there once before and had foolishly left. Now that he had Natalie in his arms again, he wasn't ever going to let her go.

Her long, slim fingers slid beneath his shirt. A groan left him when her nails skimmed his back. She'd always known how to touch him in ways that heightened his senses and had him begging for more.

He broke the kiss long enough to jerk off his shirt before he was back in her arms. Owen braced his elbows on either side of her as he held her face between his hands.

As he gazed into her eyes, he was taken back to a time when the future was stretched before them, uncharted and unexplored. He wanted that again.

He needed that.

He lowered his head and kissed her gently. Her hands roamed over his back and shoulders. He ached to be inside her, to feel her heat surrounding him once more. But he refused to rush it.

He wasn't going to take anything for granted. This might be his only night with Natalie, and he was going to make love to her as she deserved.

Kissing down her neck to her chest, he slid down her body, touching her with his hands, lips, and tongue so that his scent was branded on her.

He shifted to one elbow and flattened his palm on her stomach before he caressed to the junction of her thighs. He parted the blond curls and glided his fingers into her.

She moaned, her back arching. His cock jumped, demanding that he take her right then. He held on to his control and closed his eyes as he felt her slick, wet heat.

He pumped his finger slowly within her. Her chest heaved, and her hands clenched the covers. He'd never seen anything so beautiful.

He could still remember the first time he'd brought her to orgasm. It had been a gorgeous sight, but it was nothing compared to the striking woman who lay in his arms now.

He removed his finger from her body and swirled it around her clit. A cry fell from her lips as her legs fell open. He looked up to see her watching him with hooded eyes. Her legs trembled as her nipples hardened beneath his gaze.

She rocked, grinding herself against his hand. He moaned, his balls tightening.

"Owen," she called breathlessly. "I need you."

He settled between her legs and grinned. "Not yet, baby."

Natalie wasn't able to string a coherent thought together once his tongue touched her. He knew just where to lick to make her cry out and have her hips rocking.

He knew the right amount of pressure to apply to make her shiver. With just a few swipes of that amazing tongue of his, Natalie felt the tightening low in her belly.

The climax rose up, swallowing her quickly. She shouted Owen's name as her body tensed, then jerked with the force of the orgasm.

She cracked open an eye when she felt the bed dip, and watched as Owen yanked his jeans off. Natalie held out her arms for him, her body still convulsing from such a strong climax.

"I love watching you peak," he said as he placed a kiss on her nipple.

She smiled at him. God, how she'd missed being in his arms. Even at a young age, Owen had been a good lover. But he'd honed his skills in their years apart.

She pushed at his shoulder as she sat up, rolling him to his back. She straddled him. His smile was sexy, his gaze darkening. As if she would forget one of his favorite positions.

She rose up on her knees and took his cock in hand. Natalie wrapped her fingers around him snugly. Then she stroked his long shaft until he groaned.

As soon as he did, she halted. His eyes narrowed, but one side of his lips was still curved in a grin.

"Tease."

It was her turn to smile. She guided him to her entrance so that the head of his cock slid inside her. His large hands were suddenly on either side of her hips.

He attempted to push her down, but she refused. She raised a brow then shook her head at him. She was going to do this at her speed, because all too soon, Owen would take over. It's what she wanted. She craved his dominance in bed, for him to show her he was in control.

But for now, she was all his.

Gradually, she took him deeper inside her. She felt her body stretching for him, and it made her legs shake. When she had taken half of him inside, she straightened until just the tip of him remained.

The only warning she had was a slight tightening of his fingers before his hips rose and he plunged inside her. Her head dropped back as her eyes closed.

He felt so good. She wanted to stop time and relish the moment. Then he began to thrust, and she once more lost all train of thought.

Owen watched her, his desire heightening with each second. Nat's long, blond hair fell behind her in a thick curtain. Her exposed neck made him itch to kiss and lick it. Her hands were braced behind her on the bed so her breasts were thrust out.

He held her hips still as he plunged deeper. Her soft cries were growing louder with each minute. His gaze lowered to the sight of his cock entering her. It was an erotic picture that nearly tipped him over the edge.

The sight of her breasts bouncing made him groan. He cupped them, tweaking her nipples. That caused her to moan low in her throat.

He'd denied himself any kind of relationship through-out the years, but in his dreams and fantasies, it had always been Natalie. Now that he had her in his bed, he wanted to savor every second.

He flipped her onto her back and rose up over her. His hands were braced on either side of her head. He pulled out then thrust back in, hard and deep.

Her eyes rolled back in her head, and her nails sank into his back. It made him smile. He set a driving tempo that had sweat glistening over their skin in short order.

Their breaths were harsh, their moans loud. Her ankles were locked tightly around his waist. He plunged harder, deeper.

Natalie opened her eyes. He got lost in the green depths as their bodies joined in a dance as old as time. All that he wanted was in his arms. It was never clearer than in that moment how much Natalie was a part of his past, present, and future.

There was no use denying it. He'd done that for long enough. If he didn't grasp what was before him, he'd end up lonely and alone.

That thought made his heart skip a beat. The idea that the tragedy that brought them together might be the last time he saw her was sobering.

He stopped moving. He touched her face before he kissed her passionately. Her arms came around him, holding him tightly. Only then did he begin to move again.

She tore her lips from his on a cry as he buried himself deep. Their bodies rocked, one sliding against the other. He felt her legs tighten around him and knew she was close to peaking a second time.

He began to plunge in long, hard thrusts that he knew

always sent her over the edge. As her cries grew louder, he watched the pleasure cross her face.

As soon as her body tightened around his cock, his orgasm rushed through him. He thrust once more, burying himself deep as his seed emptied inside her.

He gathered her in his arms and rolled to the side with their bodies still joined. He could feel her heart pounding in her chest, matching the wild beat of his own.

With their legs entwined, a bubble of ecstasy surrounded them. The time was theirs. Nothing and no one were going to interrupt them.

CHAPTER TWENTY-SIX

Natalie was determined not to make a big deal of her night with Owen. The thing was, it was huge. She couldn't remember the last time she'd been so nervous. It was silly. Especially since this wasn't the first time they had slept together.

But it was the first time in years.

She was glad she'd woken to find him gone to take the truck to hide it again. His absence allowed her time to think. Unfortunately, that thinking only made things worse.

A little thrill of excitement filled her stomach when she spotted him on one of the cameras. He let the alert sound, which meant he hadn't hidden from the cameras like before.

He was giving her time to prepare for his return.

She smoothed her hands over her hair and jumped up, looking around. A glance down at her jeans and shirt made her wish she'd chosen something different, something . . . sexier, maybe. She looked helplessly at her duffle bag of clothes.

"It's fine," she told herself. "I'm fine. No reason to be anxious."

None at all.

Except that she'd slept with the man she wanted to keep at arm's length.

"Way to go," she mumbled.

The door to the base opened and Owen came down the steps. He paused when he saw her, a sexy grin tilting the corners of his lips. "Hey."

"Hey." Could he be any more gorgeous?

"I got food," he said and held up the bag.

She grabbed the bag, suddenly famished. Only then did she realize she hadn't eaten anything since yesterday at noon. She smiled when she saw the breakfast burritos and quickly gobbled the first egg, bacon, and cheese burrito slathered with picante sauce before reaching for a second.

"I didn't want to wake you when I left," he said after he swallowed his bite.

She shrugged and put more picante sauce on her burrito. "It's fine."

"I didn't want to leave that bed."

Despite telling herself not to gaze into his chocolate eyes, she did just that. But she didn't know how to respond, not when she was still so mixed up about it all.

"Do you have regrets?"

She swallowed and looked away before she stood. "No. We have needs that must be met."

"Needs? That's how you're going to handle this?" he asked, a hard bite to his words.

"There's nothing to handle." She had expected this

reaction, but it didn't make it any better. "We're consenting adults."

"Consenting adults."

Him repeating her words wasn't a good sign. Especially when his eyes began to narrow. A sure signal that he was getting frustrated or angry—or both.

"That's right. You don't have to worry about me having any expectations," she replied.

"Expectations."

She inwardly winced. There was no denying the thread of anger in his voice now.

"I want more than last night. I want you," he stated.

Shit. There went her appetite. It was all out on the table now. The very thing she'd tried to avoid. She should've known better with Owen.

He was Mr. Confrontation. If there was an issue, he wanted it talked about right then. There was no putting it off. The problem was, she wasn't sure how she felt about their night together.

Had it been great? It had been wonderful. Beautiful. Earth-shattering.

But that didn't mean she wanted a relationship with him. No matter how great it was to be in his arms, it was what happened outside of sex that reminded her how things would be.

She dropped the last half of the second burrito onto the paper and wadded it up. "Please don't."

"Is this because I left you after graduation?"

"It has something to do with it, yes." Natalie blew out a breath. Confrontation, here she came. "I'm in a good place."

His eyes hardened a fraction. "And you don't want me in it."

"It took me years to get over you, and then came my disastrous marriage and subsequent divorce. I don't want any man," she declared.

She cleared her throat, giving herself a moment to calm down. The words had come out easier than she expected. She hurriedly—and brutally—tamped down any emotion that favored Owen.

It didn't matter that he'd touched her so tenderly or brought her such ecstasy. Owen Loughman was bad for her in every way. He'd destroyed her world with one act. It had left her with a scar. It was one only she could see, but it had shaped her life and every decision.

For once, she was being selfish—callous even—by thinking of herself. She wouldn't put her heart out there again to be trampled upon as if she meant nothing.

She didn't trust love or the entanglements that came along with relationships. She hadn't lied. She was in a good place, and intended to remain there.

No amount of charm, seductive drawl, or mind-numbing kisses would change that.

He might know how to play her body to perfection, but Owen was horrendous at handling affairs of the heart. He'd once been selfish, thinking only of himself, uncaring about how his actions would affect her.

It seemed only fair that he was getting a taste of his own medicine.

"Perhaps we turn the subject elsewhere. Irina Matveev," he said tightly.

She was excited to have a change of topic. It wasn't

as if she could walk away from him. Not now, at least. Her life depended on him. It was better if they could move past things. "What do you have?"

He pointed to the conference room. "Maps of the part of downtown Dallas we'll be in."

She rose and walked into the room to see the table covered by maps and detailed plans of multiple escape routes.

Just what time had he gotten up?

"As I said yesterday, we'll have several alternative means of getting away if the Russians attack. Whether they work for Irina or not, we need to be prepared," he explained, coming up beside her.

"I see that," she said as she noted the different routes in various colors.

"Learn the maps inside and out. You need to be able to know which one to take at a second's notice." He held up a tiny, flesh-colored device. "This will be in your ear, and I'll talk to you through it."

Natalie took the earpiece. "Will I be able to talk to you, as well?"

"I'll hear you and those close to you, so yes, I'll be able to answer."

That made her feel a little better. She looked at the maps. "Where will you be?"

He circled an area with his finger. "This is where you'll intersect with Irina. I'll be here."

She followed the line of his finger to a building that would have direct line of sight to her.

"The sixteenth floor is under renovation for a law firm that's moving in. I'll set up there and keep watch."

"It looks like a good vantage point. If we have to take

the red, blue, or purple escape routes, you'll be right there."

Owen tapped the map where he'd be watching. "Even if we must use the yellow, green, or orange routes, I'll still be able to get to you here," he said and pointed to a location two blocks away.

If there had been even a smidgen of doubt as to Owen being qualified to keep her alive, that was now gone. She listened as he explained how she would get away from Irina or anyone else, where she could hide, and the places where they could meet up depending on which escape plan was used.

One strategy had them going into the drainage ditches. Another had them using public transportation to "blend" in. There were several others she would need to memorize, as well. The truck would be waiting for them to make their final exit from Dallas and return to the ranch.

When Owen finished going over things thirty minutes later, she pulled out a chair and sat. "What do Wyatt and Cullen think of this?"

"Wyatt doesn't think we should do it alone. I've not been able to get ahold of Cullen."

She rocked back in the chair. "And you think all of us need to stay apart?"

"Callie has confirmed that Cullen was seen at Dover AFB in Delaware. He should've met up with Mia by now and be tracking their own leads. Wyatt is attempting to keep up with Callie, who is following a clue she has yet to share with him."

She blew out a breath, nodding. "And we've got our thing. It's going to take all of us to find Orrin."

"And stop the hit on you," he added.

How could she forget that? "And that, as well."

He stared at the map for a long moment. Just when she thought he had nothing more to say, he lifted one of the maps and pulled out a picture frame hidden beneath.

She leaned forward to see it was a family photo of the Loughmans when Melanie was still alive. It must have been taken months before her death, and by the genuine smiles everyone wore, they had been a happy family.

"Dad kept this down here in his office," Owen said.

She raised her eyes to him. "Why wouldn't he? It's his family. Despite losing his wife and his sons ignoring him, this was a time when everything was going right."

"You mean when we were happy."

"Yes."

He drew in a deep breath and slowly released it as he looked around the base. "I still recall the day we came home from school in a torrential rainstorm. There was a smell I didn't recognize about the place. It's burned into my memory, though. It was the smell of death."

Her gut clenched because Owen *never* spoke of his mother's murder. None of the Loughmans did. It was forbidden and completely off-limits to everyone. So she wasn't sure why he was telling her now.

"Wyatt ran to the barn and grabbed the rifles while I hid Cullen. Even at ten years old, I knew something wasn't right. Everything was too quiet. I know it sounds weird, but it felt as if the elements were in an uproar."

Her eyes burned with unshed tears. She fought to keep them from falling as she listened.

Owen looked down at the table. "I cocked the shot-gun and trailed Wyatt into the house. We followed the smell up the stairs. The storm ceased suddenly, and the quiet was eerie."

He paused, and she saw his hands grip the edge of the table so tightly his knuckles turned white. It was everything she could do not to reach over and touch him, to offer comfort.

"We found Mom in her room, lying on the bed. At first, we thought she was sleeping. Then we walked closer and saw her eyes open, staring at the ceiling."

She clasped her hands together in her lap. Then drew in a shuddering breath, blinking rapidly. Her heart hurt to think of a ten-year-old Owen finding his mother in such a way.

"I still see the vivid bruising around her neck from the strangulation in my dreams sometimes." His eyes slid to her. "I stood guard over Mom while Wyatt checked the rest of the house and the barns. Then we kept Cullen from seeing anything by sending him to the neighbors' for help."

The "neighbors'" was a house miles down the road.

"He rode one of the stallions, who was a handful, but the fastest horse on the ranch. Cullen didn't argue about us getting the horse ready for him. He held on with a death grip and wide eyes. The stallion seemed to know something was wrong. He didn't fight the bit or the saddle as he usually did. He stood still as stone while Cullen used the fence to climb on him. Then they took off in a flash."

A tear escaped and rolled down her cheek. Everyone in the small town knew of Melanie's murder, but all she'd ever heard were rumors. She supposed that the only ones who knew this part of the story were the brothers.

For a long moment, Owen stared at her in silence. Then he blinked, as if remembering what he was doing. "The police finally arrived. Wyatt and I were quickly shoved out of the way. Cullen remained at the neighbors', which was for the best. I still think how odd it was that everyone who entered the house whispered. I thought it was because of us, but now I know it was because of Mom."

Natalie had met Mrs. Loughman several times at school functions. Melanie had been a beautiful, kind woman, who always had a smile on her face and time to spare for anyone who needed it. She never missed an event with her boys, and she was always ready with a hug and a kiss for them, no matter if they wanted it or not. She was one of those rare people who didn't have an enemy.

Owen dropped his chin to his chest. "There was no blood, but death doesn't need such displays to leave its mark. We were sitting on the porch steps when Dad arrived. He'd been on his way home on leave. The storm raged again. The lightning was horrible, and the rain torrential. He ran past us and into the house, not even seeing us. He was looking for Mom, but they'd already taken her body."

She hastily wiped away another couple of tears that escaped.

"It took six deputies to restrain him. He broke the sheriff's nose and someone else's arm." Owen grew quiet, contemplative for a moment. "There are some things I'll never forget about that day. The quiet, the smell of death, the sight of my mom with the bruises. And the sound of my father's grief as he bellowed her name over and over again."

By this time, she couldn't hold back the tears. They flowed freely. She sniffed quietly, unable to move, her gaze locked on Owen.

He lifted his head and reached over to wipe at the tears on one of her cheeks. "Just a few days ago, I arrived to that same stillness, that same smell of death. The difference was, there was blood this time. Lots of it. Death had once more left its mark on this house, and it was ghastly and horrific. I lost two more members of my family. Then they went after you. I tell you all this, Nat, so you'll understand why I need you safe. Why I will do whatever it takes to keep those men from getting to you. Because I can't lose anyone else. Especially you."

She blinked, her throat clogged with emotion too thick to work through. With no words available, she put her hand atop his and squeezed.

He stood straight and gazed at her with his dark brown eyes. "I'm not going to let them near you."

"I know you won't."

His word wasn't something Owen gave lightly, and once you had it, it was as binding as a vow.

He turned and walked from the conference room to the armory. She stood on shaky legs and made her way to the sleeping quarters before she sank onto her bed and buried her head in her hands as she cried.

Now that she knew details of Melanie Loughman's murder, as well as Wyatt's and Owen's involvement, she cried even harder. The boys had suffered so much.

It explained a lot about the Loughmans.

Especially Owen.

CHAPTER TWENTY-SEVEN

The rest of the day was spent gathering the weapons. Natalie was never far, but Owen was all too conscious of the wall she'd erected around herself.

He checked the Glock 19, moving the slide back and forth a few times before returning it to its holster. He then palmed two more magazines and set them beside the pistol.

Besides the Glock, he also had a Beretta M9 and a Colt that would be tucked into his boot. Not to mention the two knives hidden on his person.

He also tested the sights on a sniper rifle and three other semi-automatic rifles. While he worked on the weapons, he thought over what he'd told Natalie. He wasn't sure why he'd shared the memories of that life-changing day. He had never even spoken to his brothers about it.

Returning to the ranch brought everything back in living color. A reminder of how much life had sucked after his mother's murder.

Knowing what he did now, he was surprised Orrin hadn't gone after those responsible for his mother's death. Then again, for all he knew, his dad had. It wasn't as if he kept in contact with Orrin.

He began putting bullets in the magazines. It had been easy to stay away from the ranch and the memories. Yet, it also brought home a painful reminder—he only had one parent.

And Orrin was in the hands of the Russian military.

There was no doubt he and his brothers had done their father wrong. All of them had handled Melanie's murder their own way, but it pulled them apart instead of bringing them together.

If his mother were alive, she'd be grossly disappointed in all of them. And he found he was disappointed in himself.

He set down the magazine and closed his eyes. If he and his brothers had felt the loss of Melanie, then their father had been hit even harder.

Not only had he lost his wife, but also the mother of his children. Their father had become a single parent while dealing with his own grief. Owen didn't even want to think of how he might've handled things in his father's shoes.

"We're going to find him."

His eyes snapped open at the sound of Natalie's voice. He turned his head to find her standing in the doorway to the armory, but he couldn't hold her green gaze. He looked to the magazine clip in his hand, now full. He set it aside and began to load a second.

"Being back is hard, isn't it?" she asked.

"Yeah. I think that's why I kept away for so long."

"It wasn't just because of your dad?"

He gave a shake of his head. "I've been thinking of

him a lot. Growing up, I was lost in my misery. I'm only now comprehending that he had his own grief to overcome while trying to raise us."

"I can't imagine."

"Hating him was easy. He left us with Virgil and Charlotte to go back to the SEALs. I know it was his job, but it made it easy to blame him for everything. He was rarely here."

She leaned against the doorway. "Do you still hold him responsible for your mother's death?"

"I've always believed he was the cause of it. I know that with certainty after being a SEAL. No matter how deep undercover or unseen we think we are, someone always discovers our identities."

Owen finished the second magazine and started another. To his surprise, Natalie walked to him and laid a hand upon his, stilling him. She took the clip and began to fill it herself.

He searched her face, but she simply gave him a small smile. It wasn't just memories of the past that stirred something within him. It was Natalie, as well.

Being with her again, recalling how hot the passion burned between them and how good they fit together had pulled back the curtain of his life.

And he didn't like what he saw.

He thought he didn't need anyone, but the truth stood before him now. It was Natalie. It had always been her. How empty his life had been without her, how meaningless everything was.

Without a doubt, he knew he wanted her in his life—forever. He wanted her by his side, living, fighting, and loving as only they could.

The chances of that happening were slim, but regard-less of the outcome, she had a right to know the real reason he'd left her fourteen years earlier.

"It was because of Mom," he said.

Natalie's brows rose. "What was?"

"My leaving you graduation night."

Her hands stilled. She blinked up at him, her eyes giving nothing away. Finally, she set the bullets and magazine down and ran a hand through her long, light brown tresses.

Owen took that as his cue to continue. "I never doubted love existed. I saw it with my parents. I also saw how my father suffered after her death. More than anything, I knew what it was to walk into a room and find someone I loved murdered. The military was where I was born to be. I recognized and accepted that from an early age. What I wouldn't accept was bringing my work home and it affecting my family."

Her gaze lowered to the floor for a heartbeat.

"It's dangerous work I do. I never wanted to worry that some vermin would come after you while I was on a mission. I refused to have my children come home and find you as I found my mom. The only way I could guar-antee that wouldn't happen was to leave."

For long minutes, Natalie didn't respond. Then she re-sumed loading the magazine. "Now that I know how you found Melanie, I understand it all now. You should've talked with me, though. Leaving as you did was a dick move."

"It was," he said, trying to hide his smile. "I'm sorry."

"As I told you already, it's in the past."

"Is it? Seems it's still very much a part of current things."

She cut him a look. "Only because you keep bringing it up."

"Don't you see we have a second chance here?"

She set down the magazine once more and faced him. "You want me now? Now that you've gone about your life as you wished?"

He hesitated because he knew by her tone any way he answered would be wrong. "Yes."

"Too damn bad. There was a time I would've crawled through Hell and back again to get you back. I'm not that girl anymore."

She turned and left him standing there, wishing he could change the past.

All he had was the here and now. Not even the future was guaranteed in his line of work. It didn't matter if he had five minutes or fifty years, he wanted that time with Natalie.

All he needed to do was come up with a way to convince her of that while making up for the mistakes he'd made before.

An hour later, he walked up to the barn and stared over the land. With the sun nearly set, the sky was a vivid array of oranges, reds, and pinks.

Being at the ranch was just as hard as he'd always known it would be. It wasn't just the memories, but the sorrow of not having his mother there to share it with.

From the paddock, the mare snickered at him while the filly flicked her tail, watching him intently with dark, soulful eyes. He stilled when he heard Natalie walk up the steps.

She passed him without a word and walked straight to the mare. While he watched, he saw the smile on Nat's face as she whispered to the horses, rubbing the mare's head all the while.

Those lips of hers were more tempting now than ever before. He craved Natalie with a fire that threatened to devour him. All those years thinking he was living the life he wanted had been nothing but a joke.

What he wanted—what he needed—was Natalie.

And he had his work cut out for him if he intended to change her mind about them. There was no way she could respond to his touch as she had and *not* feel something.

She might not love him anymore, but there were still feelings there. That gave him all the hope he needed that he could get her to fall in love with him again.

The filly pranced around the pen, staying just out of reach of Natalie. He slowly walked to them, stopping a few feet from the fence.

"She's warming to you," he told Natalie.

Nat turned her head slightly to him. "She's the most beautiful thing I've ever seen."

"Master Ben did his job, but it's the mares who really give us such beauties."

Natalie squatted down and held out her hand, whistling softly. He held his breath while the foal hesitantly took a few steps toward Natalie before hastily backing away.

But Nat didn't give up. She called again. This time, the filly came close enough to stick out her nose and sniff Natalie's hand. After another minute, the foal took that last step.

He listened to Natalie talk to the filly while petting her neck and head. "You always had a way with the horses."

"I expected to feel odd showing up here that first time after so many years, but I didn't. This place has always felt . . ." she trailed off.

"Like home," he finished.

She nodded, shooting him a brief look. "Why would you stay away from such a beautiful place?"

"Memories. They're in every facet of this ranch."

Natalie stood when the foal turned to the mare to feed. "Good and bad memories. Don't focus on just the bad. It doesn't do your mother justice. Your father needs you. Remember that."

"I'm trying."

"Try harder."

He hesitated when he saw her looking at the oak tree. Was she remembering the story he'd told her of watching his parents there? She'd thought it romantic, and it was.

He hadn't done anything like that for her, and he regretted it tremendously. Now wasn't the time to make such a gesture with everything going on. But that didn't mean Owen couldn't plan something when this was all over.

He didn't want to think about the odds of them winning. Yes, they had the bioweapon, but for how long? Whoever betrayed his father would figure out soon enough that it was in their hands. And then they—along with the Russians—would come for it.

It was bad enough to have the assassins after them,

but an unknown enemy, as well? Then there was finding Orrin before he was killed.

The odds were stacked against them at every turn. And truth be told, it scared the hell out of Owen because Natalie was involved.

"You're thinking of Orrin," she said.

Owen nodded, keeping his thoughts about her to himself.

She stuck her hands in the back pockets of her jeans. "Tomorrow could give us something new."

Or end it all with her death. But he kept that to himself, as well. "We should get below now that it's getting dark."

He walked to the stairs as Nat gave the mare and foal one last pat. He made his way down with Natalie behind him. She slipped on the last step. Instinctively, he grabbed her, yanking her against him.

Her green eyes clashed with his as their faces came close. He wanted to kiss her so badly it took all of his willpower to hold back.

She had no idea how much he hungered for another taste of her, how he yearned to sink into her tight body once more.

He reluctantly released her. Then held his breath, hoping she would reach for him. Instead, she walked around him toward the kitchen area to begin fixing her dinner.

It was going to be a long-ass night.

CHAPTER TWENTY-EIGHT

Natalie swallowed past the nervousness the next morning as she stared in the mirror. She had done no more than doze the entire night, thinking about confronting Irina Matveev—and Owen's presence.

She was conflicted. She wanted to hate him for what he'd done. Time had dulled the heartache so that she had to keep reminding herself how badly she'd been hurt.

Could she really hold a man accountable for his actions as a teenager?

There was no doubt she wanted to, but it wasn't as easy as that. Sleeping with Owen had only complicated things to the extreme. She'd told him they were consenting adults, but the reality was that she'd wanted him.

After their kiss, she knew she was going to give in to the passion between them. When it came to Owen, she had never been able to resist his enticing kisses or his touch.

He'd had power over her body that seemed almost otherworldly from the very beginning. And nothing had changed that.

If she hadn't been staring at his ass, she never

would've tripped and wound up in his arms again. All she'd wanted to do was remain there. But no good could come of them together again.

She'd managed to walk away, but it had been close. With him so near, it was all she'd been able to think about.

His hands, his mouth. His thick cock filling her.

She closed her eyes and fisted her hands, trying to bring her body under control. Her sex throbbed, eager to have Owen inside her again, thrusting hard and fast.

Natalie shook her head to clear it of such thoughts—or at least push them aside for the moment. She opened her eyes, looking over herself in the mirror.

The tan corduroy jacket fit as if it had been custommade, and it was one of her favorite pieces. She paired it with a cream shirt, jeans, and brown boots—without a heel. She was going to be prepared if she had to run.

Satisfied, she walked from the bathroom to find Owen double-checking her pistol in her purse.

"Ready?" he asked.

"As I'll ever be."

"You have the knife in your boot?"

She bent and pulled out the knife far enough so he could see the handle before shoving it back down.

He gave a nod. "Don't reach for your gun unless you have to."

"We've been over this."

"And we're going over it again. I'll have you covered. The gun is there for an emergency."

She shot him a wry look. "If you have to open fire, I'd say it's an emergency."

His gave her an equally droll look. "You're supposed to run, remember?"

"I will. Don't worry about that."

Pleased with her answer, Owen checked the monitors one more time. "Let's go."

They left in the dark once more. She longed for the days she could walk out of her house and get into her car without having to hike for an hour first.

She was glad they didn't talk on the way to the truck. Silence allowed both of them to hear everything, but she also didn't have to worry about keeping up with the conversation.

After she climbed into the truck, her hands shook as she fastened the seatbelt. When she lifted her gaze, Owen was staring at her.

"You'll be fine," he said. "I'll have you covered."

"I know."

He started the truck and put it in drive. She looked behind them as they rolled away.

"Tell me the exits, starting at A," Owen said.

She took a deep breath, grateful to have something for her mind to focus on. One by one, she went through the exit strategies and where she would wait for him.

Anticipating his next question, she went through each scenario if she got trapped from one exit and how to escape if it happened. By the time she'd finished, the Dallas skyline was in sight.

"If anything happens, you won't have time to think," he said. "It's why I wanted you to memorize all of that. You'll have to trust yourself to know where to go."

"And if I forget."

He took the exit toward downtown Dallas. "Get to the truck. Wait there for an hour. If I've not made it back, drive away and call Wyatt."

"You'll make it back."

Owen glanced at her and pulled off the highway. "Of course, I will."

He was just saying that to appease her. She suddenly wanted to turn the truck around and head back. This was a stupid idea. One or both of them could get killed.

"Let's forget this and return to the ranch," she said.

Owen reached over and grasped her hand, squeezing it. "We've come this far. Besides, you were right, we need information."

They turned sharply and slowed before turning again to pull into the parking garage. Owen steered the truck to a ground floor spot near the exit and shut off the engine. They would leave the truck there and make their way, separately, to their places.

He pulled the keys out and sighed. Then he turned his head to her. "If you want to go back because you're scared for me, then I'll sit here and talk you out of it. If you want to return because you're afraid for your life, then I'll start the truck and we'll get back on the freeway."

She opened her mouth to answer, then hesitated. Her father had died of a heart attack when she was five. She hadn't grown up with a father figure around, but that didn't mean she didn't understand the connection.

She thought about how she might feel if it was her dad who had gotten kidnapped. There was nothing she wouldn't do to find him, and she didn't have the skillset that Owen did.

Her initial reaction to find Irina Matveev and speak

with her was because they had to know who con-
trolled the assassins. Leaving now would mean they
still had nothing.

In answer, she reached for the door. Owen's hand
stopped her before she could open it. She looked at him,
brow raised in question.

"Here," he said and handed her the earpiece.

She had completely forgotten about that little piece
of tech. She took it and stuck it in her ear.

"Testing," Owen said after he put his in.

She gave him a thumbs up and smiled. "Loud and
clear."

Owen's chuckle helped her to relax. She blew out a
breath and pulled down the visor to check her hair.
When she'd finished and pushed up the visor, she clasped
her hands in her lap and looked at him.

With a nod, Owen climbed out of the vehicle. The
plan was for him to get in place first and check everything before she walked to her designated position.

She watched him leave, suddenly feeling more apprehensive than ever. Natalie closed her eyes after he'd
turned the corner and took deep, even breaths to stay
calm.

It was going to take him about forty-five minutes to
get all the guns in place. He carried the black duffle bag
casually, as if he'd done this kind of thing a million
times.

Natalie drummed her fingers, she played I Spy With
My Little Eye (which was hard to do with just one person), and she sang *Bohemian Rhapsody* by Queen twice.

Then she leaned her head back and went through
each of their escape routes one by one as she had on the

way to Dallas. There was no room for screw-ups, no chance for her to make the wrong decision.

Finally, Owen's voice came through her ear. "I'm in place."

Now it was her turn. She sat up, her stomach pitching violently. She was going to be sick. Adventure wasn't her cup of tea. She liked sedate and cautious.

This was the opposite in every way.

"Nat?"

"I'm here," she hurried to reply.

There was a pause. Then he asked, "You about to be sick?"

"How did you know?"

"This is serious shit. I'd be worried if you weren't."

That made her smile. Owen would be in her ear the entire time, looking at her through a scope. If there was one person she trusted above all others—it was Owen.

No matter what, when he gave his word, he didn't go back on it. And he'd promised he would keep her safe.

"Do you want to leave?" he asked.

She grabbed the keys and opened the door. "Absolutely not."

"Good."

She slung her purse strap over her shoulder and shut the door before hiding the keys behind the back driver's side tire. Then she straightened and began her long walk to her spot.

The sun was up in the clear, blue sky. The nip in the air would last until about noon when the Texas heat would push it back until nightfall.

Her strides were long and sure as she crossed street after street, winding her way to downtown. Just as planned, she got on the Dallas Area Rapid Transit or DART train and rode for a small ways.

Once she exited, she walked another four blocks before she was in the downtown area. She saw her designated location ahead and slowed.

She veered off to get a coffee at a stand outside some office buildings. She ordered a latte and took a seat at one of the tables, giving her a view of the area.

It was still a long time before Irina was due to make an appearance. Natalie settled in and took a sip of her coffee.

"Got you in my sights," Owen's voice said in her ear. "Pretty sure getting a latte wasn't in the plan."

She kept the cup by her lips and grinned. "I wasn't going to stand around doing nothing. Everyone gets coffee."

"Point taken."

She glanced at her watch. Forty minutes until Irina would make an appearance. The gorgeous day, cool temperatures, and sunshine all had Natalie wanting to relax. But it was the farthest thing from her mind.

The assassins could be lurking behind any building. They could be watching her now. Any of the people around her could be after her.

It set her nerves on edge. How in the hell did spies do this for a living? Every sound made her jump. She watched everyone around her, waiting for them to make a wrong move or look as if they were coming toward her.

"Easy, Nat. You're safe."

She snorted. "Don't lie to me. I'm far from safe."

"No one will get within ten yards of you if I think for one instant they mean you harm."

The cold tone in his voice told her he meant every word. "I wish you were beside me."

And she meant it. She realized she'd taken his presence the last few days for granted. He might be watching her, but she still felt utterly alone.

"I'm beside you. And above you. I see everything. You're my focus."

She fisted her hand, wishing his fingers were threaded through hers. Damn it! Was Owen somehow worming his way back into her heart?

No. That wasn't possible. She was frightened. And when she got scared, she clung to what she knew was safe—Owen.

He was the only man who'd ever made her feel completely secure. She knew he would guard her, protect her with his very life. He'd always made her feel as if she could conquer the world as long as he was with her.

She tried to think of all the exit strategies once more, but her mind kept returning to the night she'd spent in Owen's arms.

It had been heavenly. Blissful.

Amazing.

But she didn't need him—or any man for that matter. She was in a good place.

Why did she keep telling herself that? Was she stating a fact, or trying to convince herself?

That was the question, and she couldn't seem to find an answer.

CHAPTER TWENTY-NINE

Owen stared through the scope of the sniper rifle, studying everyone in the area. So far, none looked like a threat to Natalie, but he knew from experience that it could change in a heartbeat.

Before he'd returned to Texas, he couldn't think of doing anything besides being a SEAL. Now, he was seriously considering resigning so he could be with Natalie.

They belonged together. No one could touch his heart and soul the way she did so effortlessly.

He always assumed he'd retire from the military, but Natalie had him rethinking everything. He was tired of being alone. Though he never liked to talk about it, he was lonely. It hit him particularly hard at times, and when that happened, his mind always pulled up memories of Natalie.

For so long, he'd lied to himself that the loneliness didn't matter. But it did. Coming face-to-face with Natalie again had proven that.

She made him feel again. His love for her that he'd buried deep down so long ago had rushed to the surface, consuming him. It demanded he feel it, that he open himself up to it.

Now that he had, there was no turning away. Looking back now, he wondered how he'd ever left her.

As the time approached for Irina to appear, the more vigilant he became. He tried to calm his racing heart. Not even during his first mission or first kill had he felt so apprehensive. The reason sat in a chair, pretending to drink a latte.

It always came back to Natalie. No wonder everyone called him a fool. He was the biggest one of them all to leave something as precious as her behind.

He'd always thought his life was fulfilling, even if it was dangerous. Maybe it was because he was back at the ranch. It might even be because Orrin had been kidnapped. Perhaps it was because Natalie needed him.

Whatever the reason, his bleak future of endless missions with no one to come home to seemed desolate and grim now.

What he wanted—what he *yearned* for—was Natalie.

If something didn't change, he knew exactly what his future held for him.

And he refused to be like his father and end up alone.

CHAPTER THIRTY

Sklad . . .

"*Orrin.*"

Melanie. He missed her so much. Her death had left a hole inside him that could never be filled. But she was standing before him now.

She leaned over him, a soft smile on her lips as her long, black hair fell over one shoulder. There was a light behind her, making it appear as if a glow encircled her head. He quickly forgot about that as he looked into her hazel eyes.

"You're back," he said.

"Shhh." She put her finger to his lips. "Let me care for you."

"Melanie, our boys are in trouble."

The smile vanished. "So are you, my love."

"I failed you. I won't fail them."

Her hands smoothed over his face. Her fingers combed his hair. "Fate took me from you. It was always destined to be so."

"No. We were supposed to grow old together. I bought those rocking chairs for the porch, remember? We were going to sit there, watching our grandkids."

She leaned down and placed her lips on his for a tender kiss. "We will."

Orrin didn't understand how Melanie was with him, but it didn't matter. Her gentle touch soothed him, comforted him so that his mind could clear. She'd always had such an effect on him.

"Tell me who hurt you, honey," he begged. "I need to exact my revenge."

"You will," she assured him. "It's not time yet."

"I've waited too long already."

"You need to pay attention, Orrin. Listen."

He frowned, not understanding. "I am listening to you, sweetheart."

"Not to me. Everyone else. The truth is right before you."

"I know Yuri betrayed me."

Her eyes were sad as she gazed at him. "I'm sorry."

"I should've seen it. Why didn't I see it? He's not that good. And I'm usually not that trusting."

"*Listen*, Orrin. Look between the lines. Hear what isn't being said."

His hands reached out and grasped her arms as she sat up. "Baby, don't leave me."

"I'll never leave you."

"You did."

"I was always beside you. Every step of the way."

Orrin's gaze clouded with his tears. How many times had he cried out for her during the night? How many times had he begged God to give him some sign that Melanie was at peace?

The tightness in his chest eased when she rested her

head upon it. He let her thick hair run through his fingers like he'd done a thousand times before when they'd lain in just such a position.

"It's not time for you to leave this world yet, Orrin. Our sons need you. Callie needs you."

He stared up at the ceiling. "Our boys have never needed me."

"They're stubborn, just like their father. They're also honorable and dedicated. They're looking for you."

"But they're smart," he argued. "They were taught well. They won't make the same mistakes I did."

Melanie took a deep breath. "And Callie?"

Callie. The daughter they'd never had. She had a tough shell, but beneath it, she was barely held together. She was so sensitive, always thinking of others before herself.

"She's going to need you," Melanie said.

The boys could look after her. Then he thought of the awful way Wyatt had treated her before he'd left for college. Perhaps assuming his sons would step up and help Callie was wrong. They had no idea how he'd taken Callie in years ago.

"Yuri isn't just targeting our sons. He's going after anyone close to them."

He frowned at her words. "The boys should've never been dragged into this. This is my mission, my doing."

"But they're our sons."

"Yes, they are."

"Your enemies will go after Mia."

He felt the weight of so many lives he was responsible for. He already carried the heaviness from the members of his murdered team. Not even revenge for what was done to them would release his burden. But that's what happened to men like him.

His arms tightened around her. "I'm so tired."

"You can do this."

"I'm not so sure anymore."

She kissed his chest. "You don't have a choice."

No, he didn't. He'd paved his path, and he would reap the consequences.

"Remember, my love. *Listen*."

She faded away, even as Orrin fought to hold her. He cried out, anger and fear consuming him once more.

Yuri stood over Orrin's prone form with two men on either side of him. "He has a fever. Find a doctor immediately. I will not allow Orrin to die until he has seen what I plan for his sons."

CHAPTER THIRTY-ONE

All too soon, the forty minutes was up for Natalie. Her train of thought regarding Owen died when she spotted Irina Matveev.

Irina looked very much like her photo. She was a tall woman with fierce eyes and chin-length black hair just beginning to gray. Irina walked with purpose from the building, wearing an off-white jacket and gold tank paired with black pants. Irina had a stunning figure for her age.

Natalie stood and walked to the trash to throw away the coffee she hadn't drunk, which had grown cold long ago. The plan had been for her to bump into Irina, but the more she thought about it, the more she realized that wouldn't work.

She adjusted her purse and walked directly toward Irina with purposeful steps.

"Natalie," Owen said in her ear.

"Trust me," she whispered.

And then she was standing in Irina's path. "Hello, Ms. Matveev," Natalie called with a smile.

Irina's gaze was unswerving, penetrating. "Do I know you?"

"No." She lowered her gaze to the ground before looking demurely back up at Irina, all the while, searching to see if there was a shred of recognition in the woman's face. "Forgive me. My name is Natalie Dixon. I've heard so much about you that I had to meet you."

"Me?" she asked suspiciously.

She nodded. "I love languages and learned Russian first."

"*Ti govorish po russkie?*"

Did she speak Russian? Natalie wanted to snort. "*Kogda mogu,* as often as I can."

Irina smiled. "*Ti ochen horosho govorish.*"

Of course, her Russian was very good. Spending those years in Russia had only developed her skill even more. "*Spacibo*, thank you."

In her ear, Owen's voice spoke. "Either she doesn't know you, or she's hiding it very well."

In other words, there was no way to tell. She glanced around but didn't see any hulky Russians lurking about. She was going to have to take a chance, and she prayed it worked.

"Tell me again why you wanted to meet me," Irina demanded.

"I worked in St. Petersburg for a few years before returning home. I like to keep up with the Russians in the area. I know how you've immersed yourself in all that is Dallas. You're respected and admired. I'm curious why you decided on Texas as your home after you left Russia."

"I don't usually like to answer such questions, but you've intrigued me, Natalie. Walk with me a moment."

As if knowing her fear, Owen was quick to say, "I've got you."

Natalie tossed him a smile. She was really going to have to be careful or she just might fall in love with him again.

"I traveled a bit when I was younger," Irina said as they strolled slowly. "I'd visited America before in New York and again in Chicago. But I'd always dreamed of seeing Texas."

"So it was a natural decision?" Natalie pressed.

Irina smiled softly and nodded. "It was. I looked at Austin, but it was much too dry there for me. I also visited Houston, but when I came to Dallas, I knew this would be my home."

"Where in Russia did you live?"

"The village where I grew up was very far from the cities. It was small and isolated. When I was seventeen, I moved to Moscow to find a job."

Natalie smiled, slowly making her way to her true questions. "What kind of work did you do in Moscow?"

"Anything I could find in order to buy food. I even worked for the KGB for a short time."

She couldn't believe Irina would admit to it so freely.

"You looked shocked, dear," Irina said with a tilt of her head.

"It's interesting. And scary."

Irina laughed as she came to a halt and faced her. Irina's gaze was intense and probing. "That was during the Cold War. Every day, I thought we'd go to war with America."

"And yet you chose to live here."

"I worked for a communist government. Anyone who could leave, did. There was a new life waiting here in the Land of the Free."

"Even with your country becoming democratic?"

"Nothing happens overnight, as we all know. Just because the USSR became Russia with a simple name change didn't mean the government was going to change as quickly."

"Very true."

For the next five minutes, Irina spoke of her childhood and hunting for food with her father in the cold. It was mindless chatter, but Natalie let her talk instead of cutting her off.

"It sounds like your village was close-knit. Do you still have ties to anyone in Russia?" she asked.

"Yes," Irina answered. "You never really leave Mother Russia. But Dallas is my home. I love it here. The winters are mild with only a few inches of snow that is quickly gone. The people are welcoming, and I've put down roots. Any Russian would be happy here."

"What about the Russian mob?" Natalie asked.

Irina smiled politely, a dark brow raised. "I have nothing to do with that group. Anyway, I doubt they're in Texas."

"Nat," Owen said in her ear. "A black Mercedes CLS just pulled up to your left."

She spotted it—and the driver, who had gotten out and was staring directly at them. Natalie shifted and turned her back to the car.

"I'm very sorry, but I have an appointment I can't miss. I like you, Natalie Dixon. Let me give you some advice. Your questions were smart, but they weren't the one you really wanted to ask."

She stared at Irina, unsure of how to respond. Finally, she decided on the truth. "No, they weren't."

"You found me because of a snafu that occurred in my home country."

"What do you know of that?"

"Not nearly as much as you might think. The problem is, you're looking in the right direction, just at the wrong person. I'm not in charge of the team sent here."

"Why should I believe you?"

Irina's smile was sad. "Long ago, they wanted me to continue working for them, but I wanted out. In exchange, they killed my husband. I managed to escape, or so I thought. But as I said, no one ever really leaves. So now I do what I have to. Just as you are. Do you understand what I'm telling you?"

"I believe I do," Natalie answered. "Is there anything you can tell me?"

"I've already said too much as it is. Be careful, but know you are looking in the right direction. Don't find me again." Then she smiled widely and gave Natalie a wave. Beneath her breath Irina said, "Walk away now, dear. *Dasvidaniya.*"

"*Dasvidaniya.*"

Natalie's heart was hammering because she had a feeling that whoever was in the Mercedes was somehow involved. However, she didn't want to stick around and find out.

"Exit four," Owen said in her ear. "Be calm. Wait until you get around the building and then run."

Her knees were knocking as she made her way to exit four. Thank God Owen had made her memorize them, because her head was too full of what just happened to recall exactly what she needed to do. But her subconscious did, just as Owen had predicted.

"Almost clear," he said in his smooth voice.

As soon as she reached the corner and turned, Natalie started running.

Owen waited until Natalie was gone before he swung the rifle back toward the CLS and Irina Matveev. When Irina approached the car, the door opened and a man in a blue suit stepped out—along with the blond giant Owen had fought at Baylor.

"Fuck," Owen murmured when he saw the face of the man in the suit.

His gut clenched, a sign that things were about to get much worse. He wished he could hear what they were saying, but no doubt the duo was speaking in Russian. A moment later, Irina got into the car and they drove off.

But the Russian giant remained behind. He wasn't alone long. Two more joined him. Owen could pick them off from there. It would eliminate three risks to Natalie, but in the process, he'd be hunted by every branch of law enforcement there was.

He took his finger off the trigger. He watched them talk amongst themselves for a moment before they branched off in different directions.

None followed Natalie, but that didn't mean they weren't going after her. He hurriedly packed up the rifle and put it in the duffle before making his way out of the building. Once outside, he paused, looking around.

Part of him wanted to follow Natalie in case they trapped her. But she had a head start. She knew where to hide, where the weapons were located, and where to wait for him.

Owen had to trust that he'd trained her well enough in the small amount of time they had. He turned to the right and walked away.

There wasn't enough time to retrieve all the weapons he'd left, but Wyatt could gather the rest once he had Natalie back at the ranch.

He blew out a breath. Natalie had been right. Seeking out Irina Matveev had been smart. They'd learned something. The hard part now would be getting out of Dallas without the men locating Natalie.

"Owen?" she asked through the comm.

He ducked into an alley and recovered a handgun, which he then dumped in his duffle. "Yeah."

"You said fuck."

"Yeah." He really didn't want to have this conversation with her over the comm.

"You aren't going to tell me, are you?"

He walked back out onto the sidewalk and lengthened his strides. "Nat, listen to me carefully. There are three men walking the streets. One is that giant from Baylor."

"Oh, damn."

"They didn't follow you, but stay vigilant."

"Okay."

He could tell she was running again by the sound of her breathing. He asked, "How far are you from the truck?"

"Still a ways," she huffed.

He turned a corner and came face-to-face with the giant. Owen glanced around to find that this part of the street was all but deserted. "Get there as fast as you can. If you can't, then find one of the hiding spots and arm yourself until I can get there."

"Owen?"

There was no time to answer as the giant swung at him. Owen ducked, tossing aside the bag and rolling. He came up on his feet and let loose two punches into the giant's left kidney.

The Russian grunted and rammed his knee into Owen's face. He staggered backward and pulled one of his knives out. The giant was good enough to block many of his attacks, but he got in several deep slashes that soaked the Russian in blood.

In response, the giant let out a bellow and made a grab for the knife. Suddenly, they were each trying to thrust the blade into the other's gut.

The Russian might have leverage because of his height, but Owen had something more—he had motivation.

He had Natalie.

Owen twisted to the side, causing the giant to pitch forward. Right onto the blade. Owen felt it sink into the brute's body. He watched as the life drained from the man.

There was one less of the bastards hunting Natalie. He stood, pulling the knife out and wiping the blade on his clothes.

Owen glanced around to find two homeless men

watching from an alley. He gathered his bag and made his way over to them. "Gentlemen."

"I've not seen moves like that since my time in the Gulf War," one of the men said.

A veteran. Owen pulled out his wallet and handed each of them some money for food. "If you ever find your way south of Dallas, head to the Loughman Ranch. Veterans are always hired."

"We won't say anything about that," the second man said and gave a nod to the dead man.

"Appreciate it." Then Owen straightened and started toward the truck once more.

"I should kick your ass myself," Natalie's voice said in his ear.

He smiled to himself. "You sound irate."

"I'm pissed. I heard all those grunts. You were fighting, and you didn't tell me."

"There wasn't exactly time."

"Yep. Um, hm. The thing is, Owen. One of those men seems to know I'm here."

That stopped him in his tracks. "Where are you?"

"Hiding spot number two. I can see the DART, but I'll never make it. He'd spot me."

"You still have a weapon?"

"Yes."

Owen began walking again. "Stay put. I'm coming for you."

CHAPTER THIRTY-TWO

Natalie couldn't take her eyes off the Russian. He stuck out among the Texans like a zebra in a herd of cattle. She held the gun against her chest as she hid behind a set of dumpsters, watching him through a gap.

Her heart raced a mile a minute. There was nothing that could've prepared her for this moment. No amount of descriptions, no amount of computer-generated scenarios, no amount of training.

Nothing could compare to the numbness suffusing her or the ice in her veins. That was all because the man looking for her wanted to end her life.

She plastered her back against the brick wall of the building and squeezed her eyes shut. Where was Owen? What was taking him so long?

She just wanted to get back to the safety of the ranch where she could watch everything from the cameras. She opened her eyes and blew out a breath.

Owen would arrive, and when he did, he wouldn't find her crying. She would be ready for whatever he planned to get them out.

She turned her head to look out at the Russian. When she didn't see him, she started to smile, thinking that he'd gone. Then she heard footsteps approaching.

They were slow, measured. As if whoever it was considered that someone might be hiding behind the dumpsters.

She aimed the gun, her heart pounding against her chest.

"Hey, Mister!" a deep voice shouted. "You better not be messin' with my stuff. That's my home back there!"

She looked out the gap and saw a man with salt and pepper hair, mismatched clothes, and military boots that had seen better days.

"I am not touching your things," came the thick Russian accent, rolling r's and all.

"Then get away before I call my friends."

She couldn't believe that the homeless man had somehow gotten rid of the assassin. And he wasn't stopping there. She lost sight of them, but she could still hear the man berating the Russian loud enough that everyone on the DART platform watched them.

Someone came up behind her. She jumped and swung her head around. As soon as she saw it was Owen, she threw her arms around him.

He held her tight. "It's all right. I've got you."

"We're not out of it yet."

"My new friends were delighted to help."

She pulled back. "Friends?"

"When we walk outside, you'll see about four men keeping your would-be attacker too occupied to see us get on the DART." He laced his fingers with hers. "Ready?"

"Yes." She tucked the gun back into her purse and got to her feet.

Owen was calm as he walked them from the alley, not even bothering to look to the right where the Russian was. But she did. Just as Owen said, there were four homeless men, all badgering the assassin so badly that he was doing his damnedest to get away.

She and Owen got on the DART and rolled away from the scene. Owen raised his hands to one of the men in thanks. She discreetly took out her earpiece and handed it to Owen. They didn't say a word until they reached the parking garage and got in the truck.

When she opened her mouth to talk, Owen turned toward her. He grabbed the back of her head and brought his mouth down to hers for a kiss that took her breath away.

Her arms wrapped around his neck as her fingers dug into his skin. She didn't think, didn't worry. She only let herself feel.

And it was wonderful.

When the kiss ended, both of them were breathing hard. He caressed her cheek as he gazed into her eyes. She wanted to know what he was thinking, simply because she refused to allow herself to wonder at her response to his kiss.

Owen sighed and sat back. After a moment, he started the truck and put it in reverse to back out of the spot. It wasn't until they'd exited the garage that he said, "The Mercedes I told you about?"

"What about it?"

"A man named Egor Dvorak got out of it."

"The Russian consulate? Are you sure?"

Owen nodded. "Without a doubt. I believe that's who Irina was suggesting in her remarks."

"Well, it makes sense. He would be able to track what I did on my computer at the embassy. Connections, power, and authority. All the right ingredients."

"He would also have the contacts to run a team of Russian military here."

"Let's not forget diplomatic immunity," she added. "How do you know him?"

"Because of the talks he's had with the White House."

"I know of him but haven't had any dealings with him. The man gives me the creeps, though."

"The involvement of Dvorak changes everything."

She frowned at him. "How? We knew someone was managing the team of men. Why should Dvorak be any different than Irina?"

"Dvorak was a general in the Russian army. His reputation for rooting out insurgents and getting whoever he's hunting is well known. He was also the FSB's go-to man when they had a difficult time finding people, because he always finds what he's sent for."

"Great. Right now he's using his men to find me. How long before he comes after me himself?"

"That's not going to happen."

She sighed and shook her head. "I can't hide forever."

"Nor should you have to."

"What are you thinking, then?"

Owen ran a hand down his face as he pulled onto the interstate and headed back to the ranch. "I'm still putting it together in my head."

"Could Dvorak be working for the FSB?"

"It's likely."

She dropped her head back on the seat. "And I went searching the computer for anything on Ragnarok."

"Don't beat yourself up about it," he said, glancing at her. "They were probably monitoring your home computer, as well."

Her eyes went wide. "What?"

"Nat, don't tell me you're that naïve to believe that they would hire an American and trust you with classified information."

Well, when he put it that way, she did sound naïve. "They approached me."

"It doesn't matter. You believed that by living and working in Russia, you would fit in."

So she had. Regrettably. It was why she'd returned home in the first place.

"It was different at the embassy. There were other Americans working there."

"How many?" he asked.

She hesitated. "Three."

"Did they have your level of clearance?"

"No."

"There you go."

As if that said it all. And, she supposed it did. She felt like such a fool.

"Had none of this happened, you'd never have known," Owen added.

"That doesn't make me feel any better." She didn't pull away when his hand rested atop hers. In fact, she liked it.

"I know Dvorak from a different angle than you. Tell me all you know of him," Owen urged.

She thought about Egor Dvorak. "For a man in his

late fifties, he has the face and body of a man much younger. He takes great pride in keeping fit. Women flock to him, not just because of who he is and his wealth, but also because he's considered handsome."

"But he gives you the creeps?" Owen asked with a grin.

She laughed as she lifted one shoulder in a shrug. "He just seems fake to me. But he loves women. All women."

"Men like him always do."

"What's today?" she asked and grabbed his phone to check the date. "It's tomorrow."

Owen raised a dark brow at her, his chocolate eyes curious. "What's tomorrow?"

"The gala showcasing some of the artifacts Russia is loaning the museum for a few months."

"Interesting."

"We could go after Dvorak there."

"He's much different than Irina, Nat. He'll be surrounded by security. Not to mention, everyone will know your face."

Damn. She had forgotten that for a moment.

She could see Owen was working things out in his head, so she looked out the window, letting the rhythm of the road lull her to sleep.

Owen was exhausted both mentally and emotionally. Natalie had come too close to being discovered by the Russians. She'd been terrified, and that was something that had struck him particularly hard.

He could still feel the way her body had shaken when she'd thrown her arms around him. And yet, she was talking about confronting Dvorak now.

Natalie was a walking contradiction. Then again, she always had been. It was one of the things that had attracted him to her to begin with.

When he turned onto the ranch property, he missed the activity of all the ranch hands. Callie had notified them as soon as Virgil and Charlotte were killed that they'd been given some time off.

It didn't seem right to drive up with no one there. Leaving Nat asleep in the truck, he did a quick check of the house and the barns. When he saw that it was safe, he turned off the truck and woke her.

Natalie sat up, blinking. "We're home?"

It warmed his heart to hear her say that. It was probably just a slip of the tongue, but he hoped that, deep down, she meant it.

"Let's get inside the base," he said and grabbed the duffle.

Once ensconced in the base, Natalie let out a loud sigh. "It's good to be back."

He smiled and dropped the duffle near the armory. "I need to call my brothers and update them. Feel free to listen in."

"Really?"

She seemed surprised by his offer. "Of course. Today was your idea. You've had another that I want to talk over with them. The more brains, the better."

"Count me in, then."

He walked into the conference room with her on his heels. He dialed Wyatt first before attempting to connect with Cullen. Worry began to set in that he still couldn't get ahold of his younger brother. "Wyatt? Callie?"

"Yes, if Wyatt will move his big ass over," Callie grumbled.

Natalie chuckled. "All right, you two."

"I still can't reach Cullen," Owen said. He hadn't worried about Cullen in a long time, but that concern was back—tenfold.

Wyatt released a loud sigh. "Us either. Let's give him a little more time."

"Agreed. Any progress?"

"We still haven't been able to locate where Orrin might've sent the formula. How about you?"

Owen exchanged a look with Natalie. "It started out fine. Nat spoke with Irina, who told us she wasn't controlling the Russian military here, but that we were on the right track."

"Did she say who that right track was?" Callie asked.

"I saw him." Owen dropped down into a chair. "Egor Dvorak."

Wyatt was suspiciously quiet.

Owen knew how he felt. "There were three men there. I killed one, and another got entirely too close to finding Nat."

"Is she okay?" Callie asked.

Natalie was smiling as she leaned toward the speaker. "I'm in one piece."

"Nice to hear," Callie replied, a smile in her voice.

"You obviously called for more than an update," Wyatt said to Owen.

Before he could respond, Natalie said, "There's a gala tomorrow night in Dallas, and I know Dvorak will be in attendance."

"Nat wants to confront him," Owen explained.

"Because Irina led me to believe Egor is controlling the assassins."

"On the off chance it isn't Egor running things, I'll bet he knows who is," Wyatt stated.

Callie made a sound. "A man like Egor likes to keep connected to everything. He'll know one way or another. Nat's idea is good."

"But I also know why Owen is hesitating," Wyatt added.

Natalie held Owen's gaze. "Me."

"Yeah, it's you." There was no use denying it. He wanted her to know how much he cared—how much he loved her.

"This could save your father," she said.

"Or kill you."

She shrugged, grinning. "It could save the world."

He rose and raked a hand through his hair as he turned away. Natalie didn't understand. He would die if something happened to her. His father knew the chances of getting caught. Every military member did.

It didn't mean he wanted to leave Orrin behind, but Natalie wasn't in the military. She was a civilian caught in the middle of a war that had already come too close to her multiple times.

"Owen," Wyatt called. "You might also want to think about how many times you've been gone from the ranch."

He halted and turned back to the table. "I've checked every camera. No one has come on the ranch."

"They don't have to."

"I've taken precautions in hiding the truck." Except for today. It still sat outside. "You think the group might raid the ranch again?"

Wyatt blew out a breath. "It's what I'd do."

"I know some men who could come to the ranch and watch it," Callie offered. "They've worked with Orrin before."

"What if one of them is in with the Russians," Natalie asked. "Y'all did say someone betrayed Orrin."

Owen drummed his fingers on the table. "She's got a point. If those men worked with Orrin, they know about the base. Continuing to leave the vial would be pointless."

"Dammit," Callie said. "I swore to your father that as long as he was alive, I wouldn't reveal this to you, but he has a secret safe in the base. Put the bioweapon there. Until now, only me and Virgil knew of it."

Owen wondered why he was so surprised. If he'd built a base like this, he'd make damned sure to have multiple spots no one knew about.

"Where is it?" he asked.

"The bunk room."

Now that came as a shock. "Seriously? Not Dad's office?"

There was a smile in Callie's voice when she said, "I asked him the same thing. His response was that everyone would look in his office. No one would look where the bunks are."

"Where exactly?"

"Third bunk to the left," Callie said. "Lift the right side of the footboard three times."

Owen waited for her to finish. When she said no more, he asked, "Is that all?"

"That's all. I hope y'all get the significance of the threes."

He did, but he wasn't going to get into that now. "If we go, we've got the ranch and Ragnarok covered. It still doesn't change the fact that everyone will know Natalie's face."

Natalie shot him a wide smile. "It's perfect actually. They'll never expect me to be there."

CHAPTER THIRTY-THREE

Natalie left Owen alone for a while after the phone call. She knew he wasn't keen on confronting Dvorak, even though it was a solid plan. It was because she was involved. Perhaps she should stay behind.

She found Owen feeding the horses. For long minutes, she watched him interacting with the animals. How could she have forgotten how they gravitated to him?

They loved the sound of his voice. The filly she'd worked so hard to coax just to sniff her hand walked right up to Owen and let him stroke her back.

Then again, she didn't know many females who could refuse Owen Loughman and that seductive voice of his.

She leaned against the side of the barn as the light began to fade. Owen's love of the outdoors, of the ranch, showed in the way he treated the animals and tended to the land.

He belonged on that ranch.

Where did she belong?

At one time, she thought it was by his side. Then she thought in Russia. Then at the embassy. Now? She wasn't sure.

Her life had circled back around to the very place it had all begun. Was fate trying to tell her something? Did she continue to lock him out?

Did she dare to open her heart again?

It had been mended so many times, she wasn't sure it could be put back together properly.

As if he knew she was thinking of him, Owen looked up from the horses. He gave her a smile and finished pouring the last of the feed.

Before she knew it, he stood in front of her. "You look pensive."

"Did life turn out like you wanted?"

He kicked at the dirt. "Does life turn out like anyone wants?"

"Please answer the question."

"Yes and no. I'm a SEAL, just as I always wanted. I've saved lives and kicked terrorist ass."

She swallowed. "But."

"I don't have you."

Was that what she wanted to hear? Because it sounded pretty damn good. The way her heart fluttered, told her it was exactly what she needed to hear.

"And you? Has life turned out like you wanted?" he asked in a low, husky voice as he closed the distance between them.

"Yes and no. I left here and saw part of the world."

He took another step, his body pressed against hers. "But?"

The words wouldn't come. She opened her mouth, but they locked in her throat.

The disappointment that flashed in Owen's dark eyes

was like a kick in the stomach. He didn't press her. Instead, he slowly lowered his head.

Her eyes slid shut as she eagerly awaited his kiss. Just before their lips touched, he pulled back. Her eyes snapped opened to find him holding his hand out to her.

"I want you," he said. "I want you so bad it hurts. But I'll not force you to say anything you aren't ready for."

She looked down at his hand. "And this?"

"Come with me and find out."

She didn't hesitate to place her hand in his. He took her down to the base, locking the door behind them. Then he continued on to the bunk room—or so she thought. He walked past them to a room behind them that must be Orrin's.

She thought of earlier that day when the assassin had almost found her. All she'd wanted was Owen. And when he had arrived, she'd clung to him as if he were the only thing that could save her.

No longer did she know for sure what to do. The one thing she did know was that she wanted Owen.

Natalie walked to him, sliding her arm around his neck. In the next instant, their lips were locked as the fires of their desire soared.

Clothes were ripped in an effort to get naked. He lifted her so that her legs wrapped around his waist. Her breaths came faster, her hands clawing to get him closer.

His kiss was savage, and yet tender at the same time. He held her tightly, yet gently.

There was something different about this time. It wasn't desperation but . . . the frantic and very real need to come together.

To become whole. One.

Owen ended the kiss, his breaths harsh and loud. "I need inside you."

"Yes. Now," she gasped.

She felt his thick head against her sex. Then he slid inside. She screamed his name as he filled her fully.

And then he was pumping fast and hard. All she could do was hold on as he took her on a wild ride of rapture as only he could.

In his arms, the world made sense. She wasn't searching for anything, because she had her arms locked around him. There was no need for lies or half-truths—because her heart knew what it wanted.

A tear slipped from Natalie's eye as the truth unfolded before her. A truth she wasn't prepared for.

Those thoughts melted away as her body tightened and the climax neared. As she hurtled into ecstasy, she heard him shout her name as he joined her.

For long moments after, they remained locked together, unmoving. His head was buried in her neck as she smoothed her hand down his hair.

"Take me to bed," she whispered.

He leaned back to look at her. Then he turned and carried her to the bed. They crawled beneath the covers together, and when she was wrapped in his arms, she closed her eyes, content.

CHAPTER THIRTY-FOUR

Owen wasn't sure what would happen when Natalie woke. He was loath to leave her, because the woman in his arms was the Natalie of old.

He smiled as he thought of their lovemaking. No way could she deny the passion between them or how much she enjoyed it. But that's not how he would have to get through to her heart.

His smile dropped. How did he get to her heart? At one time, he knew everything there was to know about her. Now, he couldn't say that.

A glance at the clock showed it was just after four in the morning. After several bouts of lovemaking, she slept like the dead.

The SEAL in him wanted to get up to see if Callie had worked her magic and gotten him and Natalie an invite to the gala, albeit with a name change for both of them.

Instead, he remained in bed, holding his woman.

He thought of the previous day. As dangerous as that had been, the gala had the potential to be even more so.

That's where Callie and Wyatt would come in with the Ritz-Carlton's floor plans.

It would give him time to look over exits and where to hide guns. Callie was also booking a room at a nearby hotel for them under another name so they couldn't be easily traced.

Owen wasn't worried about the ranch. The six men Callie had spoken about would be there long before he and Natalie left. Two were snipers and would set up long distance. The remaining four would be scattered about.

"I swear I can hear you thinking," Natalie said sleepily. She sighed and lifted her head to look at him.

He gave her a grin. "Habit."

"I'm starving anyway. Come on," she said as she threw off the covers and pulled on his t-shirt.

Owen held back a groan as she walked in front of him with her breasts swinging and the barest glimpse of her ass peeking out. He rose and yanked on his pants, not bothering to button them as he followed her.

While she went to the kitchen for food, he checked email. The invitation for the gala would be delivered by courier to their hotel. Though Owen wasn't surprised. Callie was a true genius when it came to working computers.

"Anything new?"

He glanced at Natalie as she walked in with a large glass of milk and a bag of Oreo minis. She held the bag out to him, and he took a handful.

"Our way into the gala is confirmed, as is our hotel room." He checked another email to find that Callie had sent over the hotel floor plans.

Natalie leaned over and saw them. She sat back with a laugh. "This should keep you entertained for hours."

"I can't help it. I love figuring this stuff out." Not to mention, it was keeping Natalie safe.

Six hours later, they were headed back to Dallas. Though it was hastily planned, everything was in order. But he knew better than most that things could go sideways at any second.

He and Natalie kept an easy conversation on the ride to the city while occasionally going over details of the night. The closer they got to Dallas, the more nervous she appeared. And she had every right to be.

When they pulled up at the Hilton, he walked her to their room and then left her to get ready. Since the Russians were everywhere, and Natalie couldn't leave to shop, he had the shopping come to her.

All the while, Owen was going to scope out the Ritz for himself. Besides, he needed to see what security was like before they arrived.

There was no time to think over her emotions about Owen now that she was in Dallas. And a part of Natalie was thankful for that. It was too much to take in when she'd fought so hard to keep him away.

He'd been gone hours, but she'd expected that. She stared at herself in the full-length mirror and smoothed her hands down the black dress that fit to perfection.

The sleeveless gown hit her mid-thigh with a small two-inch slit showing more of her left leg. The dress plunged low, but delicate black lace covered her chest and rose up to her neck.

Her long hair was pulled back in an array of twists with just enough wisps of hair about her neck to look messy. She was finishing off her look with a pair of diamond stud earrings when the hotel door opened and Owen strode in.

He came to an immediate halt, his gaze traveling up and down her twice. "I've never seen anything more beautiful in my life."

"Thank you." She couldn't have been more pleased by his reaction. She may have had to dress for the gala, but she wanted to impress him.

"The security is as tight as expected. It's going to be dangerous," he warned.

"You'll be beside me this time, right? Not just in my ear?"

He came to stand before her and pulled her against him. "Beside you."

"Then we can do this. You'd better get dressed," she said and nodded to where his tux hung, waiting.

With a wink, he walked away. She followed him to the bedroom and stood in the doorway.

"I found a place we can stash Dvorak as we have our little chat," Owen said.

She raised her brows. "Really? That's good. Have you figured out how we'll get him there?"

He paused, looking up at her from buttoning his shirt. "I'm loath to say it, but you."

"He does want me dead. But why wouldn't he just send his men?"

"You'll promise to give him something he wants."

She chuckled as she realized the plan. "The bio-weapon."

"Exactly. Once we're alone with him, we'll do what we must to get information."

She grabbed his tux jacket and held it out for him to slip his arms into the sleeves. Then she smoothed her hands along his shoulders once the jacket was in place. "Ready?"

"Are you?"

"I wish I had a weapon."

He nodded in understanding. "They'll be checking."

She glanced at the clock. It was time. Owen thought it wise for them to arrive well before Dvorak to get the lay of the land—and hope no one spotted either of them.

Owen threaded his fingers with hers. Then they walked from the room. In two blocks, they arrived at the Ritz. Owen handed the security guards their invitations.

With a nod, another guard motioned them through metal detectors. And then they were inside the gala with the upper crust of Dallas society in attendance.

She grabbed a glass of champagne from a passing waiter while they walked the perimeter, pretending to look at the exhibits for the next twenty minutes.

"I've counted six guards in tuxes while the others are in the customary black suits," Owen said.

She nodded to passing couples. "I spotted one holding some kind of device in his hand."

"A jammer. There won't be any cell phones working."

Which meant there was no calling for help. She and Owen really were on their own. She searched for anyone she might know from the embassy. So far, luck was on her side.

Owen led her up the stairs. She was grateful to have

a hold of his arm, because with every Russian guard they passed, she expected one to reach out and grab her. It was Owen's reassuring strength beneath her hand that kept her steady.

They halted near the railing at a semi-secluded spot overlooking the floor below. She leaned close to Owen, a smile in place.

"So far, so good," he murmured.

"Have you been in situations like this?"

He glanced at her, a wealth of meaning in his chocolate gaze. "Something similar, but I didn't have such precious cargo to look after."

Two days ago, she would've waved away his words. Now, she couldn't. She ran her fingers through his deep brown locks at his temple. Just as she started to speak, there was a murmur that went through the continually growing crowd.

"I think Dvorak has arrived," Owen said.

She briefly closed her eyes. This was it. The time of no return had arrived. This was for Owen, Orrin, and the others.

Not just because they'd saved her from the killers. But because they were family.

People milled around them, wanting to get a look at Dvorak as he strolled into the gala with a gorgeous woman on each arm. He smiled and waved, enjoying the attention.

Someone bumped into Natalie in an attempt to get to the railing. Instantly, Owen navigated them out of the crowd. She drained the champagne to help steady her nerves.

Owen took the empty glass without a word and

handed it to a waiter. His hand remained on her back, comforting and warm. He leaned in close, his mouth near her ear. "Dance with me."

His words were so unexpected that she swung her head to him. It was that crooked smile of his, the one that always made her heart skip a beat that said her reaction was just what he wanted.

"Yes," she replied breathlessly.

The lights were dimmed except for the spotlights on the exhibits, as the music grew louder. Together, they strolled down the stairs to where other couples already danced.

Owen led her to the floor. And then she was in his arms, moving slowly with the music.

"My God, you're beautiful," he whispered.

He gave James Bond a run for his money in a tux. And out of it. She had never felt so special as she did in that moment, in his arms. "I've never seen you look more handsome."

"I want you."

She let her lids fall shut as her blood heated. "Don't tempt me."

He leaned close so his lips brushed her ear. "Why not? There are plenty of dark corners."

It was difficult for her to remember where they were as she imagined what he would do to her in those dark corners.

"I can hear your breathing," he said huskily. "My God, what you do to me."

She gasped when he brought her close and she could feel his arousal.

"Yes," he said. "I'm hard for you."

How was she supposed to think with him saying such things? He was seducing her. She'd known it last night. And she hadn't fought it. Perhaps she was tired of fighting it. Why not give in? Why not allow herself to let someone close again?

He pulled her closer so that their cheeks were pressed together. He then whispered, "You sparkle even in the dark."

She savored the moment. The seductive music, their bodies swaying, Owen's arms holding her firmly, and his nearness. It was enchanting, entrancing.

It was perfection.

"In my worst moments," he said, "when I was pinned down in some Godforsaken country with all the odds stacked against me coming out alive, I always thought of you. No matter what you might believe, know that you were always on my mind."

Her heart warmed at his words. It gave her the courage to do the same. "I compared every man to you. Even in my marriage. No one has ever come close to rivaling you. Ever."

He pulled back so she had no choice but to meet his dark gaze. The dimmed room made it difficult for her to see him clearly. He moved their joined hands between them and touched her cheek with a finger.

"I haven't had a relationship since you."

Her eyes widened in shock. "Why?"

"Because no one was you."

The song came to an end, but they didn't stop moving. Soon another song began to play.

"I want you. Not just tonight or while I'm here. I want you forever."

Forever. How long had she dreamed of hearing those words from him? At one time, she would've moved Heaven and Earth to hear them.

And now? She wasn't sure what to think or feel. She wasn't nearly as confused about Owen as she had been before.

"Don't say anything," Owen urged. "I want you to be happy. But know this. I don't give up when I want something."

And he wanted her. A thrill went through her.

She looked down at his lips, a mouth that she wanted to lean up to and kiss. Everything she ever wanted was being offered.

His hand splayed on her back, pulling her hips against him. "You were made for me," he said. "You were always meant to be mine."

Second chances. People rarely got them, and it had practically fallen in her lap. Ignoring it would be foolish, but she was scared. Her heart had been trampled enough.

"You said you didn't want me in the military life," she said.

Owen gave a shake of his head. "I said a lot of stupid things in an effort to keep you out of this very situation. It's made me realize what an idiot I've been. I want to spend my days with you."

"Why are you telling me this now?"

"Because you can't run away."

Did he really think she would? She placed a soft kiss on his lips. "We need to talk about this—"

"But not here," Owen finished, his voice shifting deeper. "We've been spotted."

CHAPTER THIRTY-FIVE

Owen didn't take his eyes off the two Russian guards who were eyeing them. It was time for them to put their plan into action.

"Our fun is up, Nat."

She released a small sigh. "Let's get this over with."

He turned them until he spotted their target. "Dvorak is to your right and surrounded by women doing very outrageous things to get his attention."

"Stupid women," she grumbled.

He hid his smile. "Get him out to the hallway, and I'll do the rest."

Natalie gave him another kiss before they walked from the dance floor. He led her directly in front of Dvorak, who frowned as they passed.

Owen situated them behind a large group of people to hide them from the guards. "It's all up to you."

"We're here. We're going to do this." Natalie squared her shoulders before walking away.

He wanted to call her back, to toss her over his shoulder and leave. So much could go wrong, and they had no backup. He'd never second-guessed himself before. Frankly, he didn't like it.

But that's what Natalie did to him.

He moved to watch his woman. Men ogled her. And why wouldn't they? The sleeveless black dress that clung to her exceptional curves made his mouth water. The dress dipped low enough to teasingly show off her breasts that were covered with black lace, which rose to encase the slim column of her neck. The short skirt showed off her gorgeous legs. She was a sight to behold.

Luck was on their side when the two guards who had been watching them had their attentions diverted by someone else. Natalie saw it as well and made her move.

Owen shifted closer to her because Dvorak had two bodyguards standing just feet away. The two straightened when Natalie stopped in front of Dvorak.

The consulate halted talking and simply stared at her. She moved closer to whisper in his ear. At that moment, Owen shoved a man into one of the bodyguards. The second one he kicked in the side of the knee, taking him down.

In all the commotion, no one saw Dvorak leave with Natalie but him. He kept his eyes on the other guards and managed to slip out after Natalie.

"Where is it?" Dvorak demanded.

She motioned with her hand, leading him. "This way."

Owen came up behind Dvorak and knocked him on the back of the head so he was out cold. Then he hurriedly threw Dvorak over his shoulder as Natalie took off her heels and ran down the hall to the room.

As soon as he was inside, Natalie shut and locked the door. Owen dumped Dvorak in the chair and tied his wrists behind the backrest.

"Stay behind him. I don't want him to know you're here," Owen told her.

Natalie did as he requested, setting her shoes down beside her. "Do you think he'll talk?"

"We've got to make him. We don't have much time either. His guards will be looking for him."

"Perhaps you shouldn't have knocked him out," she said with a grin.

He slapped Dvorak twice—hard. Dvorak gave a shake of his head and blinked open his eyes. The consulate glared at Owen before he smirked.

"For a man held captive, you're awfully confident," Owen said.

"You will pay for this," Dvorak stated testily.

"I honestly don't care."

"Do you know who I am? I am an ambassador from Russia!"

He studied Dvorak as he spoke. "We know exactly who you are. Despite retiring from the Russian military, you still seem to have quite a hand in maneuvering men—especially here in the States."

"I know nothing of what you speak," Egor replied. His disdain faded to that of tediousness. "My men will be looking for me."

"They won't find you until I want them to." Owen pulled up another chair before Dvorak. He sat, and then said, "Where is Orrin Loughman?"

"I do not know that name." It was the subtle tightening of Dvorak's mouth that gave away the lie.

Owen nodded as he leaned forward and placed his forearms on his knees. "You have to say that, but I know you're lying. You can leave here just as you are, or you can hold out and get the beating of your life."

Dvorak began to laugh, his cocky smile large. "I have diplomatic immunity. You cannot touch me."

"I know just where to hit that will leave no evidence. I was trained to bring the hardiest to their knees, Ambassador. And I've got all the time in the world."

"You will get nothing from me." Dvorak spat after delivering that statement. "The ranch will be gone when you return."

Owen stood slowly and shoved back the chair with his foot. "You just confirmed you're commanding the Russians in Texas."

"In the entire US," Dvorak declared triumphantly. "If something happens to me, there is another ready to take my place. The instant I go missing, he steps in."

"Then they won't care if you're dead."

That caused Dvorak to pause, the truth sinking in. "They will come for me."

Owen chuckled. "You don't sound quite so confident. Tell me, *Ambassador*, did you get a thrill out of killing my aunt and uncle?"

Dvorak lifted his chin, his smile cold. "Yes."

Owen relished the sound of Dvorak's grunt of pain when he landed the first hit.

CHAPTER THIRTY-SIX

Sklad

Orrin woke on a soft bed, but kept his eyes closed. Something wasn't right. The last thing he remembered was . . . Melanie. His stomach clutched painfully. Melanie. His Melanie had been there, in his arms.

Angel or ghost, he'd spoken to her. It made his eyes burn with unshed tears, but that was a weakness he could ill afford others to see.

"Will he live?"

Anger swarmed him at the sound of Yuri's voice.

There was movement next to him, and then a feminine voice with an American accent said, "He should. His fever is gone. I set his shoulder back in place, but I left the break in his wrist, per your instructions."

"Good," Yuri said. "You may go."

The sound of quick footsteps soon faded. Orrin remained still. He didn't want Yuri to know he was awake. Not yet, at least.

"You thought you could escape the torture I have." Yuri laughed. "I will not let that happen. I have so much more planned, *stariy droog*."

Yuri's large hand rested upon his broken wrist. Orrin knew what was coming. It was years of training that kept his breathing even and his face impassive—even when Yuri squeezed.

He thought of Melanie, he thought of his sons. He imagined what his boys were doing to keep the bio-weapon safe and out of everyone's hands.

"So you are still asleep," Yuri said and released his grip. "Too bad."

He counted to a hundred after Yuri left to allow the pain to subside. Only then did he crack open an eye. He was no longer in the tiny, damp cell. He was still in the same compound if the peeling paint and yellow lights were any indication.

He held on to the pain of his arm. It was all he had. If it would keep him conscious and prepared for whatever Yuri had in store for him next, then he welcomed it.

Slowly, he moved the fingers on his good arm before attempting it with his broken one.

"You're going to cause yourself more pain."

His gaze jerked to the doorway where he found a woman. Her dark red hair was parted to one side and fell straight to brush the tops of her shoulders.

She glanced at the floor before entering the room and checking the IV in his arm. "You nearly died," she stated in a clipped tone.

"You should've let me."

Her eyes swung to him. They were a soft gray, but held all the wariness of someone being forced.

She returned to examining the IV. After a minute she said, "I didn't have a choice."

"Yuri rarely gives one." He swallowed, his throat raw and hurting.

The woman held a cup with a straw before him. "Here."

He tried to lift his head, and he was shocked at how weak he was. It took her hand behind his head to lift and hold him before he could drink.

When he finished, he dropped his head back on the pillow. If he were going to get past Yuri and however many men with him, Orrin was going to have to be much stronger.

"I thought you were Russian," the woman said.

Orrin turned his head toward her. "Where are we?"

Her forehead furrowed as if she wondered at his question. "Virginia."

Thank God. They hadn't taken him to Russia yet. He still had time to get away, because once on that plane, that was the end of him.

He licked his dry lips. "I work for the US government. Yuri killed my team. I need you to alert the authorities."

She looked away, refusing to meet his gaze while shaking her head as he spoke. "I can't."

It was the way it seemed to pain her to hear him talk that finally hit home. "Who has Yuri threatened so you'd help him?"

"My son."

"Do whatever Yuri asks. Don't ask questions, and don't look long at him or his men. You and your son should get out of this fine."

"I tried to set your wrist."

Now that surprised him. "I can do it now that my hands aren't tied."

She didn't say anything else as she pulled something

out of her pocket. Owen saw the bottle and syringe. He lifted his gaze to her and frowned.

"I'm sorry. This is all I can manage now," she whispered as she stuck it in his IV. Without another word, she left the room.

The woman wasn't a killer, so he knew she hadn't poisoned him. But what had she given him? It wasn't painkillers, that was for sure.

He lifted his broken wrist and took a deep breath. Then he set the bone back in place. It was his weaker hand, but if he didn't get out of there soon, the break might heal wrong, which could hinder him later.

He thought of Melanie and her urging for him to listen. So Orrin closed his eyes and opened his ears. It was quiet, making him think he was the only one in the building even as he knew otherwise.

Then he heard the distant rumble of voices. Men. He couldn't make out how many. They grew louder as they suddenly laughed. A moment later, a door creaked open. It sounded heavy, probably made of steel.

That's when he heard them—seagulls. They were by water.

CHAPTER THIRTY-SEVEN

Owen sent a hard jab into the ambassador's right side, directly into his kidney. Dvorak leaned over, gasping for breath.

For the past five minutes, Owen had pounded Dvorak's body without a single punch landing on his face. Though that was harder to refrain from than he'd expected. He sent another jab into Dvoark's kidney.

"All right," Dvorak gasped. "What do you want to know?"

"Everything," Owen stated. He bent over so his face was even with Dvorak's. He wanted to hit him some more, but he wasn't surprised that Dvorak had given in so easily. Men like Dvorak liked to wield power but were ultimately weak. "Where is my father?"

"I . . . I do not know," Egor answered while he struggled to breathe.

Owen stood and grabbed a handful of Dvorak's black hair and jerked his head back. "You know, and you're going to tell me."

"Kept from me for this reason," Dvorak hurried to say.

"Is he still in the States?"

"I do not know!"

Owen didn't believe him. How could he? Dvorak was known for his subterfuge. "I think that's horseshit. You'd want to know every detail."

Dvorak tried to shake his head, but Owen's hold tightened. "If Orrin's sons lived up to their reputation, I wanted to be prepared. I studied him and all of you."

"This is a goddamn game to you, isn't it?"

He glanced at Natalie to see that she was staring at Dvorak. Her eyes held a wealth of anger and purpose. Her gaze lifted to meet his.

There was something different about her, as if she saw the scene in another way. Natalie shooed him back with her hands. He stared long and hard at her before he released Dvorak.

The ambassador's head dropped forward. She moved toward him. Her hands came to rest on his shoulders before slowly smoothing over them to his chest.

Dvorak tried to turn and see who it was. Owen retreated as far as he could to allow Natalie to keep all of Dvorak's attention. If a beating wouldn't work, perhaps seduction would.

Dvorak closed his eyes and tried to turn his head away. Owen watched as Natalie ran her lips over Dvorak's neck to his ear and nipped.

"Do you like that?" she asked in a husky voice.

Owen sure as fuck didn't.

Dvorak nodded.

She unbuttoned Dvorak's shirt and spread it wide. Then dug her nails into his skin and pulled her fingers together. "I can give you pleasure to remove the pain," she whispered.

"*Da.* Please," he begged.

"You like control, don't you?"

"I do."

"You like commanding others and taking lives."

"Yes," he replied, his breath hitching when Natalie bit his earlobe.

She met Owen's gaze. That's when he realized this was her way of getting back at Dvorak for the men at her house. Owen gave her a nod of reassurance.

Natalie doubled her efforts. It revolted her to be touching such a vile man this way, but the beating was getting them nowhere. Dvorak was a man. He needed a different incentive. And what did a man like Dvorak crave? Women.

She moved to stand before him, a smile on her face. He no longer seemed to care that she was a target. His thoughts were elsewhere. She squatted in front of him, being sure to place her hands near his cock.

His groan filled the room when her hands ran leisurely up and down his thighs, coming closer and closer to his rod. She held his gaze and bit her tongue so as not to gag when she cupped him, squeezing his cock and causing him to moan loudly.

"More," he urged.

As soon as her hands stopped touching him, Dvorak opened his eyes. She smiled and lifted her skirt while she straddled his lap.

She then grabbed the arms of the chair and bent back, pushing her breasts forward. Dvorak attempted to lean forward to bury his face in her breasts, but she pulled back before he could.

"I'm in charge," she ordered.

He was panting, his eyes trained on her while her hips ground into him. "Yes."

Natalie straightened and moved as if she were going to kiss him. At the last minute, she grabbed his face in her hand. "Do you want to kiss me?"

Dvorak nodded, beyond words.

"I can allow that. If you answer my questions."

His eyes were dilated, his arousal evident. "Anything."

"Where is Orrin Loughman?"

Dvorak's face contorted as if he remembered he shouldn't talk. She redoubled her efforts by grinding into his cock.

"Yes!" he shouted. "More, please."

"There's more," Natalie told him. "Tell me where Orrin is."

"Kiss me first."

She wasn't sure if she could do it, but then she thought of Owen and all he'd done for her. She leaned forward and kissed Dvorak as if it were all she craved in the world.

After, she ran her hands through Dvorak's black hair and put her lips near his mouth again. "Do you want another kiss?" she whispered seductively and ground against his cock once more.

"Yes."

"I'll give you as many as you want, but I want something in return."

Dvorak was panting. "Anything. Ask anything."

"Tell me of Orrin."

"Virginia," Dvorak answered. "He is in Virginia. Now kiss me again."

She scored his chest with her nails, careful not to break the skin. "I give the orders."

"Please," Dvorak begged. "May I have another kiss?"

Natalie couldn't believe how effective this was. Then again, Dvorak thought he was smarter than most. To him, she was just a woman. What could she do?

Well, she was going to show him how capable she was. Maybe then she'd remind him that she wasn't alone in the room.

Natalie reached down and unfastened his slacks. Dvorak groaned loudly, his eyes wild with lust. "Who made the bioweapon?" she asked as she rubbed her breasts against his chest.

Dvorak groaned loudly, his hips rising from the chair to grind into her. "Cannot."

When he hesitated, she gave him a harsh look and slapped him. "You will submit to me."

This act was rather gratifying. To have someone like Dvorak willing to do nearly anything for sex. It made her want to roll her eyes.

Dvorak nodded eagerly. "I am."

"No, you're not. Who made the bioweapon?"

Once more, he dithered. She grabbed his cock and squeezed.

"Konrad Jankovic. He defected two days ago. But you know that," Dvorak said and attempted to kiss her.

She dodged him and put her hand around his throat. "I tell you when you can touch and kiss me."

"I told you," he said in a sulk.

Natalie caressed his face before slapping him. "You've told me nothing."

"Jankovic must be found. My men look for him now."

She pulled her skirt up higher. It caused Dvorak to groan loudly. "Is there an antidote to the weapon?"

Dvorak shook his head. "Jankovic is the only one who can create it."

She ran her finger along Dvorak's lower lip. "You've done good."

"Worth another kiss?" he asked hopefully.

She laughed and rocked her hips against him. "If you tell me how Jankovic defected."

"Your government."

Owen grabbed Natalie, moving her away. She was relieved that they had all the information they needed. Only then did Dvorak realize what had occurred.

She waved her fingers at him. "You're a sick son of a bitch who deserves the most painful death imaginable."

"One that lasts for months," Owen added.

Then he walked behind Dvorak and knocked him unconscious with a hit to the back of his head again. With that, they walked from the room.

CHAPTER THIRTY-EIGHT

Natalie was happy to leave the Ritz behind. She almost asked Dvorak to call off the hit on her, but she knew it wouldn't do any good.

They reached the Hilton without incident. She wanted to be back in a pair of jeans and on the road to the ranch within the next five minutes.

"I'm going to check us out and get the truck," Owen said.

She nodded slowly. "I'll get our things from the room."

Natalie made it upstairs. She hurriedly stuffed their clothes in the bags and decided not to change yet. The quicker they were on the road, the better.

It felt like forever before the elevator arrived. The doors opened, and she entered, setting down the bags before mindlessly pressing the button for the lobby.

She leaned against the back of the elevator as she thought about Owen. The doors were shutting when someone stuck their hand between them and stopped them from closing.

Her stomach dropped to her feet when two Russians

got in the small box with her. She knew a moment of true panic. Owen's face flashed in her mind, and she wished he were with her. But he wasn't. She was on her own.

Her gun was in her purse, which was in the bag and did her no good. Her few moves of self-defense would only do so much against two burly men.

"Where is he?" the shorter of the two men asked.

Natalie shrugged. "Who?"

"Dr. Jankovic."

She looked between the two men. Was it a coincidence that they'd just learned that name from Dvorak? "I don't know who that is."

The larger man sneered at her. "You lie."

"Get over it."

Both men crowded her. The elevator dinged as it reached another floor. She saw the doors open, but she'd never make it off without them grabbing her.

It was the short one who said, "Konrad Jankovic. Tell us where he is, and we will allow you to live."

Suddenly, the large Russian fell to one knee with a loud cry of pain. Natalie looked over the man's head and saw Owen. Owen locked an arm around the big Russian's neck and punched the second one so hard he slammed against the side of the elevator.

Adrenaline jolted through her, and she kicked the big one in the nuts, causing him to bellow in pain. Owen grabbed her arm and yanked. She jumped over the man, who was now on his side, holding his balls. She stumbled out and turned to watch, her heart in her throat.

There was a flash of light on the blade of a knife in Owen's hand. Owen was swift and lethal as he stabbed the Russian twice in the side before coming up behind him and snapping his neck.

The doors to the elevator kept trying to close, but the big man's leg prevented it. She shouted Owen's name when she saw the smaller man lift a gun.

Her hand covered her mouth as she watched in horror as the man and Owen struggled a second. There were two soft retorts from a silencer, and then the Russian fell to his back, red blooming over his chest.

She could hardly draw breath as she watched the blood. Owen was alive, and for that she was thankful, but there was so much death.

She forced her gaze to Owen. He stood and adjusted the sleeves of his shirt beneath his tux jacket. He grabbed their bags and punched a button inside before kicking the Russian's leg back into the elevator before he stepped out. The doors shut behind him.

Then he came to stand before her.

She looked into his dark eyes as he raked a hand through his hair to comb it back into place. He hadn't even broken a sweat.

He was terrifying. And brilliant.

"Don't ever scare me like that again," he stated as he took her hand and gave her a kiss.

She nodded, because there were no words. Her heart still pounded in her chest with the force of a jackhammer as Owen walked her down a flight of stairs and outside to the truck.

They drove off before anyone else could stop them.

"I'll have to call in a favor," Owen said. "There are cameras in the elevator. They'll see both our faces."

Oh, God. She hadn't even thought of that. "Will you be arrested?"

"That's the favor I'm calling in. Did the men say anything?"

"Oddly, they asked where Jankovic was."

"Interesting."

"Yes."

She kept reliving the scene at the hotel over and over in her head as they drove back to the ranch. She wrapped her arms around herself. It was going to take a case of bourbon to get the taste of Egor Dvorak out of her mouth. Not once did she regret doing what she'd done to help Owen. It surprised her how easily it had come.

How effortlessly she'd used her body to gain information. Because they had to get answers.

Owen's large hand covered hers and squeezed. She blinked and looked around as the truck slowed and turned. They were already back at the ranch?

She gazed at Owen to find the light from the dashboard showing a portion of his face. He smiled reassuringly, his grip firm.

"We're home."

Home. She liked the sound of that. "And it's still standing."

"I'm going to regret not killing Dvorak when I had the chance."

"Leaving him alive was smart."

Owen snorted. "It won't take them long to discover he's spilled their secrets. I give him a week to live."

She was glad he still held her hand. With Owen, she became a different person. Stronger. Balanced. Happy.

Being with Owen seemed as natural as breathing. She feared she might have fallen in love with him again, but it didn't scare her as it used to. If she'd ever *stopped* loving him.

Perhaps that's why she'd thought she managed to forget about him. Though no one disregarded a man like Owen Loughman. He was utterly unforgettable, entirely extraordinary.

Absolutely astonishing.

He stopped the truck in front of the house and turned off the engine.

It felt good to be back at the ranch. It was one place she knew was heavily guarded. The Russians would have a hard time getting to them. And hopefully, they wouldn't try.

There had been too much death and fighting at the ranch. It was time for peace. Time for love.

She gazed at Owen. Yes, it was time for love. It was time for her to admit what she yearned for, what she needed more than anything—Owen.

Natalie cleared her throat, suddenly nervous. "It seems quiet."

"I think we're all right on that front."

"You expected an attack tonight?"

He gave a nod. "I did. It was the perfect time. I would've done it."

"Perhaps they know it's pointless."

"I hope. We should get inside and get some rest."

"Agreed."

His smile took her breath away. "Come on, then."

She watched as Owen opened his door and stepped out of the truck. Blowing out a breath, she opened her door and slid to the ground. The temperature had dropped, causing her to shiver. She wanted a cup of coffee in hand ASAP.

That's when she remembered they were nearly out at the base. "I'm going to grab some coffee from the house."

"Be quick."

She was on the porch when she heard her name. Natalie turned her head over her shoulder and met Owen's gaze. His smile was slow, seductive. It caused her stomach to flutter and her heart to miss a beat.

It was on the tip of her tongue to tell him that she loved him, but she hesitated. It was something she wanted to say while seeing his face, not something to yell in the dark. Not yet anyway.

Her smile was huge as she walked into the house. Whatever happened, there was no denying her feelings.

She'd tried that. She'd even tried to ignore him, and that had been a joke. There was no more denial, no more lying. She was going after what she wanted.

Owen made a round of the house, his mind occupied with all things Natalie. He'd run the range of emotions tonight from desire, jealousy, fury, fear, and astonishment to admiration. Then again, Natalie always had a way of affecting him in such a way.

She had no idea how remarkable she was in everything she did. She had a spine of steel that had her standing up for whatever she thought was right.

When Owen glanced at the barn, he was surprised at how quiet everything was. Then he listened. There wasn't a sound—not even the wind blowing.

He had no comm to check in with the men Callie had sent. He briefly thought of heading to the base. Then he looked at the house.

Natalie.

Every instinct yelled at him to get her to the base immediately.

His blood ran cold. He kept low and ran to the truck to get a weapon. His heart thumped painfully in his chest as he ripped off his suit jacket.

He crawled toward the house, listening for anything out of the ordinary. He should've noticed the quiet when they'd arrived, instead of being too preoccupied with Natalie. That could very well get her killed.

He was nearly to the porch when he saw a light go on upstairs. Then he saw a dark figure move within the house. A moment later, the room lit up with the flash of semi-automatic rounds and bullets spraying the air.

CHAPTER THIRTY-NINE

Natalie's feet were like ice. She rushed upstairs and found a pair of fuzzy socks in Callie's drawer. After tugging them on, she stood, getting ready to head down to the kitchen when something stopped her.

She paused, listening. There wasn't a sound within the house. Not a squeak of the floorboards or the squeal of the screen door. So why did she feel like she wasn't alone?

Natalie looked out the window. All seemed normal at the barn. Owen wasn't rushing toward the house. There was no gunfire. No shouts.

She sighed and mentally shook her head. After the evening she'd endured, it was no wonder she imagined things that weren't there.

With a laugh at herself, she turned toward the door when she caught a glimpse of the barrel of a gun. Without thinking, she dove to the floor by the time the gunman opened fire.

Bullets sprayed the room. She covered her head with her arms, squeezing her eyes closed. Something whizzed past her head, moving her hair. A bullet.

That's how close it came to hitting her. She was deafened by the sound of the gunfire. Somehow, she managed to make it to the bed and get beneath it.

It offered a measure of protection, but that didn't last long. The gunman must've seen her, because the next thing she knew, bullets were hitting the mattress—and going through it.

Natalie quickly rolled from underneath the bed toward the window. There was no place for her to hide, nowhere for her to get to safety. It was only a matter of time before the shooter hit her.

She glanced at the gunman to find his gaze trained on her, a smile of pleasure on his face. Small white feathers drifted in the air from the pillows.

A spray of bullets came toward her. Natalie tried to get back under the bed so she could roll to the other side to run out of the room. Her socks kept slipping on the wood. Her tight dress hindered her movements.

It felt like ages before she was able to get back under the bed, but she didn't stop. Thankfully, the gunman walked to where she'd been in order to shoot her.

She saw the door—and freedom. She had one chance. When she stood, the shooter would have the perfect time to open fire, but for her to remain in the room was certain death.

There was only one option.

Owen.

She hoped that wherever he was, he was safe. If there was one killer at the ranch, there was more. Owen's instincts had been right. The Russians were attacking.

Natalie took a deep breath and held it as she scooted

from beneath the bed and jumped to her feet. She slipped as soon as her socks hit the bare floor.

She grabbed the door to keep herself upright, and a bullet slammed into where her head had been a second before. Natalie didn't look back. She ran out of the room.

And straight into arms she knew well.

Owen didn't say a word. He put a pistol in her hand and moved her behind him. She'd seen many of his faces. Earlier, she thought she'd seen his rage with the men in the elevator, but that was nothing compared to the violence she saw in his eyes now, the ferocity that hardened his face.

She backed away as he moved toward the bedroom. Natalie screamed when a bullet splintered the doorjamb near Owen's face, but he didn't so much as flinch.

The gunman ran out of bullets and rushed Owen. She watched as they battled each other with fists, feet, and even teeth. It was a brutal fight with Owen holding nothing back.

The beast had been unleashed.

And she was mesmerized.

A creak sounded behind her. She turned and spotted another man running up the stairs, gun raised and pointed at Owen. Natalie didn't hesitate in pulling the trigger, putting two bullets into his heart.

She watched in slow motion as the man stopped, his eyes going wide while he looked at her. Then he fell backward down the stairs.

A grunt behind her had her whirling around, ready to kill anyone who dared to harm her or those she loved. She found herself staring into chocolate eyes.

"Nat?"

She lowered the gun and walked into Owen's arms. Outside, she could hear more shooting. It was far from over. The Russians were determined to find the bioweapon and kill whoever stood in their way.

"Follow me," Owen said.

She fell into step behind him as they made their way down the stairs and out the door. She glanced behind her to see the wreckage the Russians had done to the house. It hurt her heart, and it wasn't even her home. She couldn't imagine how Owen felt.

She plastered herself against the side of the house and squatted down so Owen could look around the corner. He fired two quick shots. Then, with his gun still up, he moved to the truck.

She kept watch behind them. He moved them closer and closer to the barn where horses were screaming from the sound of the guns.

There was a gargled scream as one of the attackers fell dead from the roof of the barn.

"About time the snipers joined the fun," Owen murmured.

Two more of the Russians approached the barn.

"Dammit," Owen murmured when he noticed them.

In the next second, the men fell dead from gunshots coming from differing directions.

Owen motioned her to follow him. They ran to the barn, and she expected to feel a bullet hit her any minute. Owen was opening the trap door for her to get below when another of the attackers came at them from behind.

She turned the same time as Owen, their guns lifting, but the enemy was already firing. From behind them came a shot, killing the gunman. Natalie turned and found a man in all black.

He gave her a nod. "Get—"

The sentence was never finished as one of the Russians jumped from the hayloft and plunged a knife into the soldier's chest. Natalie was quickly knocked to the ground by Owen.

Owen leapt to his feet, and with one shot, took out their would-be killer. Natalie stared at the dead body of the man who had saved them sprawled just a few feet from her. His eyes were open, staring out the open doors of the barn, but they were empty, completely devoid of life.

Owen then did a thorough search of the barn. She felt sick. So much death that night, and for what? A weapon that could possibly wipe out the world? What was wrong with people?

The barn began to spin, the lights inside blinding her. She closed her eyes and tried to find balance. It was the sound of Owen's voice that caught her attention.

"Nat? Look at me."

She blinked up at him. "Is it over?

"Yes, sweetheart. It's over."

For now, went unsaid.

"We'll take him home," said a voice Natalie didn't recognize.

She looked up to see five men surrounding them. They were in solid black with all the tactical gear she was used to seeing Owen and his brothers in. So these were the men Callie had spoken of.

"I'm Tony," the one closest to them said to Owen.

"Orrin is our friend. If you need anything, Callie knows how to reach us."

"Thanks," Owen said.

"Me and the boys can make sure to keep an eye on the place anytime you need us."

Owen nodded.

"We all respect Orrin. Get him back for all of us." Tony clenched his jaw.

"We will," Owen promised.

Natalie accepted his help up. She no longer wanted coffee. She wanted a stiff drink. Or three.

When Owen turned toward her, she spotted the blood on his white shirt. Her heart dropped to her feet. He couldn't be hurt. Not Owen. "You're injured."

He touched his chest and looked at his body. "It's not my blood. It's . . . yours."

She frowned as he stared at her. "What?"

The next thing she knew, he lifted her in his arms and rushed her down to the base. The door slid closed, sealing them in again.

Once more safe.

He gently sat her down on the bed. Then he squatted before her and took her hands in his. He smiled at her. "It's over, sweetheart. The Russians are gone."

"They'll be back." She was suddenly very tired. She closed her eyes, wanting sleep.

"Not tonight they won't."

Why did his voice sound so far away? And what was that racket? He was mumbling to himself angrily. Natalie curled on her side.

"Natalie, honey. Look at me. Open your eyes and look at me."

It took a great amount of effort for her to do as he asked. When she did, there were lines of worry around his eyes. "What's wrong?"

"You've been shot."

Shot? What was he talking about?

Something touched her arm then, and she hissed in pain, trying to jerk away from him. Now wide-awake, her heartbeat doubled.

"It was a clean shot, went straight through the flesh," he said.

"It hurts," she said through clenched teeth. How was she just now feeling it?

"I know, baby. I'm getting to that."

She squeezed her eyes shut. Briefly, she felt the stick of a needle.

"Morphine," Owen said.

The pain began to fade almost instantly. She was able to lay still while he finished cleaning the wound. The drug was pulling her under, fast.

She didn't know how long she slept. When she woke, Owen was there beside her. There was a twinge in her arm, but it was nothing like before.

His hand laced with her good one. "I'm sorry you were alone upstairs. I should've been there. I should've checked the house."

"It's not your fault."

"It is. I know better."

She knew that stubborn streak. There was no use arguing with him when his mind was made up. "How did the Russians get on the property without being seen?"

"They didn't. Callie's men killed ten before they reached the house. It was while they were occupied with the others that those few made it to the main property," he explained.

She signed. "We found out very little."

"Actually, we scored a big win. While you slept, I called Wyatt and Callie. They're going to find the scientist. I also sent Cullen a text that Orrin is in Virginia."

"But still no formula?"

He shook his head. "If we find the scientist, we won't need it."

"What about whoever betrayed Orrin?"

Owen winced. "We'll deal with that after we find Dad. Until then, Ragnarok will remain here with us. We're holding down the fort for the others."

"I like the sound of that."

The hope in his eyes shone brightly.

No longer could she deny that she loved Owen. She needed to tell him. She bit her lip and swung her legs over the bed. Owen was immediately there to help her sit up.

When the room stopped spinning, she gazed into his eyes. "I love you. I've always loved you. Even when I tried to stop, I couldn't. You've always been in my heart, Owen Loughman. I'm sorry for pushing you away."

"Sweetheart," he murmured and brought her hands to his lips. "I was a fool for leaving you fourteen years ago. There's only been one person for me, and that's you. I love you, Nat. I'd do anything to have you as mine again. I'll even leave the service."

Tears gathered and fell as she shook her head. She knew how much serving his country meant to him. The fact that he was willing to give it up for her told her just how deep his love was—if she'd ever doubted it before.

"You can't quit. You wouldn't be you if you weren't serving," she said.

He stared into her eyes. "Fourteen years ago, I wanted to ask you to be mine. I didn't listen to my heart, but I am now. Natalie, will you marry me?"

"God, yes."

Owen held her in his arms, happier than he ever thought possible. When he'd been sent back home, he hadn't known what to expect, but it sure as hell hadn't been Natalie.

He might have been furious at one point to learn what his father had been involved in, but now he felt differently. Orrin did what they all did—protect their country the best way they could. Anger over their mother's death had put a strain on their relationship with their father.

It wasn't fair to any of them. Orrin had no more been at fault for Melanie's death than Owen was for the Russians wanting Natalie dead.

He was ashamed that he'd stayed away from the ranch. All those years he could've gotten to know the man Orrin was, but that time was gone.

All he could hope for was that they found Orrin alive. Owen had a lot to make up for, with both his father and Natalie, but this was the first time in a long while that he could remember feeling hopeful about the future.

He wasn't a fool. Going up against the group of Russians could be one of the most dangerous missions he'd ever joined, but it was worth it for his father.

It made him think of his brothers. Cullen would be happy to be a family again. Wyatt was another matter.

Wyatt's hatred for their father ran deep. So deep that

Owen wasn't sure if Wyatt could ever forgive Orrin. At one point, Owen hadn't wanted to forgive Orrin, but the woman in his arms had changed his mind.

He understood how being involved in his life put those around him in danger. Natalie hadn't asked for any of it, but she accepted the hazard. And it had nearly gotten her killed.

That's when he realized how his father must have felt all those years ago when his wife was brutally taken from him. Owen knew who was responsible for Natalie's injury—the Russians.

But who was to blame for his mother's death? For the first time, he looked at it with new eyes. Choking someone to death was personal. They had to get close to Melanie. The person could've shot her from yards away and had the same effect. So why the strangulation?

Because they wanted to get to Orrin.

Each of them long suspected Melanie's death had something to do with one of Orrin's missions. The fact that the person never touched either him or his brothers told him that Melanie's death was enough to hurt Orrin.

Owen looked down at Natalie and smoothed her hair back from her face as she smiled at him.

"I finally have you," Natalie said.

He held her tighter. "You've always had me, darlin'."

She threaded her fingers with his and gazed up at him with so much love that it took his breath away.

No one would ever hurt her again. She knew how to shoot, and she would learn hand-to-hand combat as well because he wanted her prepared.

Because she was his.

"I love you."

She smiled. "I love you."

With those three little words, his world was righted once more.

EPILOGUE

The shrill sound of the phone caused Natalie to jump in her seat before the computer. She looked up as Owen strolled toward her from his father's office, his cell phone in hand.

"It's Callie."

Natalie nodded to the phone. "Answer it."

He put it on speaker and said, "Hey, Cal."

"Is Natalie there?"

She frowned and slid off the stool at the sound of distress in Callie's voice. "I'm right here."

"You're not going to like this, Owen," Wyatt's voice came over the line.

Natalie exchanged a look with Owen. Even though they'd won against the group attacking them again, she knew this was only one of many skirmishes. Ragnarok was still in their possession—and still safe.

For the time being.

But the danger was increasing with each day. Natalie understood that, and she understood her part in all of it.

"Tell us," Owen prompted.

Callie blew out a breath. "I was finally able to do

some searching on the Saints. Guys, this is bad. Very bad. They're a shadow organization."

"Owen," Wyatt said, his voice pitched low in worry. "We can't find the head of this group. The Saints seem to be a part of every elite position within Russia."

Natalie sat back down on the stool. She was no stranger to secret organizations, having heard enough about them in college. Nearly everyone had heard of the Illuminati or the New World Order.

Most people disregarded all of it as conspiracy theories that didn't have a grain of truth. But there was always truth to them.

"We think," Callie hurried to say. "There isn't much on this group. They're very secretive. Many of the blogs or articles I read were quick to dismiss the Saints as hearsay or made up."

"But you don't?" Owen asked.

Callie hesitated for a heartbeat. "I don't. There are too many instances of power shifts within Russia that mimic someone masterminding the entire affair. I could list everything, but it's too long."

"One instance could be overlooked," Wyatt said. "A couple could be a coincidence. But when looked at as a whole, there's no doubt."

"So it isn't Egor Dvorak controlling the Russians here," Natalie said. "It's the Saints."

Callie made a sound. "I have no proof, Nat. This is a gut feeling based on what I've found—and not found. I did unearth an article nearly sixty years old about an alliance of top members of the KGB, the military, and the elite of Russia that called themselves the Saints. Someone tried to remove every instance of that article."

"But Callie found it," Wyatt said, a note of pride in his voice. "Give her more time. She might uncover more."

Natalie leaned her elbow on the table as her mind spun with the possibilities of what this group—the Saints—could do to them. Or with Ragnarok.

"Cullen needs to know," Owen said.

Wyatt said, "Already tried to call him. I still can't reach him, but I did send a text. Let's hope he gets it."

"What about calling Mia," Natalie offered.

"Did that already, but didn't get an answer from her either."

Owen's frown deepened as he stared at the phone. "When do we go after him?"

"That might be the wrong thing to do," Callie said. "Especially if he and Mia are hiding."

"And if they're not?" Wyatt asked.

Natalie held out her hand as Owen walked to her. Their fingers intertwined. She saw the apprehension for Cullen in his gaze.

"Cullen is a Loughman," Natalie said.

There was a stretch of silence where Owen smiled at her. "We'll give him another few days."

"Then we go find him," Wyatt stated.

Sklad

Orrin wasn't surprised when Yuri chained him to the bed. The bastard stood at the door, watching as the red-haired doctor checked his vitals.

Her gaze never moved to Orrin, and he didn't look at

her. He wanted to make sure Yuri believed they hadn't spoken to each other. Because if Yuri thought for a moment that the woman had helped him, her child would be dead.

"You look . . . well," Yuri said.

Orrin suspected it had something to do with whatever the doctor had injected into his IV every six hours.

Yuri clasped his hands behind his back and walked to the opposite side of the bed from the woman. He smiled at Orrin and said, "Your home has been destroyed."

He kept his face passive. The house and buildings could be rebuilt. Cattle and horses replaced. His sons and Callie, however, could not.

He waited for Yuri to tell him who had been killed. Orrin wasn't sure if he could keep himself calm if anything had happened to his family.

"Nothing to say?" Yuri asked with a smirk.

Orrin merely stared at him. He would give Yuri nothing.

Yuri shrugged. "There was quite a fight there. Lots of gunfire exchanged. I know at least one was killed and another injured."

No matter how Orrin kept his emotions from his face, he couldn't control his blood pressure. The monitor he was hooked to began to beep with the pounding of his heart.

Yuri laughed and turned on his heel. "I think I will wait to tell you who died for later. I am enjoying this entirely too much."

The real battle was just beginning.

Read on for an excerpt from the next
Sons of Texas novel by Donna Grant

THE PROTECTOR

Coming soon from St. Martin's Paperbacks

The forest was still but buzzing with sounds, making the night seem alive. It was electric, stimulating.

Stirring.

Mia searched for an excuse—*any* excuse—to stop thinking about Cullen. And found nothing.

It was disheartening to be sure. Especially when she wanted him so acutely.

That need swirled through her, slowly at first, but increasing steadily. The kernel of desire that began upon finding him in the hanger had turned into an inferno.

She used the time alone while he did a sweep of the area to try and get herself under control. When he spoke of his mother's murder and the years after, she'd been unable to keep her hands from him. And that touch had only inflamed her need for more.

In order not to throw herself at him, she had no choice but to release him. Which had been harder to do than she expected. What was it about Cullen that enticed and captivated her?

What about him persuaded her to let down her guard and invite him in?

Was it his arousing, sexy voice that cajoled and seduced? Was it his charming words that tempted and lured?

Or was it those hypnotic hazel eyes with their mysterious mix of green and gold that coaxed her?

Her stomach fluttered at the thought of giving into desire. The attraction was there, hovering around them like a cloud. She wasn't sure how much longer she could resist. So far, her mind had remained strong, but her body was turning the tide swiftly.

Not even a mundane chore like cleaning the dishes could ease the rising desire. It burned, blazed hot and relentless. Cullen was the type of man she couldn't outrun or ignore.

He demanded her attention with a simple look. The promise of pleasure in his gaze was there whenever she sought to see it. And that terrified her.

But it also exhilarated her.

With her hands braced on the sink, she closed her eyes and imagined what it would be like to give herself to Cullen. Her head rolled to the side as her nipples puckered, tingling with the need to be touched.

Chills raced over her body, her lips parted as her breaths came faster. With his name on her lips, she reached down and touched herself.

Her eyes opened. In the reflection of the window, she saw him standing behind her. Their gazes clashed as the fire popped. Desire smoldered within his hazel depths.

There was no turning back now. Mia didn't even try. The path was laid bare before her, and it was too good to let it pass her by.

She turned around. For long moments, they simply stared. She was afraid to move—and afraid not to.

The desire was so tangible that the air was thick with it. She was shaking when she took that first, tentative step toward him.

He met her midway, but even then they didn't touch. Mia was scared that once she did, the primal, savage longing for him would take over.

It was Cullen who reached out first, putting a hand on her waist and slowly drawing her closer. Instinctively, her arms bent, grasping his forearms.

Candlelight and firelight bathed them in a soft glow. She was spellbound, caught in the web of longing and need reflected in his eyes.

His head bent forward gradually, giving her time to push him away. Except she was long past that. Her face lifted, anticipating his kiss.

The first touch of his lips against hers made her breath catch. His mouth was firm as he moved against her lips, teasing and coaxing.

She willingly opened for him. When his tongue swept in and touched hers, she sighed and ran her hands up his arms, over his shoulders and around his neck.

He held her tightly, his arms like bands of steel as he deepened the kiss. Molten desire poured through her. If there were any last reservations about giving into her longing, they faded away.

Sparks of pleasure skidded along her skin as he kissed her vigorously. She melted against him, wanting—*needing*—more.

A moan roiled through her when he slid a hand into

her hair. Then he turned her, backing her around the sofa and closer to the fire.

She was the one who reached for the hem of his shirt and yanked it upward. The kiss ended long enough for him to pull it off and toss it away.

Mia's lips parted as she stared at the specimen before her. She splayed her hands over his chest, then kissed the bullet wound at his right shoulder and the other closer to his waist. On the left side, she ran her lips and tongue along the three-inch scar along his abdomen that came from a knife.

She met his gaze and smiled. The thick sinew beneath her palms strained as he fought not to touch her. He jerked when she reached between them and unbuttoned his jeans.